Archibald Clavering Gunter

Miss Dividends

A Novel

Archibald Clavering Gunter

Miss Dividends
A Novel

ISBN/EAN: 9783337349103

Printed in Europe, USA, Canada, Australia, Japan

Cover: Foto ©Andreas Hilbeck / pixelio.de

More available books at **www.hansebooks.com**

MISS DIVIDENDS

A Novel

BY

ARCHIBALD CLAVERING GUNTER

AUTHOR OF

"MR. BARNES OF NEW YORK," "MR. POTTER OF TEXAS,"
"THAT FRENCHMAN!" "MISS NOBODY OF
NOWHERE," "SMALL BOYS IN BIG BOOTS,"
"A FLORIDA ENCHANTMENT,"
ETC., ETC.

NEW YORK
THE HOME PUBLISHING COMPANY
3 EAST FOURTEENTH STREET
1892

CONTENTS.

BOOK I.

THE GIRL FROM NEW YORK.

BOOK II.

A CURIOUS CLUB MAN.

BOOK III.

OUT OF A STRANGE COUNTRY.

MISS DIVIDENDS.

BOOK I.

THE GIRL FROM NEW YORK.

CHAPTER I.

MR. WEST.

"FIVE minutes behind your appointment," remarks Mr. Whitehouse Southmead in kindly severity ; then he laughs and continues : "You see, your oysters are cold."

"As they should be, covered up with ice," returns Captain Harry Storey Lawrence. A moment after, however, he adds more seriously, "I had a good excuse."

"An excuse for keeping *this* waiting?" And Whitehouse pours out lovingly a glass of Château Yquem.

"Yes, and the best in the world, though probably not one that would be considered good by a lawyer."

"Aha! a woman?" rejoins Mr. Southmead.

"The most beautiful I have ever seen!" cries Lawrence, the enthusiasm of youth beaming in his handsome dark eyes.

"Pooh !" returns the other, "you have only been from the Far West for three days."

"True," remarks Lawrence. "Three days ago I was incompetent, but am not now. You see, I have been

living in a mining camp in Southern Utah for the last year,
where all women are scarce and none beautiful. For
my first three days in New York, every woman I met on
the streets seemed to me a houri. Now, however, I am
beginning to discriminate. My taste has become normal,
and I pronounce the young lady whose fan I picked up
on the stairs a few moments ago, just what I have called
her. Wouldn't you, if she had eyes——"

"Oh, leave the eyes and devote yourself to the oysters,"
interjects the more practical Southmead. "You cannot
have fallen in love with a girl while picking up her fan ;
besides, I have business to talk to you about this evening,
—business upon which the success of your present transaction may depend."

"You do not think the financial effort France is making
to pay its war indemnity to Germany will stop the sale
of my mine?" says the young man hurriedly, seating
himself opposite his companion, and the two begin to
discuss the charming *petit souper*, such as one bachelor
gave to another in old Delmonico's on Fourteenth Street
and Fifth Avenue before canvas-back ducks had become
quite as expensive as they now are, and terrapin had
become so scarce that mud-turtles frequently masquerade
for diamond-backs, even in our most expensive restau-
rants. For this conversation and this supper took place
in the autumn of 1871, before fashionable New York had
moved above Twenty-third Street, when Neilson was
about to enter into the glory of her first season at the
Academy, when Capoul was to be the idol of the ladies,
and dear little Duval was getting ready to charm the
public by her polonaise in " Mignon."

This year, 1871, had marked several changes in the
business of these United States of America. During the
War of the Confederacy, speculators, under the guise of
Government contractors, had stolen great sums from
Uncle Sam. In 1865 the Government changed its policy,

and began to make presents of fortunes to speculators, thus saving them the trouble of robbing it.

In 1868 it had just finished presenting a syndicate of Boston capitalists with the Union Pacific Railway, many millions of dollars in solid cash, and every alternate section of Government land for twenty miles on each side of their thousand miles of track. It had, also, been equally generous to five small Sacramento capitalists, and had presented them with the Central Pacific Railway, the same amount of Government land, and some fifty-five millions of dollars, and had received in return for all this—not even thanks.

The opening of these railroads, however, had brought the West and East in much more intimate connection. Mines had been developed in Utah and Colorado, and the Western speculator, with his indomitable energy, had opened up a promising market for various silver properties in the West, not only in New York and other Eastern cities, but in Europe itself.

One of the results of this is the appearance in New York of the young man, Captain Harry Storey Lawrence, who has come to complete the negotiations for the sale of a silver property in which he is interested, to an English syndicate, the lawyer representing the same in America being Mr. Whitehouse Southmead, who is now seated opposite to him.

As the two men discuss their oysters, champagne, partridges and salad, their appearances are strikingly dissimilar. Southmead, who is perhaps fifty, is slightly gray and slightly bald, and has the characteristics of an easygoing family lawyer,—one to whom family secrets, wealth and investments, might be implicitly trusted, though he is distinctly not that kind of advocate one would choose to fight a desperate criminal case before a jury, where it was either emotional insanity or murder.

The man opposite to him, however, were he a lawyer, would have been just the one for the latter case, for the most marked characteristic in Harry Storey Lawrence's bearing, demeanor and appearance is that of resolution, unflinching, indomitable,—not the resolution of a stubborn man, but one whose fixed purpose is dominated by reason and directed by wisdom.

He has a broad, intellectual forehead, a resolute chin and lower lip. These would be perhaps too stern did not his dark, flashing eyes have in them intelligence as well as passion, humanity as well as firmness. His hair is of a dark brown, for this man is a brunette, not of the Spanish type, but of the Anglo-Saxon. His mustache, which is long and drooping, conceals a delicate upper lip, which together with the eyes give softness and humanity to a countenance that but for them would look too combative. His figure, considerably over the middle height, has that peculiar activity which is produced only by training in open air,—not the exercise of the athlete, but that of the soldier, the pioneer, the adventurer; for Harry Lawrence has had a great deal of this kind of life in his twenty-nine years of existence.

Leaving his engineering studies at college, he had entered the army as a lieutenant at the opening of the rebellion, and in two years had found himself the captain of an Iowa battery—the only command which gives to a young officer that independence which makes him plan as well as act. But, having fought for his country and not for a career, as soon as the rebellion had finished, this citizen soldier had resigned, and until 1868 had been one of the division engineers of the Union Pacific Railway. On the completion of that great road, he had found himself at Ogden, and had devoted himself to mining in Utah.

Altogether, he looks like a man who could win a woman's heart and take very good care of it; though, perhaps his appearance would hardly please one of the strong-minded sisterhood, for there is an indication of command and domination in his manner, doubtless arising from his military experience.

As the two gentlemen discuss their supper, their conversation first turns on business; though, from Lawrence's remarks it is apparent there is a conflicting interest in his mind, that of the young lady whom he has just seen down-stairs.

"You don't think that *milliard* going to the Germans will affect the sale of the Mineral Hill Mine," asks Harry, earnestly, opening the conversation.

"Not at all," replies the lawyer. "No fluctuation in funds can affect the capital the English company is about to invest, and has already deposited in the bank for that purpose."

"Then what more do they want? The mine has already been reported upon favorably by their experts and engineers."

"They insist, however, upon a title without contest," returns Southmead.

"Why, you yourself have stated that our title to the Mineral Hill was without flaw," interjects the young man hastily.

"Certainly," answers the lawyer; "but not without *contest*. I have to-day received a letter from Utah, stating that there is apt to be litigation in regard to your property. If so, it must certainly delay its sale."

"Oh, I know what you mean," cries Harry, a determined expression coming into his eyes. "It is those infernal Mormons! When we made the locations in Tintic, there was not a stake driven in the District, but now word has been given out by Father Brigham to his followers that as it is impossible to stop the entry of Gentiles into Utah for the purpose of mining, the Latter-Day Saints had best claim all the mines they can under prior locations

and get these properties for themselves, as far as possible.
Consequently, a Mormon company has been started, who
have put in a claim of prior location to a portion of one
of our mines, without any more right to it than I have to
this restaurant.   And what do you think the beggars call
themselves ?   Why, Zion's Co-operative Mining Company."   Here he laughs a little bitterly and continues :
" It was Zion's Co-operative Commercial Institutions, and
now it is Zion's Co-operative Mining Companies.   Those
fellows drag in the Lord to help them in every iniquitous
scheme for despoiling the Gentile."

" All the same," replies the lawyer, " if you wish to
make the sale of your property to the English company
that I represent, you had better compromise the matter
with them.   I sharn't permit my clients to buy a lawsuit."

" Compromise ?   Never ! " answers the other impulsively.   Then he goes on more contemplatively : " And
yet I wish to make the sale more than ever.   You see,
the price we name for the property is an honest one.   It
is worth every dollar of the five hundred thousand we
ask for it."

" Then, why not work it yourself ? " asks the lawyer.

" Simply because I have got tired of living the life of
a barbarian—surrounded by barbarians.   It was well
enough to spend four years of early manhood in camps
and battles, three others in building a big railroad, and
three more in the excitement of mining, away from the
convenances and graces of life that only come with the
presence of refined women ; but now I am tired of it,
more so than ever since I have seen that young lady
down-stairs."

" Ah ! still going back to Miss Travenion ? " laughs
the lawyer.

" You know her name then ? " cries the captain, suddenly.

"Yes," says the other. "I happened to be impatient for your coming. The evening was sultry. I walked out of the room, looked down the stairs and saw your act of gallantry."

"Ah, since you know her name, you must know her!"

"Quite well; I am her trustee."

"Her trustee!" cries Harry Lawrence impulsively. "Her guardian? You will introduce me to her? This is luck," and before the old gentleman can interrupt him, the Westerner has seized his hand and given it a squeeze which he remembers for some five minutes.

"I said her trustee; not her guardian," answers the lawyer cautiously. "If, as your manner rather indicates, you have designs upon the young lady's heart, you had better get a reply from her father."

"Her father is living then?"

"Certainly. Last January you could have seen him any afternoon in the windows of the Unity Club looking at the ladies promenading on the Avenue, just as he used to do when he lived here, and was a man about town, and club *habitué* and heavy swell. Ralph Travenion has gone West again, however, but I have not heard of his death."

"Then for what reason does his daughter need a trustee?"

"Well, if you will listen to me and smoke your cigar in silence," says Southmead, for they have arrived at that stage of the meal. "Erma Lucille Travenion——"

"Erma—Lucille—Travenion!" mutters the young man, turning the words over very tenderly as if they were sweet morsels on his tongue. "Erma—Lucille—Travenion,—what a beautiful name."

"Hang it, don't interrupt me and don't look roman-tic," laughs the lawyer.

But here a soft-treading waiter knocks upon the door

and says: "Mr. Ferdinand Rives Chauncey would like to see you half a minute, Mr. Southmead."

And with the words, the young gentleman announced, a dapper boy of about nineteen, faultlessly clad in the evening dress of that period, enters hastily and says: "My dear Mr. Southmead, Mrs. Livingston has commissioned me to ask you if you won't come down and join her for a few moments. Oh, I beg pardon—" He pauses and gives a look expectant of introduction towards Harry Lawrence. The lawyer, following his glance, presents the two young men, and after acknowledging it, Chauncey proceeds glibly, "Awful sorry to have interrupted you."

"Won't you sit down and have a glass of wine and a cigar?" says Southmead hospitably.

"Yes, just one glass and one cigar—a baby cigar—they remind me of cigarettes. I have not more than a moment to deliver my message. You see, Mrs. Ogden Livingston has just come back from Newport, and to-night gave a little theatre party: Daly's 'Divorce,' Clara Morris, Fanny Davenport, Louis James and James Lewis, etc. Have you seen Lewis's Templeton Jitt? It is immense. That muff, Oliver, actually giggled," babbles this youth, commonly called by his intimates Ferdie.

"So, Mr. Oliver Livingston laughed? It must have been very funny," remarks Whitehouse affably.

"Didn't he, when Jitt, the lawyer, got his ears boxed instead of the husband he was suing for divorce. You want to see that play, Southmead; it might give you points in your next application for alimony."

"I am not a divorce lawyer," cries the attorney rather savagely.

"Oh, no telling what might happen in your swell clientele, some day," giggles Ferdie. "But Ollie was scandalized at the placing of a minister on the stage—an Episcopal minister, too."

"Does he expect to use an Episcopal minister soon?" asks the lawyer, suggestively.

"Not very soon, judging by the young lady," grins Ferdie. "The only time Miss Dividends——"

"What the dickens do you call Miss Travenion Miss Dividends for?" interrupts Whitehouse testily.

"You ought to know best; you're her trustee," returns the youth. "Besides, every one called her that at Newport this season, especially the other girls, she is so stunning and they envied her so. Lots of money, lots of beaux and more of beauty. If she didn't have a level head, it would be turned."

"Yes, she has got a brain like her father. Besides, Mrs. Livingston keeps a very sharp eye on her," remarks Southmead.

"Don't she though?" chimes in Mr. Chauncey. "Look at to-night. The widow invited your humble servant to take care of the Amory girl, so that Ollie could have full swing with Miss Dividends—I mean Erma. We are all having supper in the Chinese-room. Mrs. Livingston wishes to see you for a moment on business; Miss Travenion on more important business. They chanced to mention it, and knowing your habits, I thought it very probable you were at supper here. I told them I could find you if you were in the building. I roamed through the *café* and inquired of Rimmer, and he suggested you were upstairs. The head waiter in the restaurant corroborated him. It won't keep you long. Miss Travenion and Mrs. Livingston wish to see you particularly. They are very busy."

"Busy!" cries the lawyer. "What have those two birds of Paradise to do with business?"

"They are packing. They wish to know if you can possibly call on them to-morrow afternoon."

"To-morrow afternoon, Captain Lawrence's business compels my attention."

"Ah, then, to-morrow evening."

"Unfortunately I have promised to deliver an address at the Bar Association Dinner."

"Very well, to-morrow morning."

"Still this young gentleman's business," remarks Mr. Southmead. "It is important and immediate."

"Oh, very well, then," returns Ferdie; "suppose you come down to our supper party *now!* I know what Mrs. Livingston wants to say to you, won't take over three minutes, and Miss Travenion won't occupy you five. Come down and join us? We are pretty well finished."

"But this young gentleman," remarks Whitehouse, smiling at Lawrence.

"Oh, bring Captain Lawrence down with you," and before Southmead can reply to this request, which is given in an off-hand, snappy kind of a way, Ferdie finds his hand grasped warmly in a set of bronzed maniples and Harry Storey Lawrence looking into his eyes with a face full of gratitude, and saying to him, "Certainly! I will run down with you with the greatest pleasure."

"But—" interjects Southmead.

"Oh, it will not inconvenience me in the slightest. It will be rather a pleasure," cries the Westerner.

And before he can urge any further objection to Mr. Ferdinand Chauncey's proposed move, the two younger men have left the room and are walking down-stairs, and the lawyer has nothing to do but to follow after them as rapidly as possible.

The door of the Chinese-room is opened for Mr. Chauncey. As he looks in one thought strikes the mind of the mining man, and that is,—If you would thoroughly appreciate the beauty of women, be without their society for a few months. Then you will know why men rave about them, why men die for them.

No prettier sight has ever come before the eyes of this

young Westerner,—who has still the fire of youth in his veins, but whose life has kept him away from nearly all such scenes as this,—than this one he gazes on with beaming eyes, flushed face, a slight trembling of his stalwart limbs. This room, made bright by Chinese decorations and Oriental color, illuminated by the soft wax lights of the supper table, and made radiant by the presence of lovely women—one of whom—the one his eyes seek—the like of which he has never seen before—Erma Travenion.

CHAPTER II.

MISS EAST.

THE girl stands in an easy, but vivacious, attitude. She has just been telling some story, and growing excited, has got to acting it, to the derangement but beauty of her toilet, as a little bonnet made all of pansies has fallen, and hanging by two light blue ribbons, adorns her white neck instead of her fair hair, which, disordered by her enthusiasm, has become wavy, floating and gold in the light, and red bronze in the shadow.

The party having left the supper table with its fruit, flowers, crystal, silverware and decorated china, are grouped about, looking at her.

The chaperon, Mrs. Livingston, standing near the door, is a widow and forty-five, though still comely to look upon, and the girl behind her is interesting in her own peculiar style, being piquant and pretty. Though it is late in September the weather is still quite warm, and dressed in the light summer costumes of 1871, which gave as charming glimpses of white necks and dazzling arms as those of to-day, either lady would attract the eyes of men: but the glorious beauty of Erma Travenion still holds the Westerner's gaze.

2

Eyes draw eyes, and the young lady returns his glance for a second.

Then Mrs. Livingston speaks : " Why, Chauncey," she says, " I thought you were going to bring Mr. Southmead."

" And I have brought his client," laughs Ferdie. " Mr. Southmead will be here in a minute. He was engaged with Captain Lawrence and could not leave him. So I took the liberty and persuaded Captain Lawrence to join us also. But permit me," and he presents his companion in due form to the hostess of the evening.

While Harry is making his bow, Mr. Southmead enters.

" Ah, Chauncey," he says laughingly, " you have made the introduction, I see. But still, Mrs. Livingston, I think I can give you some information about Captain Lawrence which Ferdinand does not possess. He is a *rara avis*. He has not opened his mouth to a beautiful woman for eight months."

" Excuse me," interposes Lawrence gallantly. " That was before I had spoken to Mrs. Livingston."

This happy shot makes the widow his friend at once. She says : " Not spoken to a beautiful woman for eight months ! Surely there could be no beautiful women about," and her eyes emphasize her words as she looks with admiration on the athletic symmetry the young Western man displays under his broadcloth evening dress.

" Not spoken to a beautiful woman for eight months ! " This is an astonished echo from the two young ladies.

" Yes," replies Southmead laughing. " He has been in southern Utah. He only stopped over night in Salt Lake City on his trip to New York ; he comes from the wilds of the Rocky Mountains."

" The Rocky Mountains ? " cries Erma, whose eyes seem to take sudden interest at the locality mentioned.

A moment after, Mrs. Livingston hastily presents the Western engineer. "Miss Amory—Miss Travenion: Captain Lawrence."

"Not heard the voice of beauty for eight months? That is severe for a military man, Captain Lawrence," laughs Miss Amory, her eyes growing bright, for she is in the habit of going to West Point, to graduating exercises, and loving cadets and brass buttons generally and awfully.

"I was once Captain of an Iowa battery," answers Harry; "for some years after that I was a civil engineer on the Union Pacific Railway, and for the last three I have been a mining engineer in Utah."

"On the Union Pacific Railway," says Miss Travenion, her eyes growing more interested. "Then perhaps you know my father. Won't you sit beside me? I should like to ask you a few questions. But let me present Mr. Oliver Ogden Livingston, Captain Lawrence." She introduces in the easy manner of one accustomed to society the Westerner to a gentleman who has arisen from beside her.

This being remarks, "Awh! delighted," with a slight English affectation of manner, which in 1871 was very uncommon in America, and reseats himself beside Miss Travenion.

"There is another chair on my other hand," says the young lady, indicating the article in question, and looking rather sneeringly at Mr. Oliver for his by no means civil performance.

Consequently, a moment after the young man finds himself beside Miss Travenion, though Mr. Livingston has destroyed a *tête-à-tête* by sitting upon the other hand of the beauty.

Ferdie has grouped himself with Miss Amory and is entering into some society small talk or gossip that apparently interests her greatly, as she gives out every now and then excited giggles and exclamations at the young man's flippant sentences.

Mrs. Livingston is occupied with Mr. Southmead, who has just said : "You brought Louise with you from Newport?"

"Of course," answers the widow. "We have left there for the season." Then noticing that the gentleman's glance is wandering about the room, she continues : "You need not hope to find Louise here. She is only sixteen—too young for theatre parties. The child is in bed and asleep." A moment after their voices are lowered, apparently discussing some business matter.

During this, Erma Travenion appears to be considering some proposition in her mind. This gives Lawrence a chance to contemplate her more minutely than when he picked up her fan on the staircase or as he entered the room. He repeats the inspection, with the same decision intensified : she is the most beautiful woman he has ever seen ; but, dominating even her beauty, is that peculiar and radiant thing we call the charm of manner.

Seated in a languid, careless, dreamy way, as if her thoughts were far from this brilliant supper-room, the unstudied pose of her attitude, gives additional femininity to her graceful figure ; for, when self-conscious, Miss Travenion has an appearance of coldness, even *hauteur;* but there is none of this now.

Her well-proportioned head, supported by a neck of enchanting whiteness, is lighted by two eyes which would be sapphires, were they not made dazzling by the soul that shines through them, reflecting each emotion of her vivacious yet brilliant mind. Her forehead has that peculiar breadth, which denotes that intellect would always dominate passion, were it not for her lips that indicate when she loves, she will love with her whole heart. Her figure, betwixt girlhood and womanhood, retains the graces of one and the contours of the other. The dress she wears brings all this out with wonderful distinctness, for it is jet black, even to its laces,—a color which segregates her from the more brilliant decorations of the room, outlining her exquisite arms, shoulders and bust, in a way that would make her seem a statue of ebony and ivory, were it not for the delicate pink of her lips and nostrils as she softly breathes, the slight compression of her brows, and the nervous tapping of her little foot that just shows itself in dainty boot beneath the laces of her robe. These indicate that youthful and enthusiastic life will in a moment make this dreaming figure a vivacious woman.

As Lawrence thinks this, action comes to her. She says impulsively : " You must let me thank you again for the attention you showed me on the stairway."

"What attention?" asks Mr. Oliver Livingston, waking up also.

"Something you were too occupied with yourself to notice," smiles the young lady. "I dropped my fan as we entered this evening, and this gentleman, though he did not know me, was kind enough to pick it up. But," she continues suddenly, "Captain Lawrence, you can do me a much greater favor."

"Indeed ! How ?" is Harry's eager answer.

"You say that you have been an engineer upon the Union Pacific Railway. What portion of it ?"

"From Green River to Ogden, though I was employed as assistant at one time at Cheyenne."

"From Green River to Ogden ! Then you must have met my father, Ralph Harriman Travenion."

"No, I never had that pleasure," answers the young man, after a moment's consideration.

"But you must have !" cries the girl impulsively. "He was one of the largest contractors on that portion of the road."

" Your father—a railroad contractor ? " answers Harry,
opening his eyes, which appear to the young lady very
large, earnest, and flashing compared to the rather effem-
inate ones of Mr. Livingston.

" Not in New York," laughs Ollie, waving his white
hands. " When here, Mr. Travenion is one of our leading fashionables. Did you see any one dance more grace-
fully than your father did last winter, Miss Erma ?—
though I believe he did have something to do with the
building of the railway out there."

" I don't see how that was possible," suggests Lawrence. " I and my assistants figured all the cross-sec-
tionings of that portion of the work, and I know that none
were accredited to Ralph Travenion. Our largest contractors were Little & Co., Tranyon & Co., Amos Jen-
nings, George H. Smith, and Brigham Young—nearly all
Mormons."

" You are sure ? " says the young lady, knitting her
brows as if in thought.

" Certainly ! "

" This is very curious. Why, I have even had letters
from him on Union Pacific paper."

" Perhaps he was a silent partner in one of the companies," suggests Lawrence, who is very much astonished
to find a girl in New York's most exclusive set, as Miss
Travenion evidently is, connected so intimately with
one of the builders of a railway in the Far West.

" Perhaps you are right," says the young lady contemplatively. " However, I will know all about it myself in a few weeks."

" He is coming to visit you, I presume ? "

" No, but I am going to take a trip to California with
Mrs. Livingston and her party," remarks Erma, " and
en route I expect to meet him—my dear father, whom
I haven't seen for half a year ! " and the girl's eyes light
up with sudden tenderness and pleasure. " *Apropos* of

the trip—excuse me." Here she rises suddenly and passes to the family lawyer.

At his side she says: "Mr. Southmead, if you have finished your business with Mrs. Livingston, I have some for you. I want to inform you that Mrs. Livingston, her daughter Miss Louise, her son Mr. Chauncey, and myself, intend to take a trip to California, and to ask you, as my trustee, if you have any objection to the same. I presume that it is a mere form, as you are not my guardian."

"You have written to your father?" asks Whitehouse hastily.

"No," laughs the girl. "I intend it to be a surprise to papa."

"Then, let me suggest," answers the lawyer, something of a shade passing over his brow, "that you write to Mr. Travenion first."

"Impossible! We have not time : We leave in three days! Fancy—in a little over a week I shall see my father. You wouldn't deprive me of that pleasure, would you, Mr. Southmead?"

"No! but I would suggest that you telegraph him."

"I can't. I have not heard from papa for two weeks, and I do not know his address. Besides, it will be such a surprise!" Miss Travenion has thrown away contemplation from her, and is all brightness and gayety.

"Of course I can have no objections," says Whitehouse.

"Then you don't think it wise?" mutters the girl, with a pout.

"I don't say that. I have no doubt it is all right, and I know your father will be pleased to see you."

"I should think so! The idea of anything else! You know I am the apple of his eye!"

"Yes, I know that," remarks Southmead decidedly.

"Very well, then," returns Miss Travenion; "will you be kind enough to get me a letter of credit on

California and the West for—for twenty thousand
dollars."

This amount for a two or three months' pleasure
trip makes Lawrence open his eyes, and the lawyer gives
a little deprecating shrug of the shoulders.

"Oh, I don't mean to spend it *all*," cries Erma. "I
am not so extravagant as that. Still, it might be convenient. I might want to buy something in the West.
Please get it by to-morrow for me."

"Not later, any way, than the day after," interjects
Mrs. Livingston. "It is impossible to put off our
trip."

"Oh, it had all been decided before you saw me?"
laughs Southmead.

"Certainly. We didn't propose to have any objection
made to our taking Erma with us on our trip," says Mrs.
Livingston, leaving Mr. Ferdie and Miss Amory, and
placing a plump arm round Miss Travenion's waist.

The party have all now risen, apparently ready to
leave, and Lawrence and Southmead are compelled to
say "Good evening."

As he departs, however, Harry astonishes Miss Travenion. She is a little in advance of her party, and
offers him her hand cordially, saying, "Were we not in
disorder on account of our preparations for departure,
I should ask you to come and see me, Captain Lawrence."

"As it is," answers the young man, "I hope to see
you in the West."

"Ah, you expect to be there?"

"Yes; my headquarters must be in Salt Lake for the
next month or two."

"Why, *we* shall be there also," cries Erma. "You
shall show me over your city."

"Excuse me, I am not a Mormon!" answers Lawrence grimly, biting the end of his moustache.

"Oh, of course not! I—I beg your pardon. Yes; I remember now—that awful sect live there—" stammers Miss Travenion. "You'll forgive my ignorance, won't you?" Her eyes have a playful pleading in them that makes her judge very mild.

"On one condition!" he answers eagerly: "that you surely come to Salt Lake."

"Certainly," answers Miss Penitent; "it is there or in Ogden or somewhere about the Rocky Mountains I hope to meet my father."

"I also hope to meet your father some day," replies Harry, in a tone that astonishes the girl, for her beautiful eyes have made him forget he has only met her ten minutes.

She raises these to his inquiringly, and what she sees makes her cheeks grow red. A cordial grip upon her fingers is emphasizing this rapid gentleman's speech.

Miss Travenion draws her hand hastily from his; then says with thoroughbred coldness and *hauteur*, "Perhaps. Good evening!" turns her pretty back upon him and begins to converse with Mrs. Livingston and her party as if no such being as Harry Storey Lawrence existed upon this earth.

A moment after the Westerner finds himself beside Southmead strolling up Fifth Avenue, *en route* for his hotel.

"I'll go with you as far as the Fifth Avenue," remarks the lawyer. "There may be some telegrams awaiting you on your mining business."

"Delighted," says the young man. Then he breaks out hurriedly: "How the dickens does Miss Travenion, who is apparently a butterfly of New York fashion, have a father who, she says, was a contractor on the Union Pacific Railway? You, as her trustee, ought to know."

"Yes—I know!" returns Southmead. Then after a second's pause of contemplation he continues: "And

I'll tell you—it may save you getting a wild idea in your head, young man. Only don't look romantic, because the young lady we are discussing is half-way engaged to another, Mr. Oliver Ogden Livingston."

"Half-way engaged," ejaculates Harry with a sigh. Then he says suddenly, a look of determination coming into his eyes : "Half-way is sometimes a long distance from the winning post," and lapses into silence, smoking his cigar in a nervous but savage manner, while the lawyer continues his conversation.

"Miss Erma Travenion's history is rather a curious one. Her father is an old friend of mine. Her mother was an old friend of mine." This last with a slight sigh of recollection. "Both came of families who have from colonial times occupied leading positions in Manhattan society. Nearly twenty-five years ago, Ralph Harriman Travenion married Ella Travers Schuyler, one of the prettiest girls in the Manhattan set of New York society. Four years after, the young lady we are discussing came into the world. When she was about ten, her mother died, and her father concentrated his affection, apparently, on his only daughter. He was a man of very large fortune, a member of the leading clubs, on the governing committee of one or two of them, a man about town and a swell among swells.—But perhaps to forget his wife, whom I know he loved ; during the sea of speculation that came with the Rebellion, he entered largely into dealing in stocks and gold, in an easy-going sybaritic kind of a way—and Wall Street made almost a wreck of what had once been a very fine fortune. This blow to his pocket was a blow to his pride. He could not endure to live in diminished style among the people who had known him as millionnaire, aristocrat, and *bon vivant*. Shortly after he sold his horses, yacht, villa in Newport, house in town, in short, his whole extensive establishment, and placing his daughter, who was about fourteen years of age at that time, at Miss Hines' Fashionable Academy, in Gramercy Park, he went West.

"When he did so, I thought it was wholly from pride. Now I have become satisfied that it was in the hope of making another fortune, so that when she arrived at young ladyhood, Erma Travenion could assume the position in New York society to which she had been born."

"What makes you think this?" asks Lawrence hurriedly.

"Her father's actions since that time. You see, the Travenions and Livingstons had always been great friends, second cousins in fact, and it had been a kind of family matter and understanding that when Erma grew up, she should marry Mr. Oliver Ogden Livingston, who was then but a boy.

"A—ah! He is the son of the lady we met this evening!"

"Of course!" says the lawyer sharply. "It had been mutually understood between the fathers of the two children that each should settle what was considered in those days a most enormous sum upon their children, that is, one million dollars. The two fathers fondly hoped and expected in those days of smaller fortunes that this would put the young couple on the very top of New York society. When Travenion went West, Oliver's father was still alive. What the interview between the two men was, I do not know; but shortly afterwards, Livingston settled his one million dollars upon his son, and during the succeeding year died. As Mrs. Livingston was very ambitious for her son to make what is called a grand match, it was generally supposed the compact would come to nothing, when, some three years later, in 1868, Mr. Travenion returned from the West and settled on his daughter three hundred thousand dollars, making the Union Trust Company of New York and myself co-trustees. One year after that he again made his appearance here and settled two hundred thousand dollars more, and only eight months ago he once more returned and deposited five hundred thousand in addition, completing the sum of one million dollars, which the Union Trust Company and myself hold as co-trustees for his daughter. One half of the income from this is to be paid to Erma Travenion until she is twenty-five or her marriage. In case of her marriage before that time or upon her arrival at the age of twenty-five, we are to pay the full dividends of this one million dollar investment to the young lady, and at the age of thirty, we are to make the principal over to her, subject to her sole control, use and bequest."

"I am sorry you told me this," says Harry, a trace of agitation in his eyes, and a slight tremble on his moustachioed lip.

"Sorry? Why?" asks the lawyer, turning and looking at the young man.

The answer he gets astonishes him.

"Because I mean to marry her," says the Westerner determinedly, "and I would sooner have a fortune equal to that of my bride; perhaps sooner have her with nothing."

"You are a very extraordinary young man, then," comments Southmead. "But I think her father would not care about her marrying any one except Oliver Ogden Livingston."

"I don't imagine any father would care about seeing his daughter marry that young man I saw at supper," remarks Lawrence, contemplatively, between puffs of his cigar.

"And why not?"

"Because I do not think he is a man, anyway."

"Still, I think Ralph Travenion wishes his daughter to marry Oliver Livingston, because he has settled his million on her."

Here Harry astonishes the lawyer again. He says shortly : "Might not Ralph Travenion have some other reason for settling the million dollars on his daughter ?"

"By Jove !" ejaculates Southmead in astonishment. "What do you mean ?"

"I don't mean anything except the suggestion," remarks the young man. "But here we are in the Fifth Avenue," and the two stride into that great hostelry together, and go to the office, where the clerk says, "Captain Lawrence, a telegram for you." After a glance at its address Harry tears it open, and with a suppressed exclamation passes the despatch to his companion.

"Aha, as I thought," remarks Southmead, glancing over the message. "The Zion's Co-operative Mining Institution has brought suit for part of your Mineral Hill property. Unless you compromise, this will delay the English sale."

"Yes, this takes me back to Utah at once," says the young man. Then he adds with a laughing sigh : "I need that five hundred thousand dollars, or rather my share of it, as soon as possible."

"Ah ! But why this hurry ?"

"Because I'm impatient to make Erma Travenion my wife," says the young man determinedly ; "but I must go up-stairs to pack my trunk, so as to get off by the morning train." Then, after a few minutes' hurried conversation on the details of the business, he bids Southmead good-bye, adding : "Telegraph me any further information at the Sherman House, Chicago."

"You are going to Utah to compromise this matter ?" asks the lawyer, shaking the young man's hand.

"Never !" says Lawrence. "But, for all that, I am going to have a try for the girl."

With that he steps into the elevator of the Fifth Avenue Hotel, leaving Whitehouse Southmead to saunter to the Unity Club and cards in rather a contemplative, though by no means legal, mood, for he chuckles to himself : " Jove ! If that rapid Mr. West should capture rich and lovely Miss East? wouldn't it make Mrs. Livingston wild ? "

CHAPTER III.

HER FATHER'S FRIEND.

"MR. KRUGER, how do you do?" says Miss Erma Travenion, some three days after; turning suddenly from the Cerberus who stands at the gate leading to the out-going trains of the Hudson River Railroad, in the Grand Central Depot, New York, waiting to punch her ticket. Then she calls again with the bright, fresh voice of youth : "Mr. Kruger! Mr. Kruger! Don't you recognize me?" and drawing up her dainty white skirts to give her pretty feet room for rapid movement, pursues a gentleman who, in the rush of the great station, apparently does not notice her.

The ticket puncher looks astonished for a moment, and then promptly and savagely cries, "Next!"

But the "Next!" is Mr. Oliver Ogden Livingston, who has also turned from the entrance, and is gazing after Miss Travenion, an occupation his eyes have become quite used to in the last few months, since her father had finished settling his million upon her.

Livingston, after a second's pause of consideration, says hurriedly to the lady who comes immediately behind him, " Mother, you and Louise had better go to our car. Ferdie will escort you. I will wait for Miss Travenion and see her on board before the train starts."

To this, Mrs. Livingston, who, though fair, plump and forty-five, is of a nervous tendency, cries out, " My Heaven ! She's running out of the depot—she is so impulsive—if anything happens to Erma, what shall I say to her father?" And the chaperon casts anxious glances on her charge, who is still moving in pursuit of the abstracted Mr. Kruger, who is apparently looking for somebody himself.

"NEXT!" cries the ticket man savagely. "Don't block the way!"

"Ferdie, take us in," whispers Miss Livingston, who is immediately behind her mother, and is sixteen, pretty and snippy. "That gateman looks impatient."

"Quick, Louise, or the ticket puncher 'll mistake my head for a ticket," laughs the young man. Then he cries, "Come along, auntie. Don't be frightened. You don't suppose Oliver will ever lose sight of Miss Dividends?" And with a passing wink of inborn knowledge to Ollie, which is returned by a stare prim and savage, Ferdie rushes his aunt and Miss Louise past the portals, towards a private Pullman car, the last of an express train standing ready to move out to Chicago, on a bright September day, of the year of our Lord 1871.

Livingston, relieved of the care of the other ladies of his party, watches his valet, assisted by two maid-servants in caps, carrying the hand-satchels, shawls, and minor baggage of the party to the car, then turns his glance towards Miss Travenion. The savageness leaves his eyes, and a little soft passion takes its place. They follow the movements of the girl with prim rapture, as well they may.

Miss Travenion is just overtaking the man she is pursuing; her eyes, intent upon her chase, sparkle as blue diamonds. From her well-shaped head float, after the fashion of that day, two long curls of hair that would be golden, did not the sun seem to claim them as his own, and permeating them with his fire, make each hair as brilliant as his own bright rays. Above the curls, a summer hat, beneath this, waving locks that crown a marble forehead, perhaps too broad for ancient sculptors' taste, but ideal for modern artists, who love soul in woman; cheeks rosy with health, lips red and moist as coral washed by sea-spray, the upper one laughing, the under one eager; a chin that tells of resolution, a figure light as a fairy's, but with the contours of a Venus; clothed in a travelling gown that does not disguise the graces that it robes; one eager hand outstretched towards the flitting Kruger, the other grasping firmly, yet lightly, the skirt and draping it about her, plucking its laces and broideries from out the dust, and showing as she trips along a foot and ankle that a lover would rave about—a sculptor mould.

This is what makes Ollie Livingston's little heart beat one or two pats to the second more rapidly than normal, showing how small his soul, how puny his manhood, for no more charming girl has ever been looked upon than Erma Travenion, as she lays her well-gloved patrician hand upon Lot Kruger's big Western arm, even amid the crowds of this great railroad station of New York, where beauties—American beauties at that—have given forth to admiring humanity each glance and gesture, grace and tone, that allure and conquer mankind.

Mr. Kruger, also in pursuit of some one, has just found his man, and thus Erma is enabled to overtake him. As she comes up he is in such earnest conversation with a small, weazened-face, ferret-like individual that he does not note the approaching beauty.

Were Miss Travenion intent upon anything but speaking to the Westerner she could hardly avoid appreciating the peculiarity of the interview she is breaking in upon—Kruger all command, the other answering with a docility unusual among Americans, and at times saluting in almost a cringing manner the man addressing him. As Erma stands for a moment behind Kruger, she hears him say tersely and sharply to his companion: "Jenkins, there are four hundred more coming on the *Scotia*, due

to-morrow, and three hundred here now. We have contracted with the Central for the U. P. to take them at
forty dollars a head. The other crowd I will wait for."

Mr. Jenkins's reply Miss Travenion does not catch, as
she places her hand on Lot Kruger's arm and he swings
around suddenly and quickly to see who interrupts him.
His face for a moment has a startled and annoyed, perhaps
an angry, expression upon it, but as he turns and gazes
upon Erma, smiles chase sternness away from his features,
even as they did upon Livingston's flaccid face ; the
young lady's beauty seeming to have a similar effect
upon both men, though Kruger's virile passion is ten
times as strong as that of the prim New Yorker.

Miss Travenion says hurriedly : "Mr. Kruger, I saw
you here. I couldn't help following you. You have just
come from the West—you have seen my father lately?
Tell me, is he well? I haven't had a letter from him for
a fortnight."

He cries, "Miss Ermie, I am mighty glad your
daddy hain't written, for if he had, I guess I shouldn't
have heard your pretty voice, unless I hunted you up at
your boarding-school."

"Oh, you wouldn't have found me there. I have not
been at Miss Hines' for nearly ten months."

"Ah, I see : graduated in all the arts and sciences and
music and etceteras," remarks Kruger, his eyes, piercing,
though gray, looking over the exquisite girl before him,
and growing red and inflamed with some potent emotion,
as he concludes rather huskily : "I might have seen
you have left school. You have developed as be-uti-
fu-l-ly as one of the lambs of Zion," though, even as he
says this, Lot Kruger seems to repress himself and from
this time on to keep a tight rein upon some peculiarity
that is strong within him.

"But papa, papa ; you haven't told me of him," exclaims the young lady, who seems little interested in Mr.

3

Kruger's remarks, and only intent upon information as to her absent loved one, for as she speaks of her father, the girl's voice grows soft, and tender tears come into her eyes.

"Oh, your dad's all right, Sissy," goes on Kruger, in his easy Western way. "You needn't water his grave yit. Reckon your pap has had too much railroad and mine on his hands to be able to even eat for the last month. I know, for I am interested in the mine a leetle." Then he tells her quite shortly that her father has so many big enterprises beyond the Rockies that he is an "uncommon busy man."

As he does so, Erma is gazing at him and thinking what an extraordinary individual her father has found for a partner, beyond the Rocky Mountains ; for Lot Kruger, as he stands before her, would be a striking figure, even in Western America, which produces curious types and more curious individuals.

He stands six feet two in his stockings, and has proportionate shoulders and limbs, which are covered with ample black broadcloth, after the Sunday-best-clothes Southern and Western fashion of the year 1871 ; the coat of Prince Albert style, open and unbuttoned and falling below the knees of his trousers, that are cut in what was then called the "peg-top" pattern ; his shirt front as ample as his coat is large, crumpled and protruding from out a low-cut vest and adorned by a splash or two of tobacco juice ; his hat a stove-pipe, its plush rumpled and brushed against the grain,—all make him a man of mark. From off his broad shoulders rises a neck strong as that of a buffalo, and supporting a massive head covered with long red hair, and a face from the nose up that of a good-natured Newfoundland, but below the jaws and teeth of a bull-dog ; the eyes gray as a grizzly's, and steely when in anger ; while, thrown over all this is a kind of indescribable, semi-Puritanical, semi-theological air that makes one wonder, "Is this man a backwoods preacher turned mining speculator, or a reformed cowboy made into a missionary?"

At present, as he gazes at Miss Travenion, Lot Kruger's face is nearly all that of the Newfoundland dog; and Erma, though she thinks him a curious associate for her father, with his Eastern breeding and education and New York manners, still considers Mr. Kruger, though crude, very good-natured and rather meek.

Oh, these judgments of women, whose instinct *never* mistakes character,—where one out of ten women guesses the villain at sight and brags of it forever, the other nine mistaken sisters are swindled and perchance undone, and say nothing about woman's unfailing intuition, but still keep on guessing wrong until the crack of doom.

. As Erma gazes on Kruger he continues : " Bound for a summer jaunt, I guess,—some watering place where the boys and gals will have a high time—Nar-regani-set or Newport or Sarietogy, Miss Ermie. Your dad is very liberal to you, I understand,—puts up the greenbacks in wads."

" My father is generosity itself to me," returns Miss Travenion rather haughtily, for she is by no means pleased with the freedom of Mr. Kruger's remarks. " But the Newport season is finished, and I have accepted Mrs. Ogden Livingston's invitation to be one of her party. Under her charge I am going to take a run across the continent, and *en route* for California I shall drop in upon papa, and astonish and enrapture him."

" Wh—e—w ! " This would be a prolonged whistle, did not Kruger check it savagely, and cut it off in the middle. Then he goes on stammeringly, but eagerly :— " Your dad doesn't know of—of your intention ? " an amazed expression lighting up his honest gray eyes, which is forced down by his set, calm, repressive lower face.

"No, he doesn't guess that I'm coming. Won't it be a surprise to dear papa when I step lightly into his office, and say : 'Behold your daughter!'" laughs Erma.

"Yes,—I—reckon it will be a—sockdolager!" mutters her father's friend contemplatively. Then says suddenly, "You haven't telegraphed him?"

"Certainly not ; I wish to surprise him. Besides, I shall be with him almost as soon as a telegram, now that this wonderful Pacific Railway is finished," babbles the girl. "It will only take seven days to far-off California, and Ogden is two days this side of San Francisco, I understand."

"Yes, your time-table's all right," returns Mr. Kruger. Then he asks quietly, "Who's in your party?"

"Oh, Mrs. Livingston, of course ; her daughter, Louise ; Mr. Ferdinand Chauncey, her nephew, and her son, who is now just beside me. Mr. Livingston, Mr. Lot Kruger, my father's friend."

The two men acknowledge this introduction ; then Livingston says hastily, "Miss Travenion, excuse me interrupting your conversation, but the train leaves in five minutes, and I presume my mother is even now anxious—perhaps already hysterical."

"Very well, then," returns Erma. "Good-bye, Mr. Kruger. I am so glad to hear that papa is all right. Shall we see you in the West? We shall be in California two months, and perhaps on our return—" And she extends a gracious hand to the Westerner.

But Lot laughs : "You'll see me before then. I'm going on the same train. You needn't have run after me, if you had known that I go out on the Chicago · express also." With this, he gives the little gloved hand that is already in his a hearty squeeze, that makes the blood fly out of the girl's fingers into her face, and turns hurriedly to the man he had previously addressed, who has been waiting for him just out of ear-shot.

A moment after, Miss Travenion is conducted by her escort through the crowd of the great station, past the ticket man at the gate, and on board the train, where Mrs. Livingston is already in a state of animated nervous rhapsody, muttering, " The cars are moving! They *are* left behind ! What'll I say to that girl's father ? " and other exclamations indicative of approaching spasms.

" Forgive me, dear Mrs. Livingston," says Erma, apologetically. " I couldn't help asking about my father. I haven't seen him for so long, and have had no letter for two weeks."

" He's a rather curious creature, that friend of papa," remarks Ollie superciliously.

" Very," answers Erma. " But my father, in his railroad enterprises, must be thrown among men of all ranks, grades and conditions."

" Oh, certainly," assents Oliver. " You remember that individual with the free and easy manners who invited himself to mother's supper party the other night."

" If you mean Captain Lawrence," remarks Ferdie, tossing himself into the conversation, " I can tell you he didn't invite himself—I did that part of the business myself. And as to his manners being free and easy, I think, considering he hadn't spoken to a pretty woman for a year, he did very well—under the circumstances. If I'd been in his place I'd have probably kissed the ladies all round."

This assertion is greeted by a very horrified " Oh, Ferdinand ! " from Mrs. Livingston, and screams of laughter from Louise.

Miss Travenion, who remembers Captain Lawrence's last glance and hand squeeze and words, grows slightly red about her cheeks and sinks upon a seat and gazes out of an open car window.

As for Mr. Kruger, the moment he has left Erma

Travenion, he has dropped all the laziness of a New-foundland dog, and assumes the activity of a terrier. He has said hurriedly but determinedly to his satellite, " Jenkins, you stay and wait for the four hundred coming on the Scotia. Forward the other three hundred by Davis, who came from Wales with them."

" But—" Jenkins is about to interrupt.

" No time to discuss this 'ere matter," says Kruger with a snap. " I must go West on this train. It's somethin' you can't understand, but more important than all the Welsh cows that we've brought over these ten years—you do as I tell ye."

" Yes, Bishop," answers the man humbly and goes away, as Mr. Kruger, whose plans the sudden meeting with Miss Travenion seems to have changed, produces a pass from the New York Central Railway, hurries to the sleeping-car office, buys a ticket to Chicago, and boards the train almost as it begins to move out for the West, and placing himself in a smoking compartment, goes to chewing tobacco in a meditative but seemingly contented manner, as after a little time he remarks to himself, " How things seem to be coming to Lot Kruger and Zion together."

CHAPTER IV.

MR. FERDIE BEGINS HIS WESTERN INVESTIGATIONS.

THE train rattles out of New York, and crossing the Harlem, skirts that pretty little salt water river ; as Miss Travenion settles herself lazily in her seat, with a graceful ease peculiar to her, for the girl has a curious blending of both style and beauty, giving her a patrician elegance of manner that makes gracious even the slight tendency to *hauteur* in her manner and voice.

The sun shines upon her face, and she turns it from the morning beams, and gazing towards the West, thinks of her father. Her eyes grow gentle, her mobile features expectant with hope, and tender with love ; and Oliver Livingston, who is reading a New York journal, glances up from it, and noting Erma's face thinks, "She really does love me, dear girl, though she is so cold, which is much better form till we are regularly engaged," and decides to give her a chance to admit her affection to him formally before the end of their summer tour, for this prim gentleman actually adores the young lady he is looking at as much as his diminutive soul can love anything, except himself.

At present he does not know how small his soul is, but rather thinks it is large and noble and very magnanimous. He has had no occasion so far to test its dimensions, his life up to this time having been quite narrow ; and though he has travelled, it has not brought much into his brain, save some strong, high church notions he has imported from Oxford, to which university this young gentleman had been sent to complete his education after Harvard ; his mother having an idea it might get him into English society, and perhaps permit him to make a great European match. This was before Erma's father had made his million dollar settlement upon her ; Mrs. Livingston having been one of the first of those pioneers from New York who passed over to England and replaced the social chains of the Mother Country upon her,—those her grandfather and other American patriots had fought to throw off, together with the political ones of George the Third, his Majesty of glorious memory.

Upon his return to New York, Mr. Ollie had signalized his advent by dragging his mother and sister to Saint Agnes's from their old pew at Grace Church, the ritual of that place not being sufficiently Puseyitic for

his views ; his father, the elder Livingston, who had no
religion to mention save certain maxims of business and
the rules of his club, being, fortunately for his son's high
church movement, dead.

This performance of the heir of the house had made
his mother think him a saint ; as, indeed, to do the
young man justice, he wished to be ; and had Ollie Livingston elected to follow any profession, he would doubtless have turned to the ministry ; but his million of
dollars perhaps dulled his incentive for work, and after
his return from England, the young man had done
nothing ; but as Ferdie had irreverently expressed it,
"had done that nothing GRANDLY."

And why should he work ?   He had money enough to
command any ordinary luxury of life.   As for position,
was he not a Livingston, and could he add additional
honor to that old Knickerbocker name ? thought his
mother.

There was only one trouble in all their family affairs,
and that was removed by the settlement Mr. Travenion
had made upon Ollie's *fiancée*, for as such Mrs. Livingston already regarded Erma.   In order to make the
settlement upon his son, the elder Livingston had culled
his best securities and most gilded collaterals ; those
left for the support of his widow and daughter, not being
so stable, had depreciated in the last few years, and
Mrs. Livingston's income had dwindled until it was not
what she considered it should be for a lady of her station.
Now, of course, if Ollie married a very rich wife, he
could be very liberal to his mother and sister, and that
point had been happily settled by the million-dollar
settlement upon Miss Travenion.

It is some thought of this that is in Erma's mind once
or twice in her first day's journey towards the West.
The girl loves Mrs. Livingston, who had been a companion of Erma's mother, and had been very kind to the

child even after her father's reverses, and had frequently visited Miss Hines' Academy in Gramercy Park, and had the little Erma, now wholly orphaned by her mother's death and father's absence, to her great house on Madison Square, where she had been regaled *en princess* and sent back to the boarding school made happy with good things to eat and presents that make children's hearts glad.

This, Miss Travenion does not forget, now that her father's settlements upon her have made her probably as great an heiress in her own right as any girl of her circle in Manhattan society.

This peculiar position of Mrs. Livingston had been pretty well known to Erma, and it seemed to compel her to make no protest when the widow had taken her from the seclusion of Miss Hines' Academy at the beginning of the winter and brought her out, with much blowing of social trumpets and flowers and fiddling at Mrs. Livingston's Madison Square mansion—and also had chaperoned her at Newport.

Therefore, she has rather grown to consider herself set apart for Oliver's wife, and as such has turned a deaf ear to the many men who, on slight encouragement, would be more than happy and more than ready to woo a young lady who has gorgeous beauty, a million of dollars of her own and a father of indefinite Western wealth, which, magnified by distance, has increased to such Monte Cristo proportions, that it has gained for her the title, among her set, of "Miss Dividends."

Besides any notion of gratitude to Mrs. Livingston, Erma knows that this match with Ollie is her father's wish. On one of his visits to New York, she had once hinted her desire to visit and live with him in the West, and had been promptly refused in terms as stern as Ralph Travenion could bring himself to use to his daughter, for whom he seemed to have a very tender love, and in doing so he had indicated that his wishes were that she fulfil the arrangement he had made with his old-time friend, the elder Livingston.

"Marry Oliver," he had said. "He is in your rank—the position to which you were born, Erma. Live in the East. The West is, perhaps, the best place to make money, but New York is *par excellence* the place to enjoy it. Some day—perhaps sooner than you expect, I shall join you here, and settle down to my old life as club man again," and Ralph Travenion looks towards the Unity Club, upon whose lists his name still stands, and of whose smoking-room he is still an *habitué* on his visits to Manhattan, rather longingly from his parlor in the Brevoort House, at which hotel he always stopped, in contradistinction to most of his comrades from the Plains, who are more apt to register at the Fifth Avenue or the Hoffman.

It was on one of these visits at the Brevoort that Erma had chanced to meet Mr. Lot Kruger, and circumstances compelling the same, had received introduction to him.

"Ha! a new convert to Zion!" the Westerner had cried out, looking rather curiously at the beautiful girl of nineteen, who had entered unannounced into Ralph Travenion's apartments.

But her father had simply said : "My daughter, Miss Erma, let me present Mr. Kruger, a business associate of mine," and had so dismissed the affair, though several times afterward the Westerner had chanced to be at Travenion's apartments when Erma called, and once or twice he had appeared at Miss Hines' Academy, bearer, as he said, of news from her father to Miss Travenion, to the amusement, astonishment and giggles of her fellow-pupils and the dismay of the schoolmistress, who thought Mr. Kruger a species of Western border ruffian or bandit.

However, as she sits and meditates, the thought that

she is drawing nearer and nearer to her loved father, drives all else out of Erma Travenion's head, and she watches the wave-washed banks of the beautiful Hudson, and as they pass by says, "One more tree nearer papa— one more island nearer papa—one more town nearer papa," and later in the day, they having got off the New York Central, she murmurs *"One more railroad nearer papa,"* and grows happier and happier as the cars bear her on.

So the day passes. Her companions have settled down to their journey, and are passing their time in cards or novel reading, and Miss Travenion has plenty of opportunity for reflection, for Ollie notices that the girl seems to wish to be left to herself, and only ventures occasional remarks when passing objects demand them.

Mr. Kruger, awed perhaps by the private car, which was much more of a rarity and luxury in 1871 than it is to-day, does not intrude upon the young lady or her party, though Erma notices when she gets off at the large stations for exercise that Lot's eyes seem to follow her about, as if he were interested in her for her father's sake.

Thus the night comes and goes, and during the next day, the 1st of October, the party pass through Chicago, just then waiting to be burned in order that it may become great.

So, running over the prairies two days and a few hours after leaving New York, they arrive at Council Bluffs, and take ferry across the Missouri River, no bridge at this time crossing that great but uncertain and shifting stream.

During this two days' journey from New York to the Missouri, a considerable change has taken place in the minds of some of the members of the party as to their proposed jaunt to the Rocky Mountains and beyond. This has chiefly been brought about by Mr. Ferdie, who, having purchased a book entitled " *Facts About the Far West*," has been regaling himself with the same, and devoting a considerable portion of his time explaining and elucidating the knowledge he thinks he has gained from it to Mrs. Livingston, producing a very distressing effect upon that plump lady's nervous system.

These "*Facts About the West*" consist chiefly of anecdotes of the border ruffian kind, descriptions of various atrocities, Indian massacres, Mormon outrages and vigilance committees, and are of such a very highly colored and blood-curdling description that Mr. Chauncey himself remarks, as he finishes the volume : " If these are *facts* about the West, I think the *fiction* will be too rich for my blood ! " Though half-believing the same, this young gentleman imagines he has acquired in his two days between New York and Council Bluffs, considerable knowledge of the manners of the Western frontiersman, border-ruffians, stage-drivers, Indians, Mormons, and buffaloes.

A number of the more blood-curdling anecdotes he has detailed to Mrs. Livingston at odd times, enjoying her shudderings at such stories as that of the waiter in the New Mexico hotel, who shot the Chicago drummer to death because he declined to eat the eggs and said they were incipient chickens ; also, a few of the more cruel exploits of celebrated Johnnie Slade, the murderous superintendent of a division of the Ben Holliday's stage line, together with a full, true and accurate account of the atrocious butchery of one hundred and thirty three men, women and children by the notorious John D. Lee, of Utah, the Mormon bishop, and a portion of the Mormon militia, disguised as Indians, that occurred in 1857, and now known under the head of the Mountain Meadow Massacre; "The Last Shot of Joaquin, the California Bandit," etc., etc.

These revelations of Western atrocity Mr. Ferdinand is

delighted to see produce upon the nerves of Mrs. Livingston effects more demoralizing than the morphine habit.
And he would continue his narrations, with much *gusto*,
to the agitated Mrs. Livingston, did not Erma, who has
been listening indifferently to his tales of blood, suddenly, at her first opportunity, lead the chuckling Ferdie
aside, and, placing two flaming eyes upon him, whisper :
" Not another of your Western horrors to your aunt ! "
Then her voice grows pathetic, and she mutters:
"Would you frighten her so that she retreats from her
journey and takes me back to New York, and deprives me
of seeing my father—the joy I am looking forward to
minute by minute, and hour by hour."

This oration, emphasized by savage glances and made
pathetic by flashing eyes, has a great effect on Mr. Ferdinand, and he promises silence, remarking to himself :
"What a stunner that Erma is, and only out of boarding
school ten months."

As it is, when Ferdie first looks upon the Missouri
River and utters, "The West is now before me. I feel
as if I knew it very well from my guide-book," tapping
his blood-curdling volume. "Now for a practical experience of the same," adding to this one or two
attempts at Indian war-whoops, the effect of his narra-
tives has been so great on Mrs. Livingston that she puts
her plump hands over her pale blue eyes and shudder-
ingly mutters : "The West—shall I ever live to come
out of it ? " and would take train immediately for
Eastern civilization, were it not that she fears the laughter of her daughter, Louise, and the sneers of Oliver,
her son, who has several times pooh-poohed Ferdie s
anecdotes of Rocky Mountain life, and once or twice,
during his more atrocious recitals, has ejaculated
" Bosh ! "

As she descends from her car at Council Bluffs, she
lays one trembling hand on her son's arm, and makes

one half-hearted expostulation, " Don't you think, since
we are compelled to leave our private car here, we had
better end the trip and return to New York immediately ? "

This Mr. Oliver silences by a stern " What ! Our
tickets already bought for San Francisco ? Besides
that, Van Wyke Stuyvesant has just come back with his
mother and sisters, and pronounces the trip delightful,
and I don't wish Van Wyke, who is something of a brag-
gart, to be able to talk of the Yosemite and Big-trees
and I be unable to say I have been there also. Besides,
Erma is looking forward to meeting her father."

Thus compelled, Mrs. Livingston nervously accepts her
son's escort to the ferry boat, and the party cross the
Missouri River to take cars at Omaha on the Union
Pacific Railway—Mr. Oliver, calmly indifferent to his
mother's feelings, and only intent upon using some of
the chances of the journey for making his romantic
declaration to Miss Travenion.

It will give that young lady, he imagines, the opportunity she is anxiously awaiting, to accept his distin-
guished name, large fortune and small heart ; though did
he but guess it, Miss Travenion has but one thought in
her soul—fifteen hundred miles nearer papa !

Mr. Chauncey, however, is very anxious for the wonders of the border land he has read about, crazy to
see a herd of buffaloes, and determined to investigate
Western matters for himself generally, in order to have
some rare stories of frontier life with which to make
his Eastern college chums open their eyes over social
spreads at the " D. K. E.," for this young gentleman will
enter Harvard as freshman next term. An Alma Mater of
which he is already very proud *in futuro*, and in which
he is very anxious to distinguish himself, not as a reading man, but as a Harvard man—a being, who, this
young gentleman fondly imagines, has the beauty of an

Adonis, the muscle of a Sullivan, the pluck of a bull-terrier, the brain of a Macchiavelli, and the morals of a Don Juan, disguised by the demeanor and bearing of a Lord Chesterfield.

So the young man springs eagerly ashore on the Nebraska side of the Missouri, and cries out in a laughing voice : " Omaha ! All aboard for the Rockies and buffaloes and Indians and scalpings ! " exclamations which make the widow's nerves tingle and the widow's plump hands shake a little, as her son assists her across the gang-plank.

Then, his mother being landed, Ollie turns to offer the same attention to Erma, but to his astonishment he is anticipated in his act of gallantry by the Western Mr. Kruger.

This gentleman, apparently, near his native heath, has grown bolder, and as he expresses it to himself, " has been do'en the perlite " to Miss Travenion, indicating to her the various points of interest in Omaha as seen from the river, together with the Union Pacific Railway bridge, which is at this time in process of construction.

" Your daddy and I once spent four hours in winter trying to get across this river, Sissy, and were mighty nigh froze to death doing it, and if it had not been for my U. S. blanket overcoat that I picked up when Johnston was out thar invadin' us "—he checks himself shortly here and mumbles : " I reckon your old man would have given in. But here we air—Permit the hand of fellowship over the step-off ! "

This allusion to her father is received by a grateful " thank you " from the young lady, who, if she has read of Albert Sydney Johnston's campaign in Utah has forgotten the same, and she accepts Mr. Kruger's aid across the gang-plank in so easy and affable a manner that Lot proffers his further escort to the omnibus waiting to bear this young lady up the hill toward what is called the railroad depot in Omaha. Having assisted her into the 'bus with rather effusive gallantry, and noting during his attentions a ravishing ankle in silken hose that makes his fatherly eyes grow red and watery, he remarks with a chuckle to himself as he sees the New York beauty drive off : " If Miss High-Fallutin' should come to Zion in the Far West, oh Saints of Melchisedec ! " and is so overcome by his emotions that he almost misses the last transfer omnibus.

So, it comes to pass that in the course of a few minutes they all find themselves at that ramshackle affair that was, and is now, for that matter, termed the Western Union Depot in Omaha. Here the train is drawn up, ready for its race towards the West. Attached to it are two Pullman cars, in one of which Erma's party have engaged their accommodations, which consist of a rear stateroom, occupied by Mrs. Livingston and her daughter, a forward stateroom, which has been engaged for Miss Travenion and her maid. The section next his mother's being occupied entirely by Oliver, that young man always looking after his own comfort and luxury very thoroughly ; while a section in the forward end of the car, next Miss Travenion's stateroom, has been set apart for Mr. Ferdinand Chauncey in order that he may be situated so as to give Erma any masculine assistance or protection she may require.

Of course, this is by no means so convenient for the New York party as the private car, which had been placed at their service by a relative of Mrs. Livingston, one of the magnates of the Pennsylvania Railway, but it had been considered by Mr. Oliver best to submit to the more contracted accommodations found upon a general sleeping car than to the exorbitant charges of the Western railways.

Miss Travenion has already made herself comfortable

in her stateroom by the aid of her maid, a pretty French girl, who is about as useless a one as could have been selected for this trip, save in the matter of feminine toilet; when glancing into the open portion of the sleeping car, Erma gets a little surprise. She sees Captain Harry Storey Lawrence entering the same, and placing his *impedimenta* in the section opposite Ferdie's, which from its location is also next to her stateroom. She gives the young man a slight bow, which he acknowledges with military courtesy, a little red showing under the tan of the sun upon his hardy cheeks; but thinks only passingly of the matter, judging it a mere chance of travel, she having already heard the gentleman state that he was returning to Utah.

She would probably pay more attention to the affair did she know that what she considers a mere accident of travel, has been brought about on the part of the young man by deliberate design.

Lawrence having finished his business in Chicago, and his telegrams from Southmead received at the Sherman House indicating that there was no immediate hurry for his presence in Salt Lake, that young gentleman had said to himself, "Why not travel with *her?* Three days in a Pullman sleeper are equal to a voyage at sea. Before my arrival at Salt Lake, *she* shall have better acquaintance with me than a few words in a Delmonico supper room can produce." Actuated by this idea, the captain had journeyed leisurely to Omaha, and discovering the location of Erma's stateroom, had promptly selected the section next to it for the trip to the West.

Very shortly after this, with much ringing of bell and much blowing of whistle, the train gets into motion, and passing out of the Omaha depot, in a few minutes is climbing a little ascent over which it will pass into the valley of the Platte, to run along endless plains till the

4

snowy summits of the Rocky Mountains come into view on the Western horizon.

To the south, a low range of hills is bordering the river; to the north prairies, nothing but prairies; to the west nothing but prairies, save two long lines of rails that run straight as an arrow towards the setting sun till they seem to come together and be one.

Gazing at these, her eyes full of expectant happiness and hope, Miss Travenion murmurs, "At the end of these, one thousand and odd miles away, my father," and the green prairies of Nebraska grow very beautiful to her, and the soft southern wind, as it enters the car windows, seems very pleasant to her, and the rays of the setting sun ·make the green grass lands and the long reaches of the Platte River flowing over its yellow quicksands and dotted with its little cottonwood islands seem like a landscape of Heaven to her.

Then Ferdie comes in, looking eagerly out of the car window, and whispers: "Do you see any buffaloes yet? I have got a revolver and a sporting rifle to kill them." A second after he ejaculates, "What's that!"

And Erma starts and echoes "What's that?"

For it is a sound these two have never heard the like of before—the shriek of the Western train book agent— not the pitiful note of the puny Eastern vender, but the wild whoop of the genuine transcontinental fiend, who in the earlier seventies went bellowing through a car like a calliope on a Mississippi River boat.

"Bre-*own's* prize candies! Twenty-five cents a box, warranted fresh and something that'll make you feel pleased and slick in every one of 'em—Bre-own's prize candies."

Being of a speculative turn of mind, Ferdie invests in one or two of these, and he and Erma open them together and laugh at their bad luck, for Ferdie has won a Jew's harp, worth about a cent, and she is the happy possessor of a brass thimble, and the candies, apparently, have been manufactured before Noah's Ark put to sea. While joking about this, a new idea seems to strike Ferdie.

The news-boy, who has gathered up his packages after making his trades on the sharpest of business principles, is leaving the car. Mr. Chauncey asks him if he has any Western literature.

"I always have everything," cries the young man. "Give you 'The Scout of the Plains,' or 'Long Har, the Hermit of the Rockies,' for twenty-five cents."

"I don't want fiction; facts are what I'm after," says Ferdie, interrupting him.

"Then I'll accommodate also," remarks the youth, and going away, he returns after a few minutes bearing four or five bound volumes, entitled, "The Oatman Girls' Captivity among the Apaches," "The Construction of the Union Pacific Railway," "The Life and Adventures of Jim Beckworth, the Naturalized Crow Chief," "Kit Carson, the Pioneer," "Fremont's Explorations" and "Female Life among the Mormons, by the Wife of an Elder of the Latter-Day Saints."

"Facts come higher," he says, "than lies. These are bound books, and will cost you all the way from $1.50 up to $4. But you can turn 'em in at the end of the trip, if you want, and I will let you have fifty per cent. on them. I had sooner you did it that way, because then *I'll* bag the profit, not my boss."

Whereupon, Ferdie selects "Kit Carson," "The Building of the Union Pacific Railway," and "Female Life among the Mormons," tendering a ten-dollar bill, for which he receives very little change, but making the agreement for the return of the books on arrival at Ogden, much to the delight of the news-agent, who remarks oracularly, "Buck Powers is never quite left."

"Oh, that is your name, is it?" says Mr. Chauncey.

" Probably you know a good deal about the West your-self ? "

"I was born in Chicago," answers the boy proudly, "and railroaded ever since I was corn high."

" Ah, a railroad man ? "

"You bet! I've run on the C. B. & Q., I have," re-marks Buck, his voice growing proud, "and any man that has run on de boss road of the West out of Chicago, can call himself a railroad man and nothin' else."

In this exaltation of the Chicago, Burlington & Quincy, Buck was by no means alone in the early seventies, for somehow that was considered the great road west of the Mississippi, and all who were connected with it from a switchman up, seemed to be very proud of the C. B. & Q., and to run upon it into Chicago, appeared to them to be the acme of railroad bliss and happiness, which was the acme of all happiness. So they kicked off tramps with a proud kick, and they coupled freight cars with a self-satisfied air, and they received deaths with complaisance as defective couplings broke and box cars crashed together, and they made up passenger trains and ran locomotives with the haughty air of men belonging to the most prominent road in that great country which centred in Chicago, to which the rest of America, espe-cially the East, was but an attachment.

" Oh, you are a railroad man—a *Western* railroad man. Perhaps you can tell me about the Rocky Mountains ? "

" What I can't tell you about the Rockies and the U. P. ain't worth knowing," remarks Buck. "After I get through with this candy trip, and give 'em a rattle or two on books, notions and fruit, I'll come back and give you some eye-openers, because I can see you're going to be a good trader." Thus tagging on business with pleasure and self-glorification, Buck Powers proceeds on his way through the cars, shouting in a voice that drowns the roll of the wheels and the tooting of the locomotive :

"Bre-*own's* prize candies ! Twenty-five cents a package ! Warranted fresh and *genuine*, and each package guaranteed to contain a donation ! It is your last chance to-night ! Last chance to-night for *Bre*-own's prize candy and Chicago chewing gum ! "

During this interview, Miss Travenion has looked on with an amused glance. She is astounded that one so small can make so great a noise, for Mr. Buck Powers is but five feet and five inches high, and rather slight, skinny, and wiry of frame, but his voice is like that of Goliath of Gath, with occasional staccatos stolen from the midnight yelp of the coyote of the plains.

As the boy's howls die away in the next car, she says suddenly to Ferdie, "What are you going to do with those books ? "

" Amuse auntie with them."

" That I forbid you to do. No more fibs about the West to Mrs. Livingston. Do you want her to have a nervous fever ? "

" Very well," remarks Ferdinand, contemplatively. " If you object to my instructing auntie, I will keep them for my own amusement and knowledge." Then he cries suddenly, " By George, wasn't that a buffalo ? " and throws up the car window, and looks out excitedly, to the serious danger of his caput, for the train is running through a small town.

And Erma laughs and says, " No, it's a cow."

Just here the conductor comes in and makes everybody on the car alert and happy, for he cries : " GRAND ISLAND ! THIRTY MINUTES FOR SUPPEP ! "

CHAPTER V.

THE GRAND ISLAND EATING-HOUSE.

BUT with this announcement comes another sensation to Miss Travenion.

Ollie Livingston has been engaged most of the afternoon trying to make the trip comfortable for his mother, for, whatever may be his other failings, he certainly is a dutiful and attentive son.

As the train slackens its speed, he passes to Miss Travenion's stateroom, and remarks : " You have heard the conductor announce supper. Ferdie, take care of Louise and her mother. I will see to Erma." A moment after he ejaculates nervously: " I'll just wash my hands, and be with you in a moment," and moves hurriedly back to the gentlemen's wash-room at the rear of the car, leaving Erma alone.

Miss Travenion makes her own preparations in the privacy of her stateroom, and steps out to find herself cut off from the rest of her party by her fellow-passengers, who have risen hurriedly, and are crowding *en masse* through the aisles, anxious to get to their evening meal as rapidly as possible, most of them being old Western travellers and knowing that if they wish to get a good supper, it is best for them to be among the first rush upon the viands of a Pacific railroad eating-house.

The train has stopped, and caught in the crowd, Miss Travenion finds herself swept out upon the front platform of the car ; a couple of stout Western women crowd past her, shoving her nearly off the platform. The Pullman porter shouts to her to look out. She has a hurried vision of Mr. Lot Kruger rushing to her assistance in the next car, and blocked in the aisle and struggling to squeeze past Buck Powers, who has been caught in the supper rush and who is dashing about like a fiend to save his wares from destruction.

She hears a voice that is half-way familiar say incisively : " This way, Miss Travenion, at once ! " and looking down, sees Harry Lawrence's stalwart arm uplifted to assist her from the car. She puts out two little gloved hands. These are eagerly seized upon, and in an instant she is lifted lightly to the ground.

Here, blushing very slightly, she murmurs, " Thank you, Captain Lawrence ! "

" I am glad you remember my name," answers the young man in a very happy voice.

Then he continues rapidly, " Excuse me a second. Your maid does not appear to know what to do." And he assists the French abigail to alight with as much care, if perhaps not as much ceremony, as he did the mistress.

" Yes," replies Erma. " We travelled by a private car as far as Omaha, and, of course, had our meals on board of it. Therefore, Marie was rather disconcerted— as, to tell the truth, so was I."

" Ah, then, you *do* need my assistance, if you want a meal," says Harry quickly, for the gong is sounding very wildly outside the eating-house, and the throng from the long train of cars is moving bodily upon it.

Noting this, the young man cries shortly : " Indecision means hunger—at all events, the leavings. Come with me ! "

Then, perceiving that Erma is hesitating and looking towards the car from which Ferdie and Louise are just appearing, and which still conceals Mrs. Livingston and her son, he says hurriedly : " Quick ; I'll reserve a table for your party and get them a first chance at the meal. Come at once if you want your supper ! "

" Of course I want my supper," cries Miss Travenion with a laugh ; for the brisk Nebraska air, which is quite often cool toward evening, in October, has stimulated the young lady s appetite, which, like that of most healthy girls of her age, is generally a good one.

So the young lady, placing her hand upon his arm and followed by her maid, turns away from the crowd and is led to a side door, Lawrence seeming to know the by-ways of the hotel pretty well.

In front of this are lounging the station master and two or three railroad employees. These spring up with ejaculations of welcome and delight ! One cries, " God bless you, Cap ! " and another, " Harry, you're doing well." A third guffaws *sotto voce*, "You bet he is."

Returning their salutes, he says shortly, " Please let me in at the side door—before the rush. This young lady is hungry." A moment after they are in the dining-room of the railroad hotel before the crowd of passengers have entered by the main portal.

This is a large apartment filled with tables, each of which will accommodate six people, and each presided over and waited upon by a brisk moving, calico-clothed Nebraska maiden.

A moment after, Erma's escort says to a bright-eyed prairie-girl who is flourishing a feather duster to keep the flies off an as yet unoccupied table : " Sally, reserve this table for myself and party."

Then to Miss Travenion's astonishment the maid answers, giving him a look of open-eyed admiration, " Yes, Cap ! "

The next instant she finds herself seated beside him, and her maid, under his direction, taken to another table and made comfortable by another brisk Nebraska girl, who also answers deferentially, "Yes, Cap ! " Then the one employed at their table calmly but uncompromisingly waves off both flies and passengers from the tempting seats with her feather duster, remarking, " This 'ere table 's engaged ! This 'ere table 's engaged," to applying drummers and hungry cattlemen

who would make a raid upon the precious vacant chairs ;
for all the other seats in the room are by this time in use
and the viands are flying off the tables in a manner peculiar to Western appetites ; while over all this comes in
continual chorus from the waiting-girls: "Steaks—chops
—ham and eggs—tea or coffee—pie or pudding," with
an occasional variation of "stewed prunes or fruit."

In this chorus their attendant maid has already joined,
singing out in a business way, "Steaks, chops or ham
and eggs," when to Miss Travenion's awful blushes, the
girl suddenly stops her song and giggles, after the
free and easy manner of the prairies, "I know what's
the matter with you, Cap; you've been going and git-
ting married, and are bringing your wife West !" casting a look of identification on Erma as the imported
bride.

To this Harry, choking down a rising curse, mutters
in a very hoarse voice, "Steaks for two, and ham and
eggs *turned!*"

Then Ferdie inserts himself into this scene of embarrassment to the young lady, and from which she has
half risen to fly in a sudden bashful spasm, and says :
"Erma, what the deuce have you been doing? Mrs.
Livingston is almost hysterical, and thinks the Indians
have got you, when it is only Captain Lawrence and—
supper."

"Yes," answers Harry, who blesses the boy for his
interruption ; "I know more about Western eating-houses
than you do. I have rescued Miss Travenion from
the crowd, and reserved a table for the rest of your
party. Just bring them along, will you—that's a good
fellow ?"

To this, Mr. Chauncey, who has already met Lawrence
upon the train during the afternoon, answers : "Won't
I ? I have been hunting everywhere for a place for our
ladies. It was these vacant chairs that attracted me."

Then the young New Yorker, having gone in search of his party, Miss Travenion once more finds herself subject to the attentions of the gentleman beside her. But these are so very respectful that her embarrassment gradually vanishes, and she devotes herself with considerable comfort of mind to the supper which has just been placed before her, for Captain Lawrence is particularly careful from now on that his attentions to her, though effective as regards her wants, shall have not the slightest affectation of familiarity in them.

So the girl, looking at him, thinks: "Some men who might consider themselves of perhaps higher breeding than this one beside me, would have made a joke out of that awful *contretemps*, but Captain Lawrence is a gentleman, and gentlemen are very much the same all the world over," and once or twice, when he does not notice it, she turns grateful eyes upon him during pauses in the meal.

A moment after, Mr. Chauncey re-appears, followed by the Livingstons.

Mrs. Livingston mutters: "Good gracious, Erma, how you frightened me. My heart is beating yet. If anything had happened to you, what would I have said to your father?"

She would continue her emotion, did not Miss Travenion quietly say, "You owe your supper this evening to Captain Lawrence, who was kind enough to take charge of me in the crush, and also to look after your interests in the matter of chairs and vacant table."

To which Miss Louise ejaculates: "Oh, how good of you. I'm dying of hunger!" and the widow, who still remembers the fortunate compliment of the young man, remarks: "Captain, as I owe my meal to you, I will sit beside you," giving him a grateful glance and taking the chair on the young man's left hand.

Then, being compelled to it, Mr. Oliver Livingston

suddenly remembers that he has met the Westerner before,—a thing he has forgotten, though he has passed him several times upon the train, and suddenly says : " How are yer?" in an absent-minded sort of way, and seating himself enjoys the pleasures of gastronomy.

As the party's appetites become satisfied, their tongues begin to move in conversation, and Harry, taking advantage of the situation, proceeds to make himself very agreeable to Mrs. Livingston ; for this young man has been thinking the matter over during his three or four hours on the train, and has concluded that to be a friend of the chaperon's will be very useful to him in his intercourse with Miss Travenion.

" I was afraid," says the New York widow, "that Erma had been carried off by Indians."

" Indians," remarks Lawrence, " were plentiful enough about here four or five years ago, but the railroad, with its settlements, has swept them back.   In 1867 there were too many of them at times," and the young man's brow grows dark and his lips compressed with some recollection of the past.   Throwing this off, he explains lightly to Mr. Ferdie, who begins eagerly questioning him on the point, that any buffalo that may be seen will be probably far to the West of where they are now ; their best hope of catching sight of them being during the next day's journey.   "If you had wanted to see buffalo in quantities," he continues, "you should have journeyed on the K. P., one hundred and fifty to two hundred miles south of here.   There they graze, sometimes, even now, in droves of ten thousand by the side of the railway track."

" By Jove ! " cries Ferdie to this information, looking with longing eyes to the South.   " But we will return by the K. P., auntie, won't we ? "   Then he questions suddenly : " You have killed buffalo, haven't you, Captain Lawrence ? "

"A few," remarks the Westerner quietly, and from that time on he is a hero in Ferdie's eyes.

Mr. Ollie having by this time finished his meal,—a business that he has interspersed with a few curt remarks about the badness and greasiness of Western cooking and the general inefficiency of frontier waiter-girls, he arises and suggests, "If you wish to miss this train, you had all better linger a little longer over the table."

To this, Mrs. Livingston suddenly gasps, "Hurry! The passengers are all leaving the room!"

"Oh, no hurry! They are only gentlemen anxious to get at their cigars," says Harry, to whom the meal has been a very pleasant one, Miss Travenion having made it brilliant by one or two glances from her bright eyes and a few vivacious remarks.

But the chaperon suddenly cries in a voice of terror, "If we miss the train, we are here on the prairies, un-protected and ALONE!"

This pathetic remark, in a rising young frontier city of two thousand inhabitants, produces a giggle from Miss Louise. She titters, "Pooh, ma! This is a metropolis. I saw a dozen trainmen, half a hundred loafers and one or two tramps on the platform as we drew up."

But Mrs. Livingston having risen, the party saunter towards the door, that lady thanking Lawrence for some information he has given, tending to dissipate her fears of wild Western adventure on the railroad. She concludes this by saying, "You must give us a little of your aid and protection, we have had so little frontier experience, Captain,"—a request that gentleman is very glad to accede to, and he promises that he will look after them all, especially the widow, very thoroughly and very faithfully during their journey.

Harry in conversation with Mrs. Livingston has left the room, so have Ferdie and Louise, and Ollie is employed settling the score ; Erma finds herself alone.

Actuated, perchance, by a wish to learn more of the gentleman who has been kind to her this afternoon, and perhaps prompted by some curiosity to know why he is treated with so much respect under the familiar appellation of "Cap" by the Western waiter-girls, she turns back, and walking up to the bright-eyed abigail who has waited on them, says, "You seem to know the gentleman who brought me into supper this evening very well."

"Oh, Cap Lawrence?" answers the girl. "I should think so ; we all have a pretty powerful liking and respect for him about this portion of the country."

"And why ?"

"Why?" cries the Western girl. "Don't you know ? Well, five years back, when this 'ere hotel was nothin' but a log cabin and I worked giving meals to our section men, the Indians made a raid up thar at Elm Creek," she points towards the west, "and if it hadn't been for the Cap taking a hand-car and going up the track they would have wiped out every section hand to the last man. As it was, they killed five of them, and it ain't every man out here that wants to run into a lot of Sioux on the war-path, in an open hand-car, but Cap Lawrence is the man to do it. You are married to him, ain't you, Missus ?"

"No," replies Erma, growing very red. "I am married to no man," and striding away from the girl joins Ollie, though she catches a prophetic, "Wa-al, perhaps some day you will be. I seed him look at you once or twice, and you'll be mighty lucky if you catch him."

The subject of this colloquy is standing on the platform smoking his cigar ; he sees Miss Travenion pass him upon the arm of Mr. Oliver Livingston, and wonders why the girl blushes so deeply, though she gives him a pleasant nod. Then he suddenly thinks, "It is that accursed remark of that red-headed Sally in the eating-house," and does not know that Sally has done him one of the best turns that have as yet come to him. She has set the mind of the girl he loves running upon a subject that had not as yet occurred to her. As it is, Erma gives a glance at the stalwart figure of the Westerner as he stands, in athletic ease, puffing his cigar, then catching sight of Ollie's rather diminutive figure, compares the two, perhaps not altogether to the advantage of Mr. Livingston.

As Miss Travenion is assisted into the train by her escort, Lawrence looking at her himself hears a low but resonant whisper at his side, "By Jove, Cap, ain't she purty? Reckon she must come from Chicago." Looking around he sees Buck Powers standing at his side, gazing in admiration at the beauty who has caught and entranced the engineer's soul. This would make Harry angry did he not notice that the news-agent is very young, though his face has that peculiar precocity that comes from an early struggle with the world and an early battle for life and bread, and notes that the tone of the boy is as respectful and loving as his would be did he happen to speak of his divinity.

A moment after, Mr. Livingston returning from the car, Captain Lawrence accosts him and offers him a cigar.

"Awh! thanks," remarks Ollie, being compelled to the same, and accepting it, he finds it to his astonishment to be a very good one,—much better than the average weed he would get in a New York club: for this young man does not know that the Western mining man and speculator uses the very best of cigars, wines, and all creature comforts, even when his luck is hard and his pocket almost empty.

A moment after Mr. Lot Kruger passes the two, and gives Harry a by no means kindly glance, for he has noticed the attentions of this gentleman to the daughter of his old friend, and does not like them.

This feeling is perhaps also felt, though at this time in a lesser degree, by Mr. Oliver Livingston, who somehow or other has arrived at the conclusion that Miss Travenion likes to listen to the conversation of this gentleman from the West, and does not like it very much more than Mr. Kruger.

Consequently, when the engineer rings the bell and the conductor cries, " All aboard ! " Harry Lawrence has made one active and one at present passive enemy, though he is rapidly growing to be a hero in Mr. Ferdie's imagination ; and as for Buck Powers, he has loved and admired this young engineer of the Pacific Railway for years, as nearly every other employee of the same, especially those engaged in its early building, have done ever since he ran the lines in Nebraska when that State was a howling wilderness of Indians, wild animals, trappers and prairies.

Then the train, getting under headway, passes with illuminated Pullmans and flashing headlight into the night of the plains. Miss Travenion, with a new interest in her mind as to this Western gentleman chance seems to have thrown into her way, looks out of her state-room—the car is half empty, most of its male passengers being in the smoking room with their after-dinner cigars. Among them, Ferdie and Ollie.

Captain Lawrence is at the other end of the car, conversing with Mrs. Livingston and Louise.

Erma carelessly picks up a book,—one of Ferdie's purchases, the volume on the Union Pacific Railway ; and glancing languidly over its pages, sees a picture of Indians attacking a hand-car, and reads, " Elm Creek Massacre " in large type. Beneath it is an account of the heroism of Captain Harry Storey Lawrence.

Then the brakeman cries out " Elm Creek." The train pauses for a moment, and gazing out, she can see the station house on the side track. A moment after, the locomotive dashing on again, she finds herself peering into the darkness that lies upon the low stretch of prairie, and wondering exactly whereabouts the man sitting so quietly and conversing with Mrs. Livingston, made his fight ; and her imagination getting the better of her, she seems to see the stalwart figure, which is commencing to interest her, standing on a little hand-car on that lone prairie, surrounded by Indians and fighting them off, and saving the section men surprised at their work, as they drop their tools and run from their labor ; and she sees his dark eyes, that she has commenced to know very well, flashing with determination as he encourages the fleeing laborers, and getting them on the car, they make their running fight towards the station, and hears the cracking of the deadly rifles and the whoops of the pursuing savages.

She is interrupted in this fantasie by Mr. Livingston's placid voice, saying, "What are you reading, Erma ?" for she still has the volume in her hand.

"Only an account of the construction of this railway," says the young lady, and she passes him the volume.

Looking over the account of the "Elm Creek Massacre," Ollie's eyes open rather widely ; but, a moment after, he remarks sneeringly : "This fiction of the Rocky Mountains seems to make quite a hero of your friend Lawrence. I wonder if he wrote the book himself ?" And the gentleman chuckles to himself, imagining he has been rather witty.

Miss Travenion's reply rather disconcerts him.

"I am glad you call him my friend," answers the girl, a gleam of admiration in her blue eyes. "Any man who could do what is written there, is worthy to be any woman's friend."

"Oh, indeed," says Mr. Livingston, rather nettled at this ; partly because he thinks his joke is not appreciated, and partly because he does not care about Erma

Travenion showing an interest in any other man save his own small self. "I suppose you will soon make a first-class border ruffian out of your hero?" Then he utters oracularly : "I wonder how it is that some girls seem to take such interest in 'men of blood.'"

"I don't take interest in 'men of blood,'" cries Miss Travenion, rather warmly, for this remark about border ruffians is not pleasing to her ; "but I do take interest in the men of courage, determination and manhood, who are risking their lives to make this country a greater America."

But here she gets a surprise from Ollie, who, incited by the beauty of the girl, which is made greater by her enthusiasm, replies suddenly : "If I thought you would like it, Erma, I myself would become a pioneer."

The idea of Mr. Ollie's turning frontiersman, proves too much for Miss Travenion's control ; she bursts into a fit of laughter, which disconcerts the young man, and makes him retreat from her, with a plaintive, "I meant what I said. I didn't believe you would treat my expression of regard for you with a jeer."

Left to herself, however, Erma goes into more thought about this man who has risked his life for others, and even after she has gone to bed, as she turns upon her pillow, visions of Captain Harry Storey Lawrence, fighting Indians, come to her, and she wakes up with a suppressed scream, for he is about to be scalped, and finds that it is only the shriek of the locomotive, and the war-whoops of the Indians are only the outcries of the porter, announcing that they are approaching Sydney, where they have thirty minutes for an early breakfast.

5

CHAPTER VI.

MR. FERDIE DISCOVERS A VIGILANTE.

So, making a hasty toilet, Miss Travenion steps out of her stateroom to find the car empty, it having already arrived at the eating-station, and the passengers having departed from it.

On the platform, however, she is greeted by Ferdie, who cries out : "Come along, Miss Lazy Bird. All the rest are in at breakfast. I have got some news for you."

"News about whom?" says the girl lightly.

"About the Indians. There's some off there. You needn't be afraid! I've got my revolver on, and if they act nasty, I'll fix 'em as Cap Lawrence does," says the boy, and he leads her a few steps to one side, where Erma sees a Sioux buck, two squaws and a pappoose— the warrior on a pony and flourishing about in a red blanket and soldier hat, though his leggings are of the scantiest proportions.

The squaws, as is their wont, extend their hands for stray coins, though the Sioux are by no means such beggars as their more degraded cousins, the Piutes on the Central Pacific in Nevada. Looking at these unedifying redskins, Miss Travenion finds that Cooper's novels, which she had once regarded as facts, have immediately become fictions.

"I was going to get my rifle," babbles Ferdie at her ear, "but Buck Powers told me I'd be jugged if I shot at 'em. They're at peace now." Then he goes on confidentially : "I have interviewed Buck about Cap Lawrence, and it cost me about two dollars in indigestible candies and peanuts, but I got the information. Buck says the Cap is a snorter on Injuns."

"Don't use such language in my presence, Mr. Chauncey," cries Erma sternly.

"Oh, I am only quoting Buck," answers Ferdinand. "Buck says the Cap has killed hundreds of buffalo and rafts of Indians—heaps of them. Say! What's the matter with you? I thought you'd like to listen to the history of your Indian killer," continues Ferdie, surprised; for the girl has turned suddenly away from him and is passing on towards the eating-house.

Then he suddenly ejaculates, "Well, I'm blizzarded!" a queer wild notion having got into his brain. And he has guessed very nearly the truth; for Miss Travenion, for some reason, which is at present indefinite to herself, is not altogether pleased at hearing this Western gentleman's name always connected with deeds of blood.

In the dining-room she finds her party seated at a table, at which a chair has been reserved for her, but Captain Lawrence is not with them, and looking about, she sees him at another table.

Then Ferdie, bolting his food, finishes his breakfast in about five minutes, and departs in search of Western adventure and information, not on the main platform of the station, but in out-of-the-way saloons and shanty bar-rooms; methods of frontier slumming that are productive during his trip of one or two decided sensations to this young gentleman, as well as the rest of his party.

Shortly after Mr. Chauncey's departure, the meal being finished, Miss Travenion wanders with Mr. Ollie to the platform, and notices Harry smoking his cigar, and surrounded by a lot of the train men and station officials, who seem to crowd around him at every stop they make, as if anxious to do him honor, Buck Powers among the number.

A moment after, Mr. Livingston having left her, the newsboy sidles up to her and remarks, having an eye to both business and pleasure, "I've got some prime California peaches saved up for you. You weren't out when I come through the train before breakfast—two dandies

at ten cents apiece.   The Cap chewed one this morning
and said it was fine.   Ain't he a stem-winder, though ?"
goes on the boy.   " He was the most popular man on
the line when it was built.   You needn't pay for them
peaches unless they're good."

" Thank you, Mr. Powers," answers the girl, giving the
boy a bright smile, for somehow she is quite pleased to
note that Captain Lawrence seems so well liked by all
who know him.

" Call me Buck !   Side-track the Mr. Powers !   You
make me feel as if you were offish," says the youthful
news-agent, giving Erma a glance of admiration.

" Very well, Buck," laughs the girl.   " You may bring
me the peaches," and would perhaps say more to him,
did not Mr. Lot Kruger, who seems somehow to always
have his eyes upon her, casting a quid of tobacco out of
his ample mouth, approach her and suggest affably,
" Prairie air seems to bloom you up this morning, Miss."

Then her party being about her, Erma finds herself compelled to introduce the Western Lot to them
all.   These introductions are very affably received by
Mr. Kruger, who insists on shaking hands with the
whole party, an attention not very well received by
Oliver, though Mrs. Livingston, thinking from his peculiar toilet he is in some degree a Western border ruffian,
and it will be best for her personal safety to be very
polite to him, receives him with effusive but nervous
politeness, to the joy of Lot's soul.   So he seats himself
beside her, and goes into a free and easy conversation
with the widow, giving her his views of things in general
and the West in particular.

Turning from them towards her own stateroom, Erma
chances to meet Captain Lawrence, who is just entering
the car.   Allured by the bright nod she gives him,
this gentleman ignores the pleasure of an after-break-
fast cigar, and sits down to a long conversation with

the young lady, which is interrupted by occasional visits from Mr. Oliver Livingston, who comes up at odd times to ask Miss Travenion if he can do anything for her comfort, for he is getting annoyed at Erma's giving her time to an outsider, as he terms the engineer, and were it not that Oliver Ogden Livingston has such an appreciation of his own charms, intellect and social position, he would be jealous, which would be a fearful tax on his placid nerves, that are not accustomed to violent emotions.

As the train passes along, the captain incidentally mentions a few things of interest in sight from the cars, stating to Miss Travenion that they will soon be in sight of the Rockies, and this leads to the girl's asking him about the " Elm Creek " affair, which he puts away, saying that it was not much, though there were a great many wild doings, both by the Indians and the whites, during the construction of the road, and some recollection coming upon him from the past, the young man's face grows dark, and he suddenly changes the subject, saying that Indian fights are not generally half so desperate as some affairs that took place in the late war.

This produces questions from Erma, and she learns a good deal of Lawrence's early life ; how his father emigrated from Massachusetts, being a nephew of that celebrated seaman Lawrence, whose words are still remembered—" Don't give up the ship "—and of this relationship and memory the young man seems very proud.

He tells her that his father is now a large farmer in Eastern Iowa, and the girl drawing him out by deft suggestions, learns that he was educated for a civil engineer, but at the breaking out of the war, left college and went to soldiering, and became, after a year or two of fighting, captain of an Iowa battery.

The conversation goes on very pleasantly until he

suddenly cries out, "The Rocky Mountains!" and shows her snow-clad peaks looming up amid the blue sky to the west, just as the train is running into Cheyenne, where something occurs that gives Miss Travenion a great shock, and makes her change her opinion considerably about this young gentleman, to whom she has devoted so much of her thoughts in the last twenty-four hours.

Like most of the sensations of this life, it comes unexpectedly.

She has just finished a comfortable sort of dinner in the Cheyenne eating-house, and is sauntering about, watching the change of locomotives, and trying to get a good look at Long's Peak, which is so distant that she can hardly tell whether it is snow or cloud, when she is joined by Mr. Ferdinand, who shocks her by whispering these astonishing words : "Come around the corner and I'll show you a telegraph pole where Captain Lawrence hung a man."

"Hung a man ? You are crazy," returns the young lady indignantly ; then she sneers, "Buck Powers invents silly stories to incite you to buy more candy."

"Not at all crazy, but rather up to the snuff," retorts Ferdie, who apparently is strongly excited and profoundly impressed. "Besides, Buck didn't tell me this. I have just met a gambler in that bar-room over there" —he points to a shanty drinking saloon, some hundred yards down the track—"and he says Cap Lawrence hung his pard, Nebraska Bill, to a telegraph pole."

"Impossible," remarks Erma in angry scorn.

"So I thought at first, but the man showed me the telegraph pole and said that was where Lawrence had murdered his pard."

"And you believe this gambler's likely story," sneers Miss Travenion.

"Of course I do. I am prepared for anything out

here. I have been making inquiries since I got the information, and they tell me around here that Captain Lawrence was at the head of the Vigilantes out here four years ago, and used to hang up gamblers in rows, at the rate of about half-a-dozen a night," asserts Mr. Ferdie confidently. "What do you say to that?"

"What do I say to it?" cries Miss Travenion with indignant eyes. "I say that I will never believe such a thing until I have proof of it."

"And have not I proved it?" says Ferdie. "How can you prove it any better?"

"By asking Captain Lawrence," cries Erma. Then, not heeding Mr. Chauncey's expostulations that he does not think any less of the captain, and that every one around says the Vigilantes were a necessity, Miss Travenion goes hurriedly into her car and shuts herself in her stateroom, for she is very much shocked at this revelation, as any girl, brought up far away from the scenes of blood and combat and swift justice of the frontier, would be.

A few moments after this, the train, drawn by two giant locomotives, gets under way, and leaving Cheyenne, begins to ascend the Black Hills towards Sherman.

As it does so, Miss Erma's privacy is invaded by Mrs. Livingston and Ollie.

"You have heard Ferdie's awful tale?" gasps the widow.

"About the murderer you picked up on the train," interjects Mr. Livingston, waving his white cuffs, as if throwing off all responsibility in the matter.

"Picked up on the train?" cries Erma, very sternly, rising from her seat, her figure growing more erect, and her eyes becoming burnished steel. "What do you mean to insinuate?"

"Oh, nothing, of course, as regards you," replies Ollie, who is somewhat quick of speech and also hasty of retraction. " Of course you did not know who he was any more than I did when that duffer, Southmead, brought him into our supper party at Delmonico's."

" Ah, you are referring to Captain Lawrence, Mr. Livingston," says the girl, haughtily.

" Certainly. Mr. Kruger, that friend of your father, who seems very affable and pleasant, though not a highly cultured man, confirms Ferdinand's information," answers Mrs. Livingston, taking this interview out of her son's hands, as he does not seem to be succeeding very well. " This Mr. Kruger, who is acquainted with the West, has informed us that this Captain Lawrence is a very blood-thirsty individual ; that he is, in fact, amenable to the laws of this country for the crime of murder."

" Yes, cold-blooded, deliberate assassination," interjects Ollie, anxious to impress the girl. " Captain Lawrence headed the Vigilance Committee, and hung up a number of unoffending citizens."

To this Miss Travenion says shortly, " I don't believe you."

" Not even your father's friend ? " cries Mrs. Livingston.

" No, neither he nor any man else who would say such awful things of Captain Lawrence. Oh, I cannot believe it ! " Then she mutters, " The tones of his voice are as gentle as a child's," and turns away.

" So were Johnny Slade's," inserts Ferdie, who has just now joined the party and conversation. " Besides, Buck Powers says the Cap was a terror to gamblers and desperadoes out here,—though I like him all the better for it."

But here Miss Travenion astonishes them all. She says calmly, though there is a tremor in her voice :

" I refuse to give any opinion of Captain Lawrence's conduct until I have spoken to him."

" What ! You are going to—to speak to that awful

man again?" gasps the widow, turning pale. Then she suddenly whispers, "Don't tell him what I said about him. He might murder us." And seemingly frightened at the thought of the blood-thirsty captain's vengeance, she takes her departure hurriedly for her own stateroom, and locks herself in.

She is very shortly followed by Ferdie and her son, to whom his half-way sweetheart says as he departs: "Permit me to satisfy myself upon this affair in my own way!"

Then, they having gone from her, she sinks down and shudders, though all the time she does justice to the man of her thoughts, and defends him, and says, "I don't believe it. He is too gentle," and finally, having persuaded herself that it is all a tissue of falsehoods, unlocks her door and steps out into the main car, to find herself face to face with this so-called desperado, who is calmly reading one of *Harper's Monthlies*, his "deeds of blood" not seeming to hang very heavily on his conscience.

A moment after, Miss Travenion remarks suddenly: "Captain Lawrence, will you pardon me if I ask you a question?" and her eyes grow bright, but her cheeks are pale, and her lips tremble as she speaks.

"Certainly," says Harry.

As he turns to her, the girl hesitates and falters, for it has suddenly come to her, if this man is innocent, he will not forgive; but forcing herself to the ordeal, she falters out: "People tell me what I will not believe, that —that—you, while occupied here in the arts of peace, have hung up men by the dozens to telegraph poles? Is it true, Captain Lawrence?"

And he, some strange fear in his eyes, rises to her question, and though he stands apparently calm, the strong fingers of his hand tremble a little as they grasp the arm of the seat, and his face grows also pale, and there is a slight twitch on one corner of his moustache as he murmurs sadly : " And they say that of me ? "

" Yes !—Is it true ? "

Then, after a moment's pause, the young man answers firmly and perhaps proudly : " In the troublous times of 1867 and '68, surrounded by gamblers, desperadoes and cut-throats, who daily sacrificed the lives of innocent men and made a mockery of both law and justice, I did what I considered my duty as a good citizen. Do you blame me for it ? "

" You—you hung men without trial by law ? "

" Yes—do you blame me ? "

But her only answer is a frightened, " Oh ! how could you ? " and Erma has swept past him into her stateroom, the door of which closes suddenly after her.

He makes one step after her, as if to say words of vindication or defence ; then bows his head and moves slowly out of the car, steadying himself with his hand. So, standing upon the front platform, Harry Lawrence looks down on the Laramie Plains, to which the train is descending, and there are tears in his eyes. For the strong man is thinking of the last words of Curley Jack just before they strung him up for the murder of an unfortunate creature of whom he was jealous. " Some day, Cap, some woman will make you crazy with misery as I was when I shot Kansas Kate," and he wonders if the prophecy of the dying desperado is coming home to him.

His meditation must be potent, for two hours afterwards, when the train stops at Laramie for supper, and his old-time railroad friends gather around him, they wonder what has happened, and the station agent remarks, " The Cap looks as busted up as if he had lost on four aces," for he goes about in a broken kind of a way, and once or twice, seeing some neighboring telegraph poles, turns from them with a shudder.

As for Miss Travenion, she has perhaps a harder two

hours of it than Harry Lawrence, for some indefinite emotion is in her mind that makes her wildly nervous and extraordinarily excitable. Three or four times she says to herself, "Why should I care if this man has all the crimes of the Decalogue on his soul? A week ago I did not know him. Twenty-four hours back I had seen his face but once. He shall pass out of my life as quickly as he entered it." Next she remarks, "He said he did his duty as a citizen." Then she laughs: "Pshaw, I am growing nervous! I am defending this man!" and grows very angry at, and perchance unjust to, Lawrence on account of this idea.

Anxious to get away from the subject, she comes out and joins the Livingston party, and laughs and jokes with them, apparently in high spirits, though there is a feverish flush upon her cheeks; and once to the widow's remark, "Did he admit his crimes?" and Ferdie's laughing inquiry, "How many did the Cap acknowledge to swinging up?" she replies shortly:

"Enough for me to drop his acquaintance as rapidly as I made it. From this time on I shall CUT HIM!" emphasizing the last with a wave of her hand and an excited laugh, in so vigorous a manner that Ollie is quite delighted and happy, thinking that Erma will have no further thoughts of the man whom he has grown to imagine his rival—a conclusion he would not so hastily have come to had he studied Miss Travenion in particular, or the sex in general.

So the party stroll out to supper, but Erma, apparently gay, has no appetite further than a cup of tea, and hardly tastes her supper.

Declining attendance, she walks back to her car, and, seated by an open window, looks out upon the beautiful scene, gazing toward the north, where the Black Hills fade away in the distance, and wonders, as the setting sun shines upon her face, how this land, which seems to her so peaceful and which might be so happy, is the home of men who regard human life so lightly.

But even as she does so, as luck will have it, additional evidence on the subject that is racking her brain and making her head ache, though she will not admit it, comes to her.

Two men beside the track are in conversation. The breeze wafts their words into the car.

One remarks : "Cap Lawrence came in from the East to-night, and I reckon every gambler in town is hunting his hole."

"Why, are they afraid of him yet?"

"You bet! He put his mark on 'em so heavy they don't forget him. Why, I remember one morning, three years ago, seeing Little Jimmie, the bartender, hanging up as graceful as life to that telegraph pole, with his natty white handkerchief tucked in his hip-pocket, and his white sleeves, with rubber bands on 'em which held them up while he was mixing drinks. He looked so allfired natural that I called out : 'Give me a whiskey cocktail, Jim.' You see, they took James from behind his bar so quick he had no time to let down his sleeves and prepare himself for the future."

But the girl hears no more ; she has hurried to the other end of the empty car.

Had she remained to listen, she would have also heard that Little Jimmie, the barkeeper, was as bad a man as had lived or died in the West, and the night before his sudden demise he had murdered and robbed two railroad men who had just been paid off.

But not knowing this, Erma has a very stern look on her face a few minutes after, when she sees Harry enter the car. He makes a movement as if to approach and address her, but the young lady turns her head away with a sudden shudder.

Noting this, the Westerner leaves the car and commences to walk about the platform, chewing nervously the end of a cigar he has forgotten to light. Then, curiously enough, the girl peeps after him, and stands aghast, for there is indignation in his look as he strides about, his athletic figure well displayed by a loose shooting coat, and he tosses his brown locks back from his forehead, as if he were facing an enemy, and his dark eyes are gleaming so potently that Erma gasps, "Why, he looks like a Vigilante *now!*"

Soon the train is crowded once more, and they begin to run over the Laramie Plains, where Ferdie excites them all by seeing a buffalo, and would get his gun to shoot at it, did not Mr. Kruger remark: "The critter is nigh onto three miles off, and you will throw away your lead, sonny."

As for Captain Lawrence, he has not entered their car, and is now in a forward smoker, puffing away desperately, and thinking with some regrets of the early days of the building of the Union Pacific Railway, those times which tried men's souls; but after turning over the matter in his mind he exclaims to himself: "By Heaven! I am glad I did my duty, even if it loses me—" Here he clenches his teeth, and a little spot of blood comes upon his lip, where he has bitten it.

CHAPTER VII.

WHAT MANNER OF MAN IS THIS?

In the rear car, Miss Travenion, anxious to throw from her mind a subject that is distressing, wanders to the organ,—for this Pullman was supplied with one, as were many Western sleepers in those days,—and seating herself at the instrument, runs her hands over the keys and begins to sing. Softly at first, but afterwards made enthusiastic by melody, this young lady, who has been very well taught and has a brilliant mezzo voice, forgets all else, and warbles the beauties of Balfe, Bellini, and Donizetti in a way that draws the attention of her fellow-passengers.

Among them is the Western Lot, who, getting near to her, watches the lithe movements and graceful poses of the girl's charming figure, and seeing her soul beaming from her glorious eyes, mutters to himself, " What an addition to our tabernacle choir after I have made her one of the elect." For this young lady's loveliness has, of late, been putting some very wild ideas into the head of this friend of her father.

She leaves the organ, and noting that Miss Travenion is somewhat alone, for the interview of the afternoon seems to have produced a slight coolness between Mr. Livingston and Erma, and perchance also Mrs. Livingston, this Western product thinks he will devote himself to the young lady's edification during the remainder of the evening, opening his remarks by, " You're comin' to a great country, Miss Ermie."

" Ah, what is that ? " asks the girl nonchalantly but politely.

" Utah," replies the enthusiastic Lot, " whar the people of Zion have made the wilderness to blossom as a rose of Sharon."

" Oh yes, where my father is ! " cries Miss Travenion, her eyes growing bright. " To-morrow we will be there."

" Yes, in the evening," assents Kruger, an indefinite something coming in his eyes that makes the young lady restless.

A moment after she suddenly asks : " Where is my father now ? "

" How can I tell? I ain't seen your dad for nigh onto a month," returns Lot, apparently somewhat discomposed by this point-blank question.

" But you can surely make a guess," suggests Erma,
" where a telegram will most probably reach him? I
have concluded to wire him. Then he will meet me
at the station. I wish I had done so before."

" Wall, Salt Lake is the most likely p'int, I reckon,"
mutters Kruger, who does not seem over pleased at the
girl's idea. A second after he suddenly says : " You
write the message and I'll make inquiries along the
line. I reckon I'll find where he is and send it for you."

" Thank you," says Erma warmly. " I'll go and prepare it at once."

Then leaving Lot still pondering, she steps lightly
away, and in a few minutes returns with the following :

" U. P. TRAIN, Oct. 3, 1871.

" Arrive at Ogden, to-morrow, at five P.M. Will come through
to Salt Lake same night. Meet me at depot.
" Your loving daughter,
"ERMA TRAVENION."

" You'll add the right address to this when you find
it, Mr. Kruger," says the girl, handing him the message.

" Yes, I'll make inquiries at Medicine Bow," returns
Lot, taking the message, "and your dad 'll get it to-
morrow morning."

" Oh, you are going to stay up to send it? We don't
get to Medicine Bow till late, I know by my time table.
How kind you are ! Papa shall thank you for this,
also, dear Mr. Kruger," and Erma holds out a soft patrician hand, that is greedily seized in strong fingers
made hard and red by exposure and toil.

Retreating from the grip, however, this New York
young lady says earnestly, " Thank you once more, and
au revoir until to-morrow."

" Oh, thank me all you want, Sissy ; gratitude becomes
young maidens," mutters Lot, trying to get the beautiful
white fingers once more in his.

" Indeed I am grateful," cries the girl, and giving him

a look that makes his eyes grow misty and watery, Miss Travenion closes the door of her stateroom, and goes to bed thinking no more of Mr. Kruger's peculiar expression and glances, for he is a friend of her father, and at the least has fifty odd years to his credit on the book of time.

She would be perhaps more concerned about her father's friend did she see Mr. Kruger, whose knowledge of French is very limited, after pondering to himself, " What did that gal mean by O-ver ? " finally answer his query by " Guess ag'in, Lot," and betake himself to the smoking car, where, after perusing the girl's telegram several times, he slyly chuckles to himself, " What !—and spile my hopes for myself and my work for the Church ? " and with this curious but ambiguous remark places the document coolly in his ample but well-worn pocketbook, between a list of Welsh emigrants *en route* for Salt Lake City and a despatch from Brigham Young ; and shortly after that turn in and sleep the sleep of the just, making no attempt either to find her father's address nor to wire her message, either at Medicine Bow or any other point on the line.

Notwithstanding this, the next morning at Green River, where the train stops for breakfast, Mr. Kruger is on hand to help her from the car and say with paternal voice, " Sissy, Dad's happy now.   Dad's happy now ! "

" Ah, you've sent the message," exclaims Erma with grateful eyes.

" Yes, it flewed away during the early morning," mutters Lot, which happens to be the exact truth, as, thinking the thing over, he had concluded it was best not to have the message on his person, and had torn it and tossed it out of the car window to the winds of Heaven, as the train had run down those alkaline, non-drinkable waters, cursed by early emigrants and pioneers under the name of Bitter Creek.

But Erma Travenion hardly heeds him; her eyes are towards the West and she is murmuring, "Papa—perhaps this afternoon.—certainly to-night!—if not Ogden—surely Salt Lake!" and her face is so happy, and she goes to thanking Mr. Kruger so heartily for his kindness in sending the telegram, that he might have pangs of conscience as to what he intends for this Eastern butterfly, who comes with brightness on her wings into the West. had he not been used to dealing with all people sternly, even himself, when acting for the glories of Zion, and the smiting down of unbelievers.

Then being joined by the Livingstons and Mr. Chauncey, who have been looking at the surprising scenery of this river, the first water they have as yet met which flows into the blue Pacific, she goes in to breakfast; Mr. Kruger, who seems to feel more at his ease as he nears his native heath, walking alongside of Miss Beauty. Pointing to the great elk heads with their branching antlers on the hotel walls, he remarks, "Thar's any quantity of them critters up thar in the Wind River Mountains, in which this 'ere stream heads."

"You've been up there?" asks Ferdie, always excited when big game is mentioned.

"Wall rather," returns Lot. "I was up all about thar and the Rattlesnake Hills and the Sweetwater Mountains and South Pass and Independence Springs in 1857, when Johnston and the U. S. troops were comin' through, and we rounded up and burnt—" But here he stops very suddenly.

"What did you burn?" queries Mr. Chauncey, anxiously.

"Oh, nothin' to speak of—brushwood and such truck," returns the uncommunicative Lot. "But here's the dining-table, Sonny!"

Then the party being seated, notwithstanding Mr. Kruger's efforts at conversation and the delights of gas-

6

tronomy, Miss Travenion's eyes will wander about, seeking an athletic figure that she sees not ; for somehow she
misses the man of yesterday, and despises herself for it.

Towards the close of their meal there is a slight commotion outside, and the man taking the money at the
door as the wayfarers pass out, deserts his post. Ferdie,
who is so seated that he can look through the open
windows, suddenly says, " It's some accident;" next cries,
" It's Buck Powers !" and rushes from the room.

A moment after Erma finds herself outside among an
excited crowd, gazing at Captain Lawrence striding along
the platform, bearing in his arms the form of Buck, the
news-agent.

" The boy was coupling the cars, and forgot till too
late they had Miller platforms that come together," says
the captain, mentioning a kind of accident very common
on the first introduction of this life-saving invention,
which until railroad men got accustomed to it, was a source
of danger instead of safety, as it now is. Then he goes on
quite tenderly, " But I got there in time, didn't I, Buck ? "

And the news-boy opens his red eyes and gasps, " You
bet you did, pard," and there is a little cheer from the
crowd, over which Lawrence's voice is heard : " Get a
doctor, quick ! "

Then a looker-on says, " Take him to the hotel."

But Buck groans, " Keep me on the train, or they will
steal all my stock of goods and I'll be busted," and some
one suggests the baggage car.

To this Lawrence quietly says, " No, I'll put him in
my section," but on arriving there with the boy in his
arms, he finds Erma standing beside him, and whispering,
" My stateroom, please.   It's quieter in there."

On hearing her voice, the young man looks at her a
moment as if in thought ; then shortly says, " Yes, it is
best as you say. Thank you, Miss Travenion," and
carries the boy in.

She can see him very tenderly brush the matted hair from off the sufferer's face, and hears about her, from excited passengers, that Captain Lawrence had risked his life to save that of a waif of the railroad.

A moment after the doctor comes, and making a short examination, the man of science says that the boy is only generally bruised and shaken up, and will come around all right if he is made quiet and sent to sleep, and would give him an opiate, did not Buck cry out piteously, ' "Don't make me insensible, Doc. My box is open, and the train hands will eat all my candies and peanuts and Californey fruit, and bust me up in business."

"I'll attend to that, Buck," answers the captain quietly. "I'll lock up your boxes," and getting the key from the boy, he bows slightly to Miss Travenion and goes out of the car on his errand, pursued by the grateful eyes of this Arab of the railroad. A moment after the doctor puts the boy to sleep, and Erma steps out of her state-room, to find that, Harry having departed, the passengers on the car are discussing him very generally, though in low tones of voice, as if fearing to disturb the slumbering invalid.

Their conversation gives her a new idea of Captain Lawrence, for she learns the opinion of those who have lived near him and are acquainted with frontier habits and frontier methods ; and they tell her that this young man is respected and honored for the very deeds which she has condemned in him and for which she has cut him off from the smiles of her face and the words from her lips.

She hears expressions of admiration on all sides, and one man, a miner from Colorado, and at present interested in the workings of a big coal property near Evanston, says : "That fellow who risked his life to save that foolish news-boy is 'clean-grit.' He and a few others like him, made some of the towns on this railroad habitable. A man's life wasn't safe in Cheyenne, but they wiped out every desperado, cut-throat and bunco-steerer in that town, and now it is comfortable to live in."

A moment after expressing this opinion, this gentleman is rather astonished to find the beautiful young lady from the East sitting beside him and saying in anxious voice : " You think Vigilance Committees right ? You have had experience. Tell me all about them."

" They are right, if self-preservation is," he answers. Then, being a man of wide Western experience, and noting the anxious look on the girl's face, he tells her that the average frontier desperado is very careful of his own life, though very careless of that of others, and if he is certain of dying twenty-four hours afterwards, he will do no murder. And he gives her a little history of Vigilance Committees in general, and tells her how at White Pine, the first rush into that mining camp being composed of old California and Nevada miners, they had said, " This will be a red-hot place for cut-throats, bullies and blacklegs," and had organized a Vigilance Committee *before* they built the town of Hamilton ; and there had never been a murder in it, until long after the Vigilance Committee and nearly all other inhabitants left it ; and that Pioche, one hundred and thirty miles away, with a population similar to Hamilton, had averaged eighteen homicides a day, most of them wilful murders, simply because the men who committed them knew that they would not be avenged, there being no Vigilance Committee in that place ; then, warming to his subject, he goes on with the history of early Montana, when it was impossible for any man to carry gold from Helena to Salt Lake City and live through the trip ; and people wondered why none of the highwaymen who robbed, looted and murdered on that trail through Southern Idaho to Utah were never brought to justice, and that a Vigilance Committee was formed, and the first man they hung in the Territory was the sheriff, and that after that they continued their work with such success that for eight years thereafter no homicide was committed in all Montana.

Next getting excited, he winds up by saying, "The best citizens of these places were Vigilance men. There was no law, but they made peace ; there was no justice, but they made the land free from blood," and is astonished at the end of this discourse to receive a grateful "Thank you," from the young lady, whose eyes seem to have grown happier during his lecture upon the morality of Lynch law.

Then, Miss Travenion, some load seeming to have been lifted from her mind, turns to her stateroom, to watch over the sleeping newsboy. As she sits gazing at the recumbent invalid, she wonders, "Why should I be happy to hear that Harry Lawrence is not regarded as a murderer by those who have seen him kill ?" and while musing upon this, the boy opens his eyes, for the effect of the opiate has passed off, Erma's conversation with the Western man having been a long one.

A moment after, he says faintly, "If you please, Miss, I would like to go back to business. This trip ain't goin' to pay me nothing."

"You lay quiet, Buck," whispers the girl. "I'll attend to your business for you," for a sudden idea has come into Erma's head. She steps lightly out into the car, and taking off her straw hat, throws a greenback into it, and goes about among the passengers of the Pullmans, taking up a collection for the injured waif, which nets him a great deal more than the profits of his trip would have been, even were he in good health and pursuing his business with his usual keenness.

Coming in from this, she shakes the money joyfully before the boy's eyes and laughs, "What kind of a news-agent do you think I make ? There are the profits of the trip, Buck. Take some of this lemonade and go to sleep again."

To which the boy murmurs, " You would make a corker. They'd buy two-year-old peaches from you— they would,' drinks down the beverage her white hand places at his lips, and so goes to sleep again.

All this time the train, which seems to rattle along very merrily to the girl, has been leaving the valley of the Green River—that stream which flows between sandstones that, rising hundreds of feet above its banks, have the appearance of domes and mediæval castles and cathedrals, making it as picturesque as the Rhine, only much more grand ; for far below, on its course to the blue Gulf of California, its cliffs from hundreds of feet grow into thousands, and its cathedrals and domes and palaces and ruins are those of giants, not of men, for this river is really the Colorado, and its Grand Cañon is the most sublime spectacle of the whole American continent, not even excepting the tremendous mountains and glaciers of the British Northwest.

So, after a few hours' running over plateaux nearly as barren as the Sahara Desert, though they would blossom like the garden of Gethsemane could irrigation ever be brought to them, they approach the high tablelands at Piedmont, and climbing through long snow sheds to Aspen Hill, run down the valley of the Bear River, by which stream the train winds its way to Evanston, the last town in Wyoming Territory.

As they progress westward, Miss Travenion leaves the sleeping boy, and coming to Mrs. Livingston's stateroom, finds that lady in conversation with Mr. Kruger, who seems to be very happy at getting back to his Utah home.

" You will soon find yourself in a beautiful land," he says. " You see them great mountains down thar ? " He points to the Uintah Range, whose peaks go up into the blue sky at the south like a great snowy saw. "Down in thar is a valley, one of the purtiest pieces of grazing land and farming property in the whole Territory, Kammas Praharie, and I've got as pretty a ranch down there as in Utah, and lots of cattle and horses, and in my house four as nice-looking young—" He checks himself as suddenly at the last of this speech as if he were struck with a club.

Which Ferdie noticing, asks, "Why are you always snapping your jaws together before you finish your sentences? One would think you had something to conceal."

"Not much!" replies the accused, his face getting very red, however. "Any one can investigate the life of Lot Kruger, and find that he's as upright and above board as the Lot of the Scriptures, and what he has done has been did with the advice and sanction of his church, and that's more, I reckon, than you can say, young man, though you're not much over kid high yit!"

But any further discussion is stopped by the train running into Evanston, where are the great coal mines. Here they take dinner, and Miss Travenion has hopes of gaining conversation with Captain Lawrence, but she only succeeds in seeing him at a distance, and thinks he looks very stern, which is the truth, for he has just received some telegrams from Salt Lake about his mining property that by no means please him. He would doubtless brighten up, however, did he but know that the girl is very anxious to say a few words to him and even offer a generous apology to this Vigilante, — this "man of blood."

After a little, a couple of locomotives helping them over a slight grade, they come into Echo Cañon, and begin to descend to the valley of the Great Salt Lake; then going on, the Weber River comes in from the south, where the melting streams of the Uintah Mountains give it birth. So skirting the willow and cottonwood

banks of this beautiful stream, they run by the Thousand
Mile Tree and the Devil's Slide and the old Mormon
bridge ; and many little hamlets and orchards, which
seem very green and beautiful to the girl after the long,
weary stretches of desert she has just left, till they come
to the Narrows, where two great mountains of the Wahsatch appear to bar the passage. But the cliffs open,
and the train bursts through to where the valley of Salt
Lake is spread before them, and Erma sees the inland
sea she has often read about, as the cars run down
towards it 'mid green pastures and lowing cattle and
thrifty orchards, for it is where the Mormons have set
their home in the wilderness, and by the arts of peace
have made a land of plenty, in order to uphold a form
of government which, like that of the ancient Druids, is
founded on blood atonement and the sacrifice of its unbelievers and its enemies.

But here the girl suddenly thinks of her invalid, and
going back to her stateroom, finds Buck sitting up, and
again ready to battle with the world.

" You and the Cap has done me a good turn," he says.
" Some day I'll even up on you," and his gray eyes
speak more strongly than his words, that some day the
deeds of this Bedouin of the railroad will tell her more
than he mutters.

" You're beautiful enough to be a Chicago gal," he
mutters. " The Cap thinks so too ! " This compliment
drives her away from him, and she has red cheeks, though
she is laughing.

But the train is now running into Ogden, and murmuring, " My father ! " Miss Travenion darts to the platform of the car and searches with all her eyes for his
loved form and dear face. After a little, disappointment comes upon the girl, and she mutters, " He is not
here." Next she says to herself, " Only three hours
more to Salt Lake. There he must be ! "

Then Mrs. Livingston and Louise attempt consolation, and shortly after the party make their way some three hundred yards north of the Union and Central depots, to where at that time the station of the Utah Central was located, and prepare to board the train that is standing ready to run thirty odd miles to the south to the city over which the Mormon Hierarchy is still dominant, though their power is beginning to wane under the assaults of migrating Gentiles, who have come to this Territory, brought by the Pacific railroads, to search for the silver and gold in its mountains.

At this little station Captain Lawrence's cause gets another and most happy advancement in the girl's mind. Some five minutes before the train is ready, Mr. Ferdie wanders off from the party, and a few moments after Miss Travenion notices him in earnest conversation with a gentleman apparently of the cowboy order.

Exchanging a few words, the young man and his chance acquaintance walk down a sidewalk to a saloon, standing about a hundred yards from the railroad.

At this moment, Erma also notes Captain Lawrence walking rapidly over from the Union Depot, apparently having made up his mind to catch this train for Salt Lake also, and hopes to herself, " This will be my time for explanation."

But even while she does so, the gentleman upon whom she is gazing casts two quick, sharp glances at Ferdie and his companion, and instantly changing his direction and quickening his pace, makes straight for the saloon just as the two disappear behind its door.

" He will give me no opportunity for apology," says Erma to herself. " Very well, the next advance shall come from him ! " and her pretty foot tapping the platform impatiently, she turns away and watches the baggage-men loading their trunks upon the Utah Central train.

A moment after, she is aroused from her reverie by the sound of the bell upon the station, which always heralds out-going trains, and Mrs. Livingston, coming to her, gasps, "Where is Ferdie? The conductor tells us we have only a minute more. He is not here. My Heaven, not here!"

"I know where he is, and I'll find him," answers Erma, and runs hastily down the sidewalk to where she has last seen the errant youth. As she approaches, however, she pauses a moment, for the thought suddenly strikes her, "If Captain Lawrence is there, perhaps he'll think I want to speak to him."

But remembering that haste is vital, she hastily opens the saloon door, and stands appalled ; for a sight meets her such as seldom comes to a New York young lady. The signs of combat are about her—a table has been thrown over, a broken spittoon and scattered cards are lying on the floor—and Ferdie, his light suit in the sawdust of the barroom, is held down upon his back, while over him, one knee upon his chest, is a man with black sombrero and buckskin leggings and red shirt, and awful hand with uplifted bowie, ready to strike the young heart that is panting beneath his grasp, did not Harry Lawrence grasp it with his left, and with his right hand press the cold muzzle of a Colt's revolver against the desperado's forehead.

Then Lawrence's voice speaks clear as a bell : "Drop that knife! You know me, Texas Jack. I hung up your pard in Laramie. Drop that knife or I fire."

At his word the bowie-knife comes to the floor. Then Harry says coolly : "Throw up your hands and walk out in front of me," and keeping the man before his pistol, marches him out of the saloon. On the sidewalk he remarks :

"Don't look back until you have gone a hundred yards, or you are a dead man. *March!*" And Texas

Jack, his spurs clinking in the dust, and a deck of monte cards slipping from his clothes as he walks, proceeds on his way, and does not turn back till he has got out of sight.

Then the bell of the locomotive is suddenly heard. Lawrence cries : "Hurry. You'll miss the cars !" and waves Erma, who is too much agitated, and Ferdie, who is too much out of breath, to speak, to follow him. And they all run to the station of the Utah Central, where Miss Travenion gives a gasp, for the train has already run out, and they can see it making its way to the bridge across the Weber bound for the city of the Saints.

"Anyway, God bless you !" cries Ferdie, who has gained his wind. "You saved my life."

"Yes," says Harry shortly, "this time ; but perhaps the next there will be no one there to help you. And take my advice, young man : don't go hunting adventures out here, not even if they tell you there is a grizzly bear chained in the back-yard."

"Why !" says Mr. Chauncey with a little gasp, "that is just what he did tell me."

"Ah, I guessed right," says Lawrence with a slight sneer, for Mr. Ferdinand had been made a victim of the notorious bear game, as were many others about that time in Ogden. Then he goes on : "Don't play three card monte, and if they rob you, don't knock the villain down, for he is sure to be armed, and your life is pleasant to you still, I guess, young man."

With this he turns away, but Erma is after him, and puts her hand on his arm, whispering, "How bravely you saved him ! I have learned the truth about you. Forgive me !"

But the man she addresses is apparently not easy to conciliate, and he remarks curtly, "You did not give me the right even a Vigilance Committee would give !"

"What right ?"

"The right to defend myself!" And he heeds not Erma's pleading eyes.

Then she whispers, "Give me the justice I denied you. Let me explain also. How was I, a girl brought up in a land of peace, to know that men could exist like that one from whom you saved Ferdie just now ; that to protect the innocent it was necessary to slay the guilty, and *right*, too?" and then bursts forth impetuously, *"Wretches like that murderer I saw out there I would kill also !"*

But the young man does not seem to heed her ; and muttering, "You don't forgive me any more than you did the murderers," she falters away and says piteously, "And I—alone here !" And there are tears in her beautiful eyes ; for at this moment Ferdie seems very little of a protector.

This last affects Lawrence. He steps to her, ejaculating huskily, "Not as long as I am here !"

"Oh, thank you," cries the girl. "You will take care of me. How nice !" her smiles overcoming her tears.

"Certainly. That is my duty," answers Harry, still coldly, for he has been very deeply wounded.

"I don't want your duty !" answers Erma hotly.

."What do you want ?"

"Forgiveness ! Don't punish me with kindness, and still be implacable. Forgive me," pleads the young lady, her little hand held out towards her judge.

Then Miss Travenion gives a startled little "Ough !" for her fingers receive a grip that makes her wince, and as their hands meet, piquant gaiety comes over the young lady, and the gentleman begins to smile, and his eyes grow sunny.

A second after he says, "If I am responsible for you, I must look after you. You must have dinner, and so must Ferdie," and he calls cheerily to the youth, who has been brushing the sawdust of barroom floor and the dirt of combat from his light travelling suit. "You are up to a bite, young bantam, ain't you, after your scrimmage ?"

"Yes, I'm dead hungry," answers Mr. Chauncey. "But Erma, your French maid is in the waiting-room, crying her eyes out. She says my aunt left her with your hand-baggage."

"Clothes !" screams Miss Travenion. "There's a new dress in my travelling bag ! Oh : to get rid of the dust of travel," and growing very happy at this find—as what woman would not ?—she and Lawrence walk across the tracks to the railroad hotel, followed by the maid and Ferdie, who brings up the rear, stopping at every other step to examine his summer suit for rent of combat, and to give it another brush from barroom dirt, and shortly arrive at the hostelry that lies between the tracks of the Union and Central Pacific Railways.

Here Lawrence suggests that Erma send a telegram to Mrs. Livingston, and dissipate any fears her chaperon may have for her safety. So, going into the telegraph office, she hastily writes the following :

" To Mrs. Livingston,

" On train bound for Salt Lake City :

"Detained by Ferdie. We are both well, and will follow on first train in the morning. Please tell papa,—who will meet you at the depot.

" Erma Travenion."

This being despatched, she comes out and stands by Lawrence, and watches the Central Pacific train, with its yellow silver palace sleeping cars, that is just about to run for the West and California, and laughs : "In two weeks I will be once more on my way to the Golden Land."

"So soon !" says the young man, a sigh in his voice.

"Oh," says the girl, airily ; "by that time I shall have

seen papa, and we have to do California and get back
to New York for the first Patriarch's Ball." Then she
babbles, " Oh, the delights of New York society. You
must come on next winter and see how gay our city is,
Captain Lawrence, to a young lady who—who isn't
always a wall flower."

" That I will," answers Harry, heartily. A moment
after, he goes on more considerately, " If I can arrange
my mining business,"—this last by no means so confidently spoken.

As he says this, the train dashes off on its way to the
Pacific, and Ferdie coming out of the hotel, where he
has been generally put in order, the three, accompanied
by the maid, go in to dinner. The mentor of the party
registers their names, and tells the proprietor, who seems
to know him very well, to give Miss Travenion the best
rooms in the house.

At this, the young lady says, " Excuse me for a few
minutes. I have clothes with me now." And despite
Lawrence's laughing protestations that no change can be
for the better, she runs upstairs, and a few minutes
after returns, having got the dust of travel from her in
some marvellous way, and appearing in a new toilet—
one of those half dress, half every day affairs, something
with lace on it and ribbons, which makes her beauty
fresh as that of a new-blown rosebud.

Their dinner is a merry meal ; Miss Travenion coming
out afterwards on the platform, and watching outgoing
freight trains and switching locomotives, as the two gentlemen smoke. Then the moon comes up over the giant
mountains that wall in this Ogden Valley, save where it
opens on the Great Salt Lake, and shadows fall on the
distant gorges and cañons. Illumined by the soft light,
the girl looks radiantly lovely and piquantly happy, for
somehow this evening seems to her a pleasant one.

After a little, Mr. Chauncey wanders away, perhaps in

search of further frontier adventure, though Lawrence notes that he sticks very close to the main hotel, and does not investigate outlying barrcoms. Then Erma and Harry being alone, the young man's talk grows confidential, and he tells the girl a good deal of his mining business, which seems to be upon his mind. How he had expected to sell his claim to an English company, but now fears that he shall not, on account of the accursed Mormons—this last under his breath, for nearly every one in the community they are now in are members of that church.

On being questioned, he goes on to explain that a claim has been made to a portion of his mine by a Mormon company, remarking that he has bad news from Salt Lake City that day. He has learned that a Mormon of great influence, called Tranyon, has purchased nearly all the other interests in Zion's Co-operative Mining Institution, which has brought suit for a portion of his property.

"How will that affect you ?" queries Erma, who apparently has grown anxious for her mentor's speculation.

"Why, this Tranyon is a man of wonderful sagacity, —more, I think, than any other business Mormon in this country. He made nearly as much grading the Union Pacific Railway as Brigham Young himself. He has blocks of stock in the road upon which we will travel to-morrow morning to Salt Lake City. I have now money, brains and a Mormon jury against me !" says Lawrence, with a sigh.

He would perhaps continue this subject, did not Ferdie come excitedly to them, his eyes big with wonder, and whisper : "Kruger is in the hotel. Buck Powers and I have been investigating your father's friend, Erma, and have discovered that he is a full-fledged Mormon bishop."

" A Mormon! Impossible," says the young lady, with a start.

" Your father's friend ? " exclaims Lawrence.

" Certainly," replies Miss Travenion. " I met him with my father several times in New York."

To this the Western man does not answer, but a shade passes over his brow and he grows thoughtful.

Then Ferdie, who is very full of his news, says : " There's no doubt of it. I talked with the man who keeps the bar, and he said Lot Kruger was as good a Mormon as any man in Salt Lake Valley, and I asked him if he didn't think we could arrest Kruger, and he cursed me and said he'll blow my infernal Gentile head off."

Here Harry interrupts the boy sternly : " Don't you know that the man in the hotel and nearly every one else about here are Mormons ? If you make many more remarks of that kind, you'll never see New York again."

This advice puts Mr. Chauncey in a brown study, and he wanders away whistling, while Lawrence turns to Miss Travenion and asks her with a serious tone in his voice : " You are sure this man Kruger is interested with your father in business ? "

" I am certain," falters the girl. " In some way. I don't know how much."

" I am very sorry for that ! "

" Sorry for it ? How can it affect my father ? " returns Miss Travenion, growing haughty.

" That I can't see myself," rejoins her escort, and the two both go into contemplation.

A minute after the girl smiles and says, " Why, in another minute, perhaps you will think I am Miss Mormon myself." This seeming to her a great joke, she laughs very heartily.

But her laugh would be a yellow one, did she know that Lot Kruger, bishop in the Mormon Church, high up

in the Seventies, Councilor of the Prophet, Brigham
Young ; and ex-Danite and Destroying Angel to boot,
has stayed in Ogden on her account, and has just sent a
telegram to one who holds the Latter-Day Saints in his
hand, which reads :

"OGDEN, *October* 4, 1871.
"She is here. I am watching her. She will arrive in Salt Lake
on the morning train. See my letter from Chicago, due to-night."

Not knowing this, the girl's laughter is light and
happy, and seems to be infectious, for Lawrence joins in
it, and their conversation grows low, as if they would
keep it to themselves, and perhaps slightly romantic,
for there is a fire in the young man's dark eyes that
seems to be reflected in the beautiful blue ones of Miss
Travenion, as she tells him of life in New York society,
and about Mrs. Livingston and her son. This discanta-
tion on the absent Oliver Lawrence enjoys so little, however, that he turns the conversation to his own prospects
once more.

On which the girl asks him if his mine is so rich, why
does he not work it himself.

" Because I am tired of barbarism ! " he cries. " I
want a home and a wife, and I wouldn't ask any woman
to share a mining cabin with me."

" What matters," says Erma airily, "if she loved you ? "

" Do you mean that ? " remarks Harry, a peculiar ring
coming into his voice.

" Yes," says the girl, rising ; " if I loved a man I
believe I could give up for him—even New York. But
it is growing late. You tell me we have an early breakfast to-morrow morning, Captain Lawrence ? "

" Yes, six o'clock," he says shortly, and escorts his
charge to the door of the hotel, where her maid is waiting for her. Here she nonchalantly says, " Good-night.
Thank you so much ! " Then, a sudden impulse impell-

7

ing her, she steps to the man who is just turning from her and whispers, her eyes glowing gratefully, " God bless you for saving Ferdie's life ! God bless you for being kind to me ! "

Next, seemingly frightened at herself, she runs lightly up the stairs to her bedroom, where she goes to sleep ; but once she is awakened by the clanging of freight trains in the night, and this thought comes into her head : "What manner of man is this who two days ago was a stranger to me, but who has built railroads and slain desperadoes and Indians and whom I think about waking and sleeping ? " Then she utters a little affrighted cry, " WHY, HE HAS EVEN MADE ME FORGET MY FATHER ! "

The gentleman she has slighted has been under discussion on the railroad platform below.

Mr. Chauncey and Lawrence, strolling out before going to bed to take a preliminary smoke, the Captain suddenly asks, between puffs of his cigar : " Miss Travenion's father was quite a swell in New York ? "

" Was ?—is ! " cries Ferdie. " I only know him by sight, but I inspected him once or twice last year when he was in town, sitting in the Unity windows, chewing a cane, and following with his eyes any likely ankle up the Avenue. In fact, he's about as heavy a swell now as you'd want to see, though they say when he lived in New York permanently he used to be heavier."

" Ah," replies Harry, taking a long puff at his Havana, "a thorough club man ? "

" I should think so ! " returns Mr. Chauncey. " He is an out and outer. There are some curious stories extant that would make your hair stand on end about Ralph Travenion in the old days. They say——"

But Ferdie stops here in sudden surprise, for Lawrence's hand is on his arm, and he is whispering : " Don't tell me anything that would make me think less of her father ! "

"Oh, of course not, if you don't wish it," replies the boy. Then he laughingly says: "You're not going to judge of Miss Beauty up there by her paternal, are you, old man? That would be *rather* a heavy handicap." A moment later he goes on, the other not replying: "But she'd stand it. She's a good girl; even a big fortune and the adoration of Newport's smart set couldn't give her airs. She's liable to marry some fellow just for love."

"You think so?" asks Lawrence with a hearty voice.

"Certainly. Did you notice her thanking you for saving my life?" returns the boy. "Could she have shown more gratitude if you'd been an English duke? And I thank you for it also. We Harvard men are not apt to gush, my boy; but we feel just the same. If I was in love with Erma Travenion, I'd sooner have what you did to-day to my credit than a million in bonds."

"Would you!" cries the captain. "Would you!" and his clasp is so cordial as he shakes Ferdie's hand on bidding him good-night that the boy goes away and mutters, "He's got a grip like a prize-fighter—but hang it, I sent him to bed happy for saving my life—and he did save it. Good Lord, if it hadn't been for him, where would yours truly have been now? Oh ginger!" And this idea making him serious, he goes to bed and sleeps, a thing that Harry finds more difficult.

The next morning there is a very happy smile on Miss Travenion's face as she trips down to her breakfast, where she is met by Captain Lawrence and Ferdie, and the three shortly after go to the Utah Central and take train there for Salt Lake, and after running through prosperous Mormon villages and outlying farms for about an hour and a half, Erma suddenly cries, "What is that great turtle rising out of the trees?"

To this Lawrence answers, "The Mormon Tabernacle !" and a few minutes after they run into the "City of the Saints," where certain things shall come to Erma Travenion such as this young lady of New York society wots not are in the heavens above the earth, nor in the waters that are beneath it.

BOOK II.

A Curious Club Man.

CHAPTER VIII.

THE CITY OF SAINTS.

HERE they are met by Mr. Oliver Livingston, who has a carriage in waiting. To his anxious questioning as to how they had missed the train, and had fared during the night in Ogden, Miss Travenion says shortly, "First my father; is he not here with you?" and looks about the depot with scrutinizing eyes. A moment after she continues hurriedly, "Your mother received my telegram?"

"Yes," remarks Ollie. "It arrived just in time to save mamma from a fainting fit."

"And you did not communicate it to my father?"

"No," returns Mr. Livingston; "that was impossible. He was not at the station here. At all events, I did not see him, as I would undoubtedly have, if he had been waiting for you."

"Then he cannot have been in town," cries Erma, her pretty lips pouting with disappointment, for Mr. Livingston is very well acquainted with Mr. Travenion by sight, having seen that gentleman on some of his visits to New York.

While this colloquy has been going on, Ferdie and Harry have been conversing apart. Miss Travenion now turns to them, and seeing that Ollie does not recog-

nize her protector of the night before, says, rapidly, but
earnestly, "Mr. Livingston, you must remember Captain Lawrence on the train. He was very kind to me
last night and took good care of me. You should thank
him also."

The latter part of this speech has been made in some
embarrassment, for the young men are looking at each
other with by no means kindly eyes. Its last sentence makes them enemies, for Livingston, who had
already been slightly jealous of the attentions of the
Westerner to the young lady he regards even now as his
fiancée, becomes very jealous, and Lawrence, who has
somehow formed the shrewd idea that there is some
connection between Miss Travenion and the son of her
chaperon, interprets the "You should thank him also,"
for indication of engagement and future marriage
between the pair, and from this moment takes that kind
of a liking to Mr. Livingston a man generally has for a
rival who is more blessed by circumstance and position
in matters pertaining to his suit—which generally means
envious hate.

Being compelled to social truce, at least in the presence of the young lady, the two men are obliged to
recognize each other and acknowledge the re-introduc-
tion. This Livingston does by a rather snarly "How
are yer?" and Lawrence by a nod of indifference.

Then Miss Travenion gives an additional pang to Mr.
Livingston, for she says: "Captain, another request.
You know Salt Lake very well? You are acquainted
with some of the journals?"

"One only," remarks Harry. "The Salt Lake *Tribune,*—the Gentile newspaper."

"'Then you can do me a favor," returns Erma. "My
father apparently has not received my telegram. Would
you take care that a notice of my arrival is inserted
prominently in that paper, so that if papa is in town, he

will see it; if in any of the mining camps or settlements about here, it may reach his eye. The sooner I behold him, the happier I shall be."

"Any request from you will be a command to me," says Lawrence, eagerly. "The announcement shall be made in the *Tribune*, but it cannot be until to-morrow morning. If I can aid you in any other way, please do not fail to call upon me." To this he adds hurriedly: "I shall leave town early this afternoon for Tintic Mining District, but shall return in three days."

"Very well," answers the young lady. "Do not forget that we stop at the Townsend House, where I shall always be most happy to see you." She emphasizes her invitation by so cordial a grasp of the hand, and Harry returns it so heartily, that Mr. Oliver Livingston pulls down his immaculate shirt-cuffs in anguish and rage.

This is not decreased by Ferdie's admiring remark: "Ain't the Cap a high stepper!" as the party step into the carriage and drive away.

They are soon at the corner of West Temple and South Second Streets, and find themselves in front of a rather rambling two-story house with an attic attachment, at this time the principal hotel in Salt Lake City, for in 1871 the Walker House is not yet built. It has a generally yellow appearance, though its windows are protected from the sun by green Venetian blinds.

Alighting here, Miss Travenion is informed that Mrs. Livingston is not yet up, and going to her room, lies down, it being still quite early in the day, while her maid unpacks her trunks and arranges her dresses. Though fatigued by her long railroad trip, sleep does not come to Erma, for thoughts of her father are upon her; and after a little, growing anxious on this subject, she springs up, and says: "I'll look for him!"

So, making a hasty but effective toilet, robed in a dainty summer dress, the girl stepping to the window,

looks out and cries: "How pretty!" for she is gazing
upon Salt Lake City on an October day, which is as
beautiful as any day can be, save a May day, when
there is a little less dust on the streets and a little more
water in the rivulets that course through them.

All round her are houses embowered in green foliage,
and broad streets, also planted with trees, and streams
of living water, fresh from the melting snows of the
Wahsatch, coursing by their sidewalks where gutters
would be in ordinary towns.

In these streets there is a curious, heterogeneous life,
the like of which she has never seen before. Immediately below her, in front of the hotel, men of many climes
lounge about the unpaved sidewalk, most of them seated,
their feet against the trees that line its side, each man
smoking a cigar, the aromas of which, as they float up
to her, seem to be pleasant.

Most of these are mining speculators from California,
the East, and Europe; as their voices rise to her, she
catches tones similar to those she has heard in Delmonico's from travelling Englishmen. For the Emma mine
is in its glory; and much British capital has floated into
this Territory, to be invested in the silver leads of the
great mountains that cut off her view to the east, and the
low ranges that she can see to the south and west; a
good deal of it never to return to London again; for,
of all the speculators of many nations who have invested
in American securities, stocks, bonds, mining properties
and beer interests, none have so rashly and so lavishly
squandered their money as the speculators of merry
England. These have sometimes been allured to financial discomfort by Yankee shrewdness, but more often
have been betrayed by the ignorance or carelessness or
rascality of those whom they have sent from their
native isle to represent them, who have judged America,
Western mines and Yankee business methods by Eng-

land, Cornish lodes and the financial conditions that prevail in Thread-Needle Street.

Two or three hacks and carriages, such as are seen in the East, stand in front of the hotel, while in the street before her move some big mule teams, laden with bars of lead and silver, from some smelter on the Jordan, and a little further on is a wagon of the prairies, covered with the mud and dust of long travel, driven by some Mormon who has come up from the far southern settlements of Manti, or Parowan, or the pretty oasis towns of Payson or Spanish Fork or some other garden spot by the side of the fresh waters of Utah Lake, to go through the rites of the Endowment House, and take unto himself another wife; paying well for the ceremonies in farm produce.

Looking over this scene, the girl murmurs, "How peaceful—how beautiful!" and next, "How wonderful," and a moment after, gazing at the great Mormon Tabernacle, she mutters, "How awful!" for in the two hours passed upon the train coming from Ogden to Salt Lake, Harry Lawrence has told her, as delicately as a young man can tell a maiden, of this peculiar city into which she has just come, and she knows quite well the peculiar creed of the Church of Latter-Day Saints,

She has learnt how this sect, founded upon the so-called revelation from the Almighty, made to Joseph Smith, and Hyrum, his brother, in about 1847, driven out from Illinois and afterwards from Missouri, had left civilization behind them, and passing over a thousand of miles of prairie and mountain, inhabited only by savage Indians and trappers and hunters, had come by ox-teams, on horseback, by hand carts and on foot, enduring for long months all the privations and dangers of the wilderness, to this far-off valley to build a Mormon empire. For that is surely what their leaders had hoped.

The civilization of the East seemed to them so far off

a hundred years might not bring it to them, across those boundless rolling prairies and that five hundred miles of mountain country. To the West were more deserts, and beyond a land scarcely known at that time, and inhabited only by Indians, save where some Mexican mission stood surrounded by its little orchard and vineyard, in that land that is now called California.

In this hope of empire, the Mormon leaders had built up polygamy, which, having been begun for lust, they now preached, continued, and fostered to produce the power that numbers give. For this reason the order had been given, "Increase and multiply, that you may cover the land," and it was cried out from pulpit and tabernacle "that Utah's best crop was children;" and missionaries and Mormon propagandists were sent out over both Europe and America to make converts to the new religion. So, many Scandinavians, Welsh and English, were taken into the faith and came to live in the Utah valleys, and thought this religion of Joseph Smith a very good one—for they were chiefly the scum of Europe—and now had land to cultivate and plenty with which to fill their stomachs, while in their native lands they had often hungered.

For the Mormon hierarchy hoped, in the distant future, when the civilization from the Eastern States had reached them, to be increased by immigration and multiplication from thousands into millions; and peopling the whole land, from the Rocky Mountains to the Pacific, to be strong enough to dominate Mexico if she dared complain of their occupation of North California, and even to give battle to these United States of America.

And to the eyes of Brigham and his satellites came the dream of a Mormon empire, holding dominion over the Pacific, ruled over by the Priesthood of the faith of Joseph Smith and the Council of Seventies, and above them the President and Vice-President, descendants of

Brigham Young and Heber Kimball and others high in rank and power in the theocracy of the so-called Latter-Day Saints.

All of these plans might have borne fruit and have been realized had it not been that one day in 1848 gold was discovered near Sutter's Fort in California, and the rush of adventurers to the western El Dorado peopled its fertile valleys and mineral-bearing mountains and great grain-raising plains with a population who worshipped Jehovah and not Joe Smith. Then the Mexican war having given Arizona and Texas and the Pacific States to the United States, Brigham Young and his emigrants found themselves surrounded and cut off in and about the valley of Salt Lake. But still they continued to increase and multiply and make the desert about them fertile and populated, still hoping to be strong enough to resist foreign domination, for they regarded the United States as such, and treated its laws, if not as null and void, at least as secondary to the commands of their prophet and priesthood, until one day in 1862 Pat Conner and his California Volunteers marched in from the Humboldt, and crossing the Jordan, despite the threats of the Mormon leaders, set up the United States flag at Camp Douglas.

Then Mormon hopes, from that of independent empire, fell to the wish to be simply left alone, to do as they pleased in their own country, as they termed it, and to follow out the revelations of their prophets, taking unto themselves as many wives as they chose, unhindered by the United States laws.

But in 1869, when the Central and Union Pacific Railways were opened, bringing in a horde of Gentiles from all the corners of the world to delve in their mountains for gold, silver and lead, then the struggle of the Mormon theocracy became one not for power, but even for existence.

It is just in this state as Erma gazes at its metropolis.

This last great fight of the Mormon Church is being
made without the sacrifice and the cutting off from the
face of the earth of their enemies, for though the prophets
of Zion would preach " blood atonement " to their followers with as much gusto in 1871 as they did twenty years
before, when they cut off the Morrisites, root and branch,
or in 1857, when, headed by John D. Lee, they massacred
one hundred and thirty-three emigrants, men, women and
children, or in 1866, when they assassinated Dr. Robinson,
luring him from his own door on a professional errand
of mercy to a wounded man, as well as many other murders, " cuttings off behind the ears " and " usings up,"
done in the name of the Lord and in pursuit of mammon,
lust and power, at such various times and places as
seemed good, safe and convenient to the Apostles ;
still, even before 1871 the rush of Gentile immigration
and the United States troops at Camp Douglas had
taught them caution in their slaughterings.

Most of this has been explained to Miss Travenion by
her escort and mentor of the morning, but he has not
descanted very minutely upon Celestial Marriage, which
permits a man to take wives not only for this world, but
also to have any number of others sealed to him for
eternity ; the doctrine that woman takes her rank in
Heaven according to the station and glory of her husband. That under these theories, men have often taken
two sisters to wife, and sometimes even mother and
daughter. That a great part of the theory, as also the
practice, of the Saints of Latter Days, is founded upon the
social degradation of woman. All these things she does
not know, though she will perchance some day learn
more fully concerning them.

But the day is too sunny and bright for meditation,
and the soft breeze from the Wahsatch incites Erma to

action. Just then there is a light feminine knock on her door, and Louise's voice cries merrily : "Hurry, Erma ; mamma is down-stairs at breakfast and wants to see you. She has so many questions to ask. Ferdie has just told her about his being saved from death by Captain Lawrence, and is singing his praises."

Being perhaps anxious to sing the young Western man's praises herself, Miss Travenion, with a happy laugh, trips out and kisses Louise, and the two girls run down to the dining-room, where they find Mrs. Livingston still pale and palpitating over Ferdie's escape, though apparently with a very good appetite, notwithstanding Mr. Chauncey has made his narrative very highly colored, stating that he had knocked the desperado down and would have done him up if it had not been for his bowie-knife.

"All the same," he adds, just as Erma seats herself at the table, "that Lawrence is a regular thoroughbred— a Western hero, and saved my life in that barroom."

"I should think you would be ashamed of yourself," says Mr. Livingston, airily, during pauses in his breakfast, "to admit associating with barroom loafers ! "

"Barroom loafers ?" cries Erma. "Whom do you mean ? " and she looks at Ollie in so resolute and defiant a manner that he hesitates to take up the cudgels with her.

Therefore he mutters rather sulkily, "Oh, if you are going to make this Lawrence your hero I have nothing more to say," and glumly pitches into the beefsteak that is in front of him ; but, all the same, hates Harry a little more than he has ever done.

Anxious to put an end to a discussion which does her son no good in the eyes of the young lady she regards as his *fiancée*, Mrs. Livingston proposes a sight-seeing drive about the city.

"You will come with us, Erma ? " she adds.

" With pleasure," answers the girl. " Perhaps on the main street I may see papa."

" By Jove," laughs Ferdie. " You're always thinking of papa now. But you forgot him a *little*—last night at Ogden, eh ? "

To this insinuation Erma answers nothing, but rises from the table with a heightened color on her cheeks.

Noticing this, Mrs. Livingston thinks it just as well that her *protégée* sees no more of the Western mining man, and is rather relieved when Mr. Chauncey informs her Captain Lawrence has departed for Tintic, and will not return for several days.

Then they take a long drive about the city, the hackman condescendingly acting as *cicerone* to the party, and pointing out the Tabernacle and the proposed Temple, the foundations of which have just been laid, and the Endowment House and the Tithing Office, and the Beehive and Lion House, in which Brigham Young, the president of the Latter-Day Saints, keeps the major portion of his harem ; though he has houses and wives almost all over the Territory.

Next, coming down from Eagle Gate, they pass the Mormon theatre with its peculiar classic front made up of two different kinds of Greek architecture, and so on to East Temple Street, by Godby's drug store, and the great block of Zion's Mercantile Co-operative Institution, till they come to Warden Bussey's Bank, upon which Erma and Mr. Livingston have letters of credit.

So they enter here, draw some money, and are kindly received by Mr. Bussey himself, their letters from the East bringing them favor in this Gentile banker's eyes, who has just made a large fortune by speculating in Emma stock. He shows them over the new banking-house he has just erected, and tells them he is going to open it with a grand ball, and hopes they will come to the same ; remarking that Mrs. Bussey will call upon them and do all she can for their entertainment during their stay in this Western city.

Then they return to the Townsend House, but during all this drive, though Erma Travenion's eyes, which are quite far-sighted, have searched the passing crowd of speculators, Mormons and Western business men, seeking for one form and one face—her father's—she has not seen it. As the afternoon passes she becomes more impatient, and says, "I have lost a day in which his dear face might have been beside me."

Then an idea coming to her, she mutters: "Why did I not think of it before? I will go where I address my father's letters; there they will know where he is." And calling a hack, says to the driver, "The Deseret Co-operative Bank!"

Arriving there, shortly before the hour of closing, three o'clock, she hurriedly asks the paying-teller if he can tell her the address of Mr. Ralph Travenion.

To her astonishment, the man answers quite politely that he does not know the individual.

"Why, I have directed a hundred letters to him here," she says hurriedly, surprise in her voice, and a moment after asks: "Can I see the cashier or the president?"

"Certainly. The president is in."

In an inner office, she meets the head of the bank, and to her question as to whether he knows the address of Ralph Travenion, he hesitates a moment—then answers that they frequently have letters addressed to their care, though they do not always keep run of the parties who call for them.

"Very well," replies the young lady. "Would you be kind enough to give orders to this effect, that in case Mr. Travenion calls, or sends for his letters, that he is to be informed that Mr. Travenion's daughter is at present at the Townsend House waiting anxiously to see him?"

" Ah, you are Mr. Travenion's daughter," replies the
official, as he shows her politely to the door and puts
her in her carriage, a rather curious expression coming
over his face as he gazes after the beautiful girl as she
is driven away; for this bank is a Mormon one, and its
president is well up in the Church of Zion, and knows
a good deal of the counsels and doings of its leaders
and nearly every one else in Salt Lake City.

Then the evening comes, and the whole party go to
the old Salt Lake Theatre, where Mr. Ollie's dress-coat
makes a great sensation, such costume not being usual
in the Mormon temple of Thespis; this gentleman's
entrance being greeted by a very audible buzz from
the female portion of the audience.

Here they see the arm-chair that is placed conspic-
uously in the orchestra, for the use of the President
of the Mormon Church; likewise, a third of the dress
circle, which is his family's private box. This portion
of the auditorium is pretty well occupied by some of
his wives and his numerous progeny, as well as a number
of the daughters and plural help-mates of other leaders
and prophets of Zion, who drop in upon them and pass
the compliments of the season and talk of the crops and
Bishop Jenkins's last wife.

The performance on the stage is composed of a
couple of light comedies, very passably given by a
Mormon stock company, several of them being members of President Young's family, one or two of whom
have since emigrated to the Gentile stage and secured
recognition upon the boards of New York and San
Francisco.

But this visit to the theatre is not altogether an
evening of delight to Erma; to her astonishment, Mr.
Livingston has suddenly changed from the complacent,
passive suitor of former times, to as impetuous a lover
as such a man can make, and his attentions embarrass

her. This Romeo business has partly been brought about by Mr. Ollie's jealousy and partly by the remarks of his diplomatic mother.

This lady has had an interview with her son, caused chiefly by Miss Travenion's adventures in Ogden, and has given her offspring the following advice : " If you do not settle your marriage with Erma during this trip, she will probably marry somebody else."

" Impossible ! She is as good as engaged to me," cries out Ollie, hotly.

" Engaged ! Why ? Because her father and your father came to some understanding when you were children ?"

" Because Mr. Travenion has settled a million dollars on his daughter ! Why did he put that big sum apart for her sole use and benefit ? He wishes his daughter to take the position that I can give her in New York."

" Because he has settled a million dollars on her," answers his mother, "she is all the more difficult to win. It is a marvel to me that she, the belle of New York last season and of Newport this summer, has kept herself apart from entangling alliances with other men. Two months ago, if she had loved that young Polo Blazer, you would have lost her then."

" You don't mean to say she loves that Vigilante— that mining fellow ?" says Oliver, turning pale at his mother's suggestion.

" If she doesn't love him she will love some man," returns his mother grimly. " Don't you know that a girl with her beauty and her money is bound to be sought after and will be won by somebody ? "

" By me ! " cries Ollie hotly. " Hang me if she shall marry any other man ! " Then he says plaintively, " I have considered her my own for a year."

" Very well," replies Mrs. Livingston ; "you had

8

better act as if you did.   Miss Travenion's attitude to
you has been one of indifference.   She saw no one
whom she liked better.   Besides, girls enjoy being
made love to.   Perhaps Captain Lawrence last night
in Ogden in the moonlight was more of a Romeo than
you have been.   He looks as if he might be."

"Does he?" cries Ollie.   "I'll show him that I can
play the romantic as well as he," and going out, he, for
the first time in his life—for he is a good young man—
says to himself, "Damn!" and then becomes frightened and soliloquizes: "Oh gracious, that is the first
time I ever swore."

So going to the theatre and coming therefrom he
assists Erma into the carriage with squeezes of her
hand that make her wince, and little amatory ogles of
the eyes that make her blush.

Coming from the theatre, they go to "Happy Jack's,"
the swell restaurant of the city in 1871, where they
have a very pretty little room prepared for them, and
trout caught fresh in a mountain stream that day, and
chickens done to a turn, and the freshest of lettuce
and some lovely pears and grapes from Payson gar-
dens and vineyards, and a bottle of champagne from
sunny France, some of which gets into Mr. Ollie's head
and makes him so devoted in his attentions to the
young lady who sits beside him, that, getting a chance,
he surreptitiously squeezes her hand under the table,
which makes Erma think him tipsy with wine, not
love.

From this they return to the Townsend House, where
the party separating, Miss Travenion finds herself alone
at the door of her own room; but just before she
enters, Mr. Oliver comes along the hallway, and walking up to her, says, with eyes that have grown fiery:
"Erma, how can you treat me so coldly when I love
you?"

"Why, when did that love idea come into your head?"
returns the young lady with a jeering laugh.

Next her voice grows haughty, and she says, coldly,
"Stop!" for Ollie is about to put his arm around
her fairy waist. A second after, however, she laughs
again and says: "What nonsense! Good-night, Mr.
Oliver," and sweeps past him into her room, where,
closing the door, Miss Changeable suddenly cries: "If
he had dared!" then mutters: "A few days ago I
looked upon his suit complacently and indifferently;"
next pants: "Now what is the matter with me? What
kind of a railroad journey is it that makes a girl—"
and, checking herself here, cries: "Pshaw! what nonsense!" and so goes to bed in the City of the Saints.

CHAPTER IX.

THE BALL IN SALT LAKE.

THE next morning sleep leaves Erma, driven away by
the singing of the birds in the trees that front the hotel.
A little time after, church bells come to her ears, and
she is astonished, and then remembers that it is Sunday, and that there is a little Episcopal church on First
South Street that has come there with the railroad, and
is permitted to exist because United States troops are
at Camp Douglas, just in the shadow of the mountains,
over which the sun is rising, and whose snowtops look
very cool and very pleasant here in the warmer valley,
five thousand feet below them.

Coming down stairs to a nine o'clock breakfast, she
encounters Ferdie and Louise at the table, for Mrs.
Livingston and Oliver are later risers. Over the meal,
Mr. Chauncey, who has not been to the theatre with
them, but has been investigating the city, points out

some of the notables who are seated about the dining-room. Then he begins to run on about what he has seen the evening before, telling them he has joined the Salt Lake Billiard Club and paid twenty-five cents initiation fee to register his name as a member of the club, in order to wield a cue, which registry is kept by pasting a few sheets of paper each day upon a roller, and has gradually rolled up until it has a diameter of five feet, and contains the names of every man who has ever played a game of billiards in Salt Lake City from the time Orson Pratt first spied out the valley; for the Mormon authorities have refused to license billiard tables, and a club was the only way in which they could be circumvented. Next the boy excitedly tells them that he has been introduced to a Mormon bishop in a barroom. At which Miss Livingston laughs : " He couldn't have been much of a bishop to have been there."

" Wasn't he ! " rejoins Ferdie indignantly. " He has four wives, two pairs of sisters."

At which Louise gives an affrighted, " Oh ! " and Miss Travenion says sternly, " No more Mormon stories, please," for Mr. Chauncey is about to run on about an apostle of the church who had married a mother and two daughters.

But now the party are joined by Mrs. Livingston and Oliver, and shortly after, the meal being finished, Mr. Livingston proposes church.

As it is a short distance, they go there on foot, the widow and Louise and Ferdie walking ahead and Mr. Livingston attaching himself to Erma and bringing up · the rear.

As they walk up South Second Street and turn into East Temple, Miss Travenion, who has been listening to Ollie's conversation in a musingly indifferent way, suddenly brightens up and says, " Excuse me, please,"

and leaving him hastily, crosses the wide main street.
A moment after, Livingston, to his astonishment, sees
her in earnest conversation with Mr. Kruger.

This gentleman has turned from two or three square-
jawed, full-lipped Mormon friends of his, to meet her.
A complacent smile is on his red and sunburnt face,
which lights up with a peculiar glance, half-triumph,
half something else, as the girl, radiant in her beauty,
addresses him.

"Well, Sissy, I am right glad you take the trouble to
run over and see me this morning," he cries genially,
trying to take her patricianly gloved hand in his.

"Mr. Kruger," she says shortly, "I fear the telegram I gave you did not reach my father. Have you
heard anything of him? Do you know where he
is?"

"Yes," replies the complaisant Lot. "I reckon he
is in one of the outlying mining camps. If so, he won't
be here for a day or two yit, though he has been com-
municated with."

"Oh!" ejaculates the girl; "then I shall be disappointed again?"

"Indeed! How?" says the man rather curiously,
noting that the lovely blue eyes are teary as they look
into his.

"I am going to the Episcopal Church. I had hoped
to meet my father there."

"You expect—to meet your dad—thar?" gasps Kruger, as if the girl's information took away his breath.

"Yes, certainly! My father has been an Episcopalian all his life. I naturally expect to meet him at
the Episcopal Church."

"Oh—your—father—has—been—an Episcopal—all
his life," echoes Lot, apparently a little dazed. Then
he goes on genially: "Wa-all, as you are certain of
not seeing your dad among the Episcopals, perhaps

you'd better go up this morning to our great Tabernacle, where President Young will make an address
that'll learn you somethin'." He apparently now has
no wish to conceal that he is a Latter-Day Saint.

"Thank you," replies the girl, with a little mocking
smile. "I am an Episcopalian as well as my father,"
and she rejoins the wondering Ollie, who has by this
time crossed the street ; as she moves away with her
escort, she thinks she hears a low chuckle from the
genial Kruger.

Horror and rage would enter her, however, did she
catch the remark of one of his companions : "Well,
bishop, what do you think Mrs. Kruger Number Six
would say to that, if she saw it ? A new favorite in the
household, eh ? "

"Oh, no tellin'," rejoins Lot, his eyes following Miss
Travenion's light form, as do likewise those of his
companions, for the girl, robed as she is in the creation
of some New York milliner, makes a picture of maiden
loveliness seldom seen in the streets of Salt Lake City
in 1871 ; Mormon women, as a rule, not being over fair
to look upon, and the few Gentile ladies in that town
being mostly married to gentlemen whose business has
brought them to Utah.

"I am simply astonished, Erma," remarks Mr.
Livingston, as they get out of ear-shot, "that knowing,
as you know now, that this man is a Mormon, a
polygamist, you even notice him, much less address him
on the public streets."

"I merely asked him where my father was," replies
the girl rather haughtily. "I would ask any man that—
to get one minute nearer my dear papa."

Then she walks silently by his side ; Oliver sporadi-
cally attempting to keep up the conversation, until they
arrive at the pretty little Episcopal church on First
South Street, where they get such an edifying sermon

from Bishop Tuttle, who is assisted by the Rev. Mr.
Kirby in the service, that Mr. Livingston is quite delighted.

"Who would have thought it! They even have altar-
boys out here. I shall leave my card on the Bishop at
once," he remarks, as the congregation is dismissed.

"Why not see him immediately?" suggests Miss
Travenion; which they do, and she has an opportunity
of asking the Right Reverend Mr. Tuttle if her father,
Mr. Ralph Travenion, is not one of his communicants,
and is much surprised and disappointed to learn that
the Bishop has never heard of the gentleman she names.

Returning from church, after dinner Ferdie, who
is anxious, as he expresses it, to see Mormonism in its
glory, induces them to go to afternoon services in the
Tabernacle. Under its vast dome, many thousands of
the elect of Utah listen to a discourse from one high up
in the Mormon priesthood, who tells them that women
who bear not children are accursed, and goes so into
the details of the "Breeding of the Righteous," that
Mrs. Livingston whispers to Louise and Erma to close
their ears, and goes out of the place to the pealing of
its great organ and the singing of its vast choir, feeling
a loathing horror of these Saints of Latter Days.

As for Ferdie, he remarks, "Isn't this a Tower of
Babel crowd?" for it is Conference time, and Northern
Utah has sent its Swedes and Scandinavians, and Southern Utah its Huns and Bohemians, and there are Welsh
from Spanish Fork, and Cornish men from Springville,
and all are jabbering in their native tongues, English
being less heard than the others; and the men have,
generally, red faces, scaly from weather exposure, and
the women have often a hopeless look in their eyes, and
the children are mostly tow-headed in this Mormon Conference crowd of 1871.

After a time the Livingstons get to their carriage

and drive up to Camp Douglas, to the dress parade which takes place every Sunday, having been invited there by Captain Ellison, of the Thirteenth Infantry, who has been introduced to Louise the evening before, and has been very much caught by her piquant graces. Then, the parade being dismissed, this gentleman brings up several of his brother officers to the Livingstons' carriage, and introduces Lamar, a dandy, dashing lieutenant fresh from West Point, and Johnson, of the Fifth Cavalry, and several other of his brother officers, and these, looking for the first time upon the New York beauties as they sit in their carriage, offer them a hundred pleasant excursions and courtesies ; all insisting that the whole party must come to Mr. Bussey's ball, as it will be a great affair in Salt Lake society, both Mormon and Gentile ; for the banker aims for popularity, and has invited every one in the city who has a bank account or has any chance of having one.

Then they drive away, and looking at the stars and stripes which float from the flag-staff of this camp bristling with cannon and Gatling guns—for Douglas, in those days, was held rather in the manner of a beleaguered fortress than in the easy method of a local garrison—the girl cannot help contrasting the columns of blue infantry she has just seen, and the vast and motley assemblage of men in the Tabernacle, who, at the word of their president, would turn upon and assault this camp and make war upon these United States of America. For the danger of Mormonism has been and will be, not in the feeling of animosity that its masses hold to this government, for they have but little, but in their blind, unthinking allegiance to a power they hold superior to it—that of their priesthood and the officers of their Church.

Then they come down the hill into the city again for supper at the Townsend House, which takes place in the evening, dinner in that primitive country being the midday meal. Finishing this, they are called upon by Mrs. Bussey, who insists upon their not omitting her ball.

During her visit she introduces to the Livingstons a number of Gentile ladies in the hotel and a few of the gentlemen engaged in speculation in the neighboring mines, who are quartered at the house, and they pass a quiet evening in the parlor, in conversation with their new-made acquaintances, whom Miss Travenion charms with a song or two.

These are mostly plaintive melodies, for thoughts of her father will run in the girl's brain and somehow make her sad. Being full of the subject now, she questions the mining operators that she meets if they know Ralph Travenion, and receives the usual answer that they have never heard of him ; and her anxiety for tidings of him increases and would now be desperate, did not a few words she catches from one mining operator to another set her thinking of the man who has gone to Tintic.

"I am afraid Harry Lawrence has a hard row to hoe," remarks Jackson of the Bully Boy to Thomas of the Neptune. "He has got Tranyon and the Mormons against him. They will stop his sale to the English company if they do not get a goodly portion of his Mineral Hill."

"He has got one chance, however," says the other.

"Indeed ! What is that ? "

"Why, don't you know," replies Thomas of the Neptune, "that the prophet up there," he nods his head in the direction of Brigham Young's private residence, "and some of the other leaders of the Church are beginning to be afraid of Tranyon ? "

"Afraid of his business talents ? " asks the other. "He has got plenty of them."

"No, afraid of his steadfastness in the faith of Joe

Smith ; afraid that he will refuse to pay his tithing !"
laughs Thomas. "They say he made a million last
year, and he hates to give up a hundred thousand to
the Church." Then he adds very seriously : "Godby
has gone back on them, and the Walkers are no more
to be relied upon for Church dues, and this time they
feel they cannot stand another apostasy, and will take
desperate measures to stop it."

"Who knows but Tranyon some day may feel the
fist of the Church upon him as heavy as it fell on the
Morrisites ?" says Jackson, lowering his voice to a whisper, and, in spite of herself, the girl, as she listens, cannot help wishing that the hand of the Mormon Church
may smite this Tranyon, if it will be any aid to Harry
Lawrence.

But the evening passes, and next day Erma getting
to thinking of her father again, it suddenly occurs
to her to look in the directory, which she does, but
there is no Travenion in its list of names.

The latter part of this day, which is a long one to
her, she kills by a drive with Mrs. Livingston and
Oliver to the Sulphur Springs, where they enjoy the
baths. Mr. Livingston, as they return home, remarking on the softness the sulphur water has given to
Erma's hands, would become very attentive and amatory and lover-like, did the girl but let him ; but this
serves to take her thoughts from that subject they will
dwell on, though she says, "To-morrow papa must
come, and he shall take me in the evening to Mr
Bussey's ball."

And the morrow does come, but with it no father, and
the girl turns for forgetfulness to making her preparations for the evening *fête*. Once or twice, however,
she grows disheartened and mutters, "I cannot go.
Dancing to-night would be a mockery," then suddenly
cries to her maid, "The finest ball dress in my trunk,—

the light blue one that I have never worn,—the one I was going to keep for San Francisco."

A second after she directs Marie to get out what jewels she is carrying with her, and murmurs to herself, " I must look my best to-night," for Miss Volatile has suddenly remembered that three days have elapsed and Harry Lawrence may be at the *fête* this evening.

So, when the soft October night settles down upon the city, Mrs. Livingston is astonished to find her charge in excited mood.

" My, how you will delight Oliver," babbles the widow, gazing in admiration at the light, graceful beauty of the young girl as she steps forth ready for the Bussey *soirée dansante;* and she does delight Oliver, who very attentively cloaks her from the evening air, which is growing cool as the autumn progresses in this valley. Then Mrs. Livingston and Erma and Louise, who is robed in some white, float-away dress and already engaged for dances six deep, as she expresses it, to some of the Gentile gentlemen in the hotel, accompanied by Mr. Oliver, take carriage for the banker's ball.

Ferdie, the night being fine and the distance short, says he will walk, which he does in company with Lamar of the Thirteenth Infantry, and Jackson of the Bully Boy, the two latter smoking huge cigars, and Mr. Chauncey affecting the more youthful cigarette.

At the portals of the banking-house a string of carriages is depositing most of the Gentile magnates, and some of the Mormon, though the Latter-Day Saints do not, as a rule, circulate very freely in outside society, their elders fearing the influence of the Gentile youth upon the maidens of Zion, as to marriage and giving in marriage.

The third story of the building has been arranged with a view of letting it for public balls, and Mr. Bussey is utilizing it for his private one this evening. Here, in

the large dancing room, the Livingstons and Miss Travenion are received by the hospitable banker and his
wife, who are shaking hands with the stream of guests
now pouring into the ball-room, and making it look
quite bright, though very much diversified. Costumes
that would grace a Newport *fête* or Parisian ball-room
alternate with the horrors of Mormon modiste invention, which is, like the country, crude. These atrocities
of toilet are mostly worn by some pretty Mormon
girls, who have persuaded their fathers, who are connected with the Zion's Co-operative stores or other
Deseret industries, to bring them to this conglomerate
ball ; their escorts mostly being arrayed in the ample
black broad-cloth long-tailed frock coats that are
considered the proper thing in mining camps and in
extreme frontier society.

But as these latter dance with much athletic vigor
and Western abandon, they add greatly to the life of
the scene. The room is decorated with flags bor-
rowed from Camp Douglas, its large rear windows
opening onto a broad balcony, which has been made
conservatory-like by flowering plants, and lighted by
Chinese lanterns. Here Mr. Dames and his band
play the " Blue Danube," which has just become popular, and other modern waltzes interspersed with
old Mormon quadrille tunes, some of which were composed, Ferdie remarks, " before the Ark," for this gentleman has just come in, apparently very merry.

" Look and see if Kruger is not changed," he whispers into Erma's delicate ear.

" Why ? He does look different. What has he been
doing ?" answers Miss Travenion.

" He has been getting his hair cut, *gratis*," giggles
Ferdie ; " likewise his beard trimmed and his hair
shampooed. You see, Bussey, with Western hospitality,
has furnished three barbers for the use of his guests,

and Kruger, as he remarks, has just been going 'the whole hog.' He would have taken a bath if there had been conveniences in the gentlemen's waiting-room," continues Mr. Chauncey, greatly amused.

"He looks very happy over it," laughs Erma ; for Kruger's countenance seems quite bland and genial this evening. His black broadcloth frock coat has been very well brushed, and his shirt front is apparently more ample and crumpled than ever, while his large boots have been very brightly shined by the bootblack on the corner opposite, and his gray eyes, as they roam over the ball-room, have an expression of triumph in them, though they apparently seek only one object. Meeting that, Lot Kruger gives a start, for they rest on Erma Travenion.

Then his orbs grow watery and his thick lips tremble, and his jaws clench themselves, as he thinks, "If it should come to me,—all this ; for the glory of the Church of the Latter-Day Saints."

For, robed in some creation of Worth that has been imported to America to make her seem a fairy, Erma's beauty is of the air not of the earth. It is some light, gauzy, shimmering, gleaming thing, covered with tiny pink rosebuds,—thousands of them,—and floats about the girl's dazzling shoulders and gleaming neck and snowy maiden bosom, which is of such exquisite proportions and contours that it would make a sculptor's dream and an average man's ecstasy.

While over all this is a face beaming with some expectant joy, its blue eyes looking for somebody,— somebody who has not yet come.

For a moment Kruger steps forward, as if he would speak to her, but just then Mr. Oliver carries the young lady away to the dance, and sinking upon a seat, the Mormon follows Miss Beauty with his eyes everywhere she moves.

Unheeding the remark that Counsellor Smith, of the Seventies, makes to him, that his last Mrs. Smith is anxious to hear of his trip to the States, and that his (Smith's) daughters, by his first and second wives, Birdie and Desie, are quite ready for a dance, Lot drinks in the girl's loveliness as if it were new wine of such rare bouquet and wondrous flavor that he cannot take the goblet from his lips—wine upon which he will finally get drunk, perchance to his own undoing.

And the eyes of other men follow his also, for there is only one woman who approaches Erma's charm or grace that evening, and that is a young grass-widow from California, at present making a six months' sojourn in Salt Lake for the purpose of obtaining a divorce—a thing easily found in the United States courts in Utah at this time.

But all the time the girl seems languid; and Ollie, dancing with her, notices that the lightness has left her step, and she seems to dream ; which, indeed, she does, thinking of a ball during the season in New York, to which her father on his last visit had taken her, and remembering how the old beau, *bon-vivant* and club man had enjoyed meeting his former friends, companions and chums of other days, also the belles of the last decade of Manhattan society, whom he had greeted again as matrons and dowagers, and she murmurs to herself : "How happy I would be if papa were by me *now* as he was *then*."

But at this moment Mr. Livingston starts, and wonders what change has come into Erma Travenion, for suddenly new life and vigor seem to enter the lithe waist his arm encircles ; her cheek, before a little pale, becomes blushing as he gazes on it ; and her eyes, which were downcast, grow bright and radiant, and her step, which was languid, becomes light as a sylph's.

Then he follows Erma's eyes, and sees the stalwart

form of Harry Lawrence standing in the door, and looking just about the same as when he first entered Mrs. Livingston's supper party at Delmonico's; and Ollie says to himself, a second time in his life, the awful word, "Damn!"

A moment after the music ceases, and Captain Lawrence is by the girl's side, and their hands clasp; their eyes have already greeted.

"I have driven seventy-five miles to-day," he says eagerly. "Am I in time to have a dance with you?"

"Seventy-five miles," replies Erma. "Then you must be very tired."

"Not tired till I have a dance with you. Can I look at your programme?"

"Certainly," and she hands it to him.

But glancing at it, the young man remarks gloomily: "There is no vacant spot."

"No vacant spot but plenty of *crosses*. Take up your cross and follow me!" laughs Miss Travenion. Then she explains, "I always reserve a few dances by crosses for friends who come late," and something gets into her eyes which makes Lawrence very ardent and very bold.

So bold that, being borne away to another dance by Ferdie, Erma looks at her card and suddenly whispers, "Why, he has taken up *all* my crosses," but though implored by a number of gentlemen who come up afterwards to erase some one of the many H. L.'s marked upon her programme, she shakes her head resolutely and says, "No, I stick to my written contracts," much to the disgust of Ellison of the Thirteenth Infantry, and Lamar, the dashing lieutenant, and Jackson of the Bully Boy.

So, a few moments after, Lawrence coming up for his first dance, she takes his arm more happily than she has ever done, to tread a measure; though she has been the belle of many Delmonico balls and has floated about on the arms of the best cotillion leaders of New York and Boston.

A moment after, Harry Lawrence, who has lived his life in camps or on the frontier, puts his arm around this beauty of Manhattan society, and for the first time feels her heart beat against his. Then perhaps something more potent than the strains of the "Thousand and One Nights of Strauss" getting into his head, he dances with all his soul. Not perhaps in so deft a way as Ferdie, who is past master of the art, and glides the graceful Louise through the room in poetic motion, nor in the dashing manner of Lamar, fresh from cadet german and Mess Hall hops, with the California widow, but still with so powerful an arm that his partner feels confidence in him, and perhaps some emotion coming into her heart other than the mere pleasure of the dance; a very bright blush is on her cheek as they stop.

"Your step suits mine very well. You dance very nicely," she murmurs.

"Yes, for a man who has not tripped the light fantastic for years," replies the captain. Then he goes on, "But who couldn't dance with you?"

"Oh, many men, I imagine," laughs the girl. "That gentleman there, for instance," and following her eyes, Lawrence sees Lot Kruger with a very red face, damp from over-exertion, circling the room with a Mormon lady, the speed of a locomotive in his limbs and the vigor of a buffalo of the plains in his feet, bringing dismay and confusion to surrounding flounces and feminine trains wherever he goes.

Then his face grows dark.

"Don't speak of him!" he replies gloomily. "Let me throw off business for one night and be happy."

Which he does, dancing with Erma so often that

Ollie becomes very sulky, and Mrs. Livingston feels it necessary to play the chaperon, which she does very deftly, mentioning to her charge that people are talking about her dancing continually with one gentleman.

"Oh," answers the young lady. "What does it matter in this town, where we shall remain but a day or two? Were it New York it might be different." Then she continues rather maliciously, "Besides, I rather like it. It makes Oliver so sulky."

Just here, however, a practical joke of Mr. Chauncey's drives all else out of the widow's head. That gentleman approaches, bearing on either arm two quite young and rather pretty women, one apparently American, the other with the light hair and blond eyes of a Scandinavian, and presents them with considerable impressment and form as the two *Misses* Tranyon; very shortly after taking off one of the young ladies he has introduced to tread a measure.

"Ah," remarks Mrs. Livingston to the one left behind, "I hope that you and your sister are enjoying yourselves this evening."

"My *sister?*" giggles the lady, astonished.

"Of course! Mr. Chauncey introduced you and your sister as the two Misses Tranyon."

"Oh, I see. The *Missus* Tranyon fooled you!" replies the catechized one with a grin. "I am *Mrs.* Tranyon Number One, and Christine's *Mrs.* Tranyon Number Two," and is astounded to see Mrs. Livingston grow pale and fly from her, muttering faintly, "Help!"

But the explanation of the Mormon lady has so horrified the widow that she forgets all about Oliver and his jealousy, and makes an immediate attempt to take her charges home even before supper. But they will not go; for Louise is enjoying herself very greatly, and Ferdie has struck up a flirtation with the prettiest Mormon girl in the room, and is asking her with pathos in

9

his voice how she thinks she would enjoy living in New York.

"Quite well," answers that young lady. Then she giggles with the simplicity peculiar to the maidens of Deseret:

"Ain't you already married to that fair-haired blonde you are dancing with so much? Have you explained to her I am to be her sister?"—a proposition that so startles Mr. Chauncey that he dodges the Mormon maiden for the rest of the evening.

As for Erma, to Mrs. Livingston's suggestion that they leave the ball at once, she replies shortly, "What! and break *all* my engagements?" omitting, however, to state that most of them are to Captain Lawrence, and continues dancing with this gentleman, to the rage of Mr. Oliver, who goes to sulking and leaves her alone.

Mr. Kruger also noticing the same, thinks to himself, "Time for Lot to put his oar in." He has already greeted Miss Travenion at odd times when he has passed with affable nods and "How do's?" and "Having a good time, Sissy?" and such expressions of interest.

He now comes to her and says, stroking his newly cut beard, "What do you promise me, Miss Ermie, if I bring you and your daddy together to-morrow?"

"Anything," replies the girl, excitedly.

"Very well; you shall see Pop to-morrow, for one dance this evening."

"Why, my programme is already full," demurs Miss Travenion.

"Well, steal one for me. Perhaps that Lawrence chap could spare one. Reckon he's down on your card a few times more," he guffaws.

"Very well," says the girl hurriedly. "Take the Virginia reel," for she is desperately afraid of dancing a waltz with the athletic Lot, whose feet must go somewhere and have very little respect for the toes of his partner. Then she adds : " But remember, if I keep my promise this evening, you will keep yours to-morrow ? "

" Oh, sure as boys like to kiss," cries Lot merrily. This compels an explanation to Captain Lawrence, which is not received very well, that gentleman growing Hector-like and muttering, " So you rob me for the benefit of one of my enemies ? "

" One of your enemies ? "

" Yes, this man Kruger is part owner in the Mormon company that is fighting for my mine,—he and that villain Tranyon," he explains, " and you dance with *him ?* "

" Why not," says the girl, growing haughty. " Have I not been generous to you this evening ? " Then she pouts, " You've had *all* my dances. What more do you want ? "

" Supper ! " cries Harry decidedly.

" Supper ? Of course I want some also," laughs Miss Travenion merrily. " It's going on now," and she places her fingers on Lawrence's arm, though she is very well aware that the privilege of escorting her to midnight refreshment will be considered by Ollie as his " very own." But Erma is just tasting of the fruit called " first love," and will eat it, though it cost her as much as the apple did Mother Eve.

So, seated in a shady nook made by two flowering shrubs on the balcony, she watches and admires the athletic figure of the gentleman she has made her hero ever since she saw him save Ferdie's life, as he forages for her. This he does with as much vigor as one of Sherman's bummers on the March to the Sea, and with such a curious knowledge of her tastes that the girl wonders how he guesses all her pet dainties,—not knowing that the gentleman now her escort had had his eyes upon her during every meal she had taken between Omaha and Ogden.

"Why, this is marvellous—just what I wanted. How did you guess?" laughs the young lady as he places his spoils before her, and the two sit down together to make a very quiet but delightfully *tête-à-tête* meal, strains of music coming faintly to them, and the Chinese lanterns throwing but little light upon them.

Then their conversation, which is becoming low and confidential, is suddenly broken in upon by Mr. Livingston, who approaches, saying with a savage tone in his usually placid voice, "Erma, I've been looking for you everywhere. Mother has been waiting to take you to supper with us for an hour!"

"Thanks to Captain Lawrence," replies Miss Travenion, who likes this gentleman's tone little, but his interruption less, "I am already very well provided for."

"Ah—with both supper and flirtation," laughs Oliver sneeringly.

"Not at all," cries the young lady. "A flirtation is where they say a great deal more than they mean."

"But here," interjects Lawrence, whose heart is very full of the loveliness upon which he gazes with all his might, "I mean a great deal more than I have said." This remark, emphasized by a very telling glance of his dark eyes, brings furious blushes upon Erma and consternation upon Oliver, who loses his head and gasps, "Why, it is almost a declaration!"

"Would you like me to make it stronger?" asks Harry quite pointedly, his remark to the gentleman, but his eyes upon the lady.

But women in these social crises have generally more *savoir faire* than men. Miss Travenion says coolly, "I fear we must postpone this *jeu d'esprit*. I see Mr. Kruger looking for me. The Virginia reel is beginning. Mr. Livingston, will you take me to him?"

So, meeting the Mormon bishop, he demands his dance, and the music playing its most lively jig, Erma sees such high kicks, such double shuffles, and such gymnastic graces from Lot, who, being anxious to make a display before his partner, dances with the vigor of a Mormon boy of twenty, that she does her share of the lively contra-dance betwixt spasms of laughter.

This display rather amuses Lawrence, who comes to her at the close and says, "You were right in choosing your partner, Miss Travenion. I yield the palm to him in cutting pigeon wings." Then he goes on sullenly, "There are two of the wives of my enemy Tranyon," and laughs a little unpleasantly, sneering, "I suppose he's got so large a family he has to obtain other men's goods to keep them all."

"Oh, no doubt," whispers Ferdie. "I imagine from his possessions Tranyon must have a dozen or so. He has only been a Mormon eight or nine years, I hear. It must be awful curious to live a life of continual orange blossoms."

Then he goes on. "The beauty of the Mormon part of this ball is that the married men are all eligible for matrimony. The girls need fear no one is not serious in his attentions. Every man goes!"

"Stop making such jokes," cries Erma, sternly. Then she continues, "It's time to go home. Good-night, Captain Lawrence," and going into the dressing-room, she gazes meditatively at the two Mormon ladies, wondering what such a life as theirs can be.

The dark one—the American—she notes is a woman of more decided character than the Swedish Christine, though neither seems to be over-well educated or intelligent. Then she thinks, "What a wretch that Tranyon must be! He is robbing Harry to put gewgaws upon these women!" for both are dressed much more expensively and in better taste than is usual with

Mormon women, even the wives of their apostles and rulers.

From this musing she is suddenly awakened by voices outside the dressing-room.

Ollie is remarking, "As Miss Travenion's guardian, I must insist upon escorting her to her carriage."

"Her guardian?" This is in Harry's tones. "Who made you such?"

"Her father!"

"WHAT?"

"Certainly, her father," continues Oliver's soft voice. "He has constituted me her guardian until she becomes my wife—next winter."

This easy falsehood makes Erma at first frightened, then angry, and a minute after, coming forth cloaked and hooded, she meets Mr. Livingston, Captain Lawrence having apparently gone away.

"Mother is waiting," he whispers, and takes her down.

But on the sidewalk outside she sees Harry standing despondently, and striding up to him, gives him words that make him happy once more.

"To-morrow at two I wish to see you," she whispers, then laughs lightly, "Fairy stories for girls; men don't believe them!"

With this she steps into her carriage, and whispers to Livingston: "Don't dare to tell any more of your fibs about me!" for she is angry with herself now, and cogitates: "What will that man think of me? I have done an unmaidenly thing, and that immaculate gentleman opposite me, gossiping so easily with his mother and Louise, made me do it."

CHAPTER X.

"PAPA!"

MISS TRAVENION rises quite late on the morning after the Bussey *fête*, dresses hurriedly, and runs down-stairs into the dining-room of the Townsend House, to find that she is at lunch, not at breakfast. There she meets the rest of the Livingston party, who have arisen before her, and are discussing, in semi-excited tones, a piece of news Mr. Ferdie, who has been up and out, has just brought in to them.

"Do you know, Erma, that your gallant of last evening has come to grief?" remarks Oliver in placid triumph after the usual salutations have been exchanged.

"It is an infernal shame!" cries Mr. Chauncey. "They say Lawrence is ruined."

"Ruined! How?" asks the girl, growing pale in spite of herself.

"Why," answers Ferdie, "as near as I can make out, not claiming to be a mining expert, though I have seen enough ore specimens to make me a geologist, since I have been here—this Tranyon, who is a wily old Mormon speculator, and whose company only claims a *part* of Lawrence's mine, has just obtained an injunction to prevent him working *any* of it. Consequently, our friend will not be able to extract any more of his ore, and, running short of money, will hardly have the sinews of war for a prolonged legal fight, and Zion's Co-operative Mining Institution, which has plenty of shekels to hire legal talent and pack juries, will have a good deal the best chance. Anyway, that's the talk about town—I give it you as it comes to me."

"But this injunction can be dissolved," says Miss Travenion excitedly.

"Yes, if he puts up a big bond," suggests Livingston, triumphantly.

"Oh, that will not be difficult. Everybody is Captain Lawrence's friend," cries Erma, enthusiastically.

"Everybody is Captain Lawrence's friend until they have to put up their money to aid him," answers Oliver, who seems to get angry at the girl's interest in the matter. "Besides, everybody is not his friend; old Tranyon and I, for instance," he sneers.

"And you link your name with that miserable Mormon?" cries Erma, a flush of defiance coming upon her face. Then she goes on rapidly: "I should think you would be ashamed of yourself. This struggle, as I understand it, is that of Gentile against Mormon, and I stand up for my crowd." Here Ferdie cries "Bravo!" and she covers her agitation by a little laugh.

To this, Mrs. Livingston, whose business had been to pour oil upon the troubled waters for the last day or two, says suddenly: "Oliver, I am going shopping. Won't you accompany me?" and the young man, having some little idea that perhaps he is not advancing his cause very much by this battle, rises to go with her. As he goes, he cannot refrain from firing a parting shot.

He says, "Ask Ferdie what mining men say about your friend's prospects." And so goes away, while Miss Travenion turns a face that is anxious upon Mr. Chauncey.

"Well," says the boy, "all agree that, though Lawrence owns the mine, he will be ruined for lack of money to grease the wheels of justice."

"This shall not be!" cries the girl, in so strange a tone of voice that Ferdie gasps, "What do you mean?"

"I mean that it shall not be!" answers Miss Travenion.

Then one of those ideas that are called Quixotic by

the world, but which make it nearer to heaven, coming into this young lady's bright mind and generous heart, she looks at her watch and says, " I am going for a walk."

" Take me for an escort ?" suggests Ferdinand, who is always happy to promenade the streets by the side of Miss Beauty, for he knows that it makes others envy him.

" No," says the girl shortly, " I am going alone. I have a little business errand," and so departs, straight for the business portion of the town, her eyes big with purpose, though there are tears in them as she mutters, " Alone in his trouble, but I'll help him defeat that villain Tranyon."

Coming back from this journey, excited, dusty and tired, about half-past one, she says to her maid, " Quick ! A white gown—something cool—something breezy; I'm excited and warm!" and, curiously enough, trembles a little as she is assisted into a light summer toilet. Then inspecting her watch she murmurs, " Two o'clock. He should be here ; " next thinks, " What shall I say to him ? I must make this a business interview," and racks her brain for some business to talk about.

A moment after blushes come to her, for she gets to thinking of her remark about fairy tales of the night before, and mutters to herself, " Good heavens ! Will he think me unwomanly ?" and once or twice hopes he will not come, and looking at her watch finds it is after two, and is very much disappointed that he has not called.

So, after a time, getting very much excited over this matter, Erma goes down into the general parlor of the hotel, where she will be compelled to receive Harry Lawrence, for at that time the Townsend House had very few rooms *en suite*. But at the door, chancing to see a sparkling thing on the third finger of her left

hand, she gasps, "My!" and tears it off. Then she
laughs, "How lucky! He might have thought it an
engagement ring, and Oliver's horrid fib a truth," and
so pockets the bauble, going to the window of the room
to look out upon the sidewalk and see if her swain is in
view.

She is interrupted in this by the gentleman himself, for Captain Lawrence comes in, a flush of excitement upon his brown cheeks, dragging with him by the
arm Ferdie, who seems nervous also : as he well may
be, for Harry is laughing like a frontiersman, and every
now and then giving Mr. Chauncey little surreptitious
pats and nudges that from his athletic arm are agitating.

"I am glad you have come," says the girl, "for I
have a little matter of business to talk to you about.
When we were in Ogden the other day, you expended
some money for me, which I did not have opportunity
to return you. How much was it ?" and she is very
glad she has thought of this matter since Ferdie is here,
and it seems to her to be a reason, if not a very plaus-
ible one, for her having asked the captain to call.

To her question Lawrence, after looking for a moment astonished, says, all the while keeping his grip on
Mr. Chauncey, who manifests several times a desire to
edge out of the parlor :

"Yes, I believe I did spend some money for a telegram for you and a newspaper. It was fifty-five
cents."

Then the girl handing him the money, he mutters :
"Thank you," and suddenly bursts out, "I am in luck to-
day. That is not the only sum I've received. Friends
are pouring gold upon me !" in a nervous way which is
peculiar in him, for up to this moment he has seemed
to Miss Travenion to have an organization capable of
standing any shock.

A moment after he appears calmer, and says, " I have

a little story to tell you. It is in relation to that Ogden matter. You know that by an accident I was there permitted to save the life of a very generous little beg-gar"—here he pats Ferdie on the head, who mutters, "Don't," and blushes like a girl. "This little gentle-man," continues Harry, "for the slight service I did him in saving his noble little life, has seemed to me unusually grateful. He has sent me presents—a gold-headed cane and a silver-mounted revolver ; but hearing that I was—in what you might call hard luck, this generous boy, who has not yet learned that it is not always best to squander your money upon friends, sent to me to-day fifteen thousand dollars."

"Oh, what a whopper ! My allowance is only three thousand a year, and I am always in debt," cries Ferdie with sudden nervousness.

"You didn't send it ?" says the captain. Then he mutters slowly, "Have I made a mistake ? "

"On my honor as a gentleman," answers the boy. "But, by Jove, I would like to have had it to send you, and more too, for you did save my life, though you don't seem to like to have it mentioned."

"This is very curious," gasps Harry. "I have made a mistake. There was fifteen thousand put to my credit to-day, only an hour ago, at Walker Brothers. I made inquiry, and they said it had come as a cashier's check from Bussey's National Bank, on which I knew that your party had letters of credit. I could think of no one else who would consider himself under obligation to me,—at least, no one willing to do me such a good turn."

Then he goes on, "I must look elsewhere for the friend in need," and as he says this, some movement of the girl seems to draw his eyes, and he looks at her and notes that she is very red, and her eyes are feverish, and her small foot in its little slipper and openwork stocking, is patting the floor at the rate of about one hundred a minute.

Suddenly he gives a start, and a great red flush comes over his face, for just at this moment Louise comes in, crying, " Erma, here is your letter of credit returned from the bank ! " and with a childish idea of showing the general importance and wealth of the family to the Western stranger, remarks : " I peeped in her envelope, and Miss Extravagance has drawn fifteen thousand dollars to-day."

Then she pauses, astounded at the effect of her words, for Erma, who has risen hurriedly to receive the paper, gives a sudden cry, and sinks into a chair, covering her face with her hands, and Ferdie has suddenly ejaculated, " By Ginger ! " and would giggle did not the captain's manner awe him.

The next second Harry Lawrence takes the paper from Louise, saying gently, " I'll give this to Miss Travenion.   My business with her will be over in five minutes," and Miss Livingston, who, for a child, has quite a quick perception of social affairs, taking the hint, gives him the document and goes silently away.

Glancing at it, a debit of fifteen.thousand dollars of this day's date is indorsed on the back, and he grows very pale, FOR HE KNOWS.   Then coming toward the girl, who has half risen to meet him, he says : " Ferdie, there is a good angel in the room, my boy,—one of the kind that make men think earth is very near to heaven. Now, you just run down and play billiards, and I will join you in a few minutes, and don't you say a word of what I have told you to any one in this world."

" On my honor," whispers Chauncey, for there are two tears in Lawrence's eyes that impress him very greatly.   Then he suddenly cries, " Erma, you're a brick ! " and leaves the captain gazing at Miss Travenion, who is pale as death also.

As he does so, Lawrence suddenly comes to the girl, and says very tenderly : "God bless your noble, generous heart !"

But suddenly he seems to Erma to grow taller and tower over her, and he shakes his head and brushes his hair back from his brow, as if he were a fevered lion, and cries hoarsely : "This must not be ! Men in the West do not take money from women !"

"But you need it. What is it to me ? A few gewgaws, and jewels, and dresses, and I have more of them than I want. Take it to regain your own—to smite down this wretch Tranyon—then repay it to me."

"No, that is impossible," he answers, slowly. "This money shall be returned to you before bank hours this afternoon. But the good will that prompted it—I'll keep that, if you please, until I die." And supreme gratitude and undying love also are in his eyes, for he cannot keep them from speaking, though he may, perchance, control his tongue.

"But you need it. You must take it. It is necessary for your success," gasps the girl.

"I cannot take it, but I will succeed without it," he cries. "I cannot afford to lose. I must win ! It is not money I am fighting for, but——"

"What ?"

"What I will never tell you till I have money enough to prevent men calling me an adventurer—a fortune hunter—if I win it." And his eyes speaking to her again, she knows what he means.

A moment after, she turns to him, and says considerately :

"If I cannot aid you in this way I can in another, which I hope you will accept. My father will be here this evening. He is a very rich man. He will be more than happy to go upon your bond, to raise the injunction, which, I understand, has crippled you."

"No," says Harry, curtly. "No favors from your father of such financial magnitude."

"Why not?" queries Erma, who has made up her mind that Lawrence must be aided in some way.

"Because your father, the first time he sees me, must think me a man who can fight his own battle in this world—a man worthy to be—" He checks himself, and drives the words that are on his tongue back into his throat.

"At all events," mutters Erma, "you must see my father. He is a man of great business sagacity. His advice will aid you. Promise that you will come to-morrow and see him."

"I go to Tintic to-morrow."

"Promise!" and, being desperate, the young lady now forgets herself and whispers, "for my sake."

Then she suddenly feels her soft hand crushed in a frontier grip as he answers:

"For your sake I'd promise anything!" and, a moment after, he raises the white patrician fingers and kisses them with that reverence and chivalry that good men, who have long lived apart from good women, oft-times feel for their sweethearts, likening them unto their mothers. Then he murmurs, "Good-bye!"

But the girl cries, "Don't forget to-morrow. I will tell papa to be in at eleven o'clock. He will advise you how to conquer that Tranyon. See! a rosebud for good luck," and smiles on him. "I will pin it in your button-hole."

"No," he stammers, "let me carry it in my hand. Good-bye!" almost snatching the flower from her, for he is desperately afraid of himself, for gratitude and love have made this young lady's beauty irresistible to him.

Hurrying from this interview, Lawrence thinks, "God help me. It was hard to keep my heart from her," then

mutters morosely, " I'll not be called an adventurer,—
an heiress hunter. Her million stands up between us
more colossal than ever." Though a moment after, he
says determinedly : " By Heaven !—No one else shall
ever have her—my angel ! "

At this moment he hears behind him, "A word with
you, sir ! " and turning, sees Mr. Oliver, who has just
noticed the end of the parlor interview with agony and
rage.

" Certainly. Half a dozen," answers Lawrence.
Then he laughs and says, " I am so happy I could even
give you five minutes."

" Very well,—come with me," whispers Ollie, and
getting to a retired part of the hallway he turns upon
the captain and remarks oracularly and severely, " I
forbid you to call again upon the young lady who is
under my charge."

" Your authority ? "

" Her father's." ·

" The young lady under your charge," remarks the
Western man sarcastically, " hinted to me last evening
that you told fairy tales ; that you have no authority whatever in the matter ; that she is her own mistress."

" The young lady," returns Livingston, pulling down
his cuffs in a nervous manner, " knows that her father
wishes me to control her life till she marries me."
Then getting excited, he bursts forth, " Good Heavens !
You don't suppose that Ralph Travenion, who was in
his day the greatest club man and swell in New York,
would permit his child to marry a frontier Vigilante
like you,—almost a mur—" Here Mr. Livingston
suddenly checks himself and shrieks out desperately
and wildly, " Don't strike me ! I was once to have
studied for the ministry ! "

" Oh, very well," says Harry, laughing. " As to

the young lady's father, he can say to me what he pleases. I am to see him to-morrow by appointment," and he carelessly smells Erma's rosebud, and continues : "But you had better keep a civil tongue. I am too happy to hit you, for if I did, I might kill you ; but I'll take you by your aquiline nose and lead you twice around the nearest barroom, if you are not as polite and as mild and as fragrant as this rosebud," and he walks out, leaving Oliver pale with rage and perspiring with agitation—for Lawrence's laughing mood and his remark that he sees Miss Travenion's father by appointment to-morrow, have frightened Mr. Livingston almost to death.

So, coming out from this interview, Harry Lawrence draws his check at Walker Brothers, has it certified, and walks over to Mr. Bussey's Bank, to restore Miss Travenion's money to her letter of credit.

Chancing on his errand to meet Bishop Kruger, that gentleman looks at him and chuckles to himself, remembering the ball of the evening before : "You play a strong game, young man, but I rather think I hold the hand on ye this deal," and being reminded of his promise to Miss Travenion, proceeds to hunt up Mr. Ferdie upon Main Street, remarking, "That cigarette boy will play my next chip for me right 'cute."

He does not tell him this, however, on meeting, but says affably, "How de, Mr. Chauncey ? I think I can furnish a leettle amusement for you and your party."

"As you did last night, dancing the double shuffle ?" laughs Ferdie, who is not particularly in love with Lot.

"No, I kin do better than that. Your party are out here studying the manners and customs of us natives, I take it. Now, if you will bring your crowd up to the Twenty-fifth Ward meeting to-night, you'll see a Mormon Sunday-school celebration. Please tell Miss

Ermie that I will see her thar ; I ain't forgot my promise, and her dad's to be in town to-night."

" I'm delighted to hear that ! Miss Travenion has been looking anxiously for her father," replies Ferdinand. " I will give her your message, and if you will promise to cut a pigeon wing, I'll come up myself," and with this leaves the genial Lot, who, cursing his impertinence under his breath, mumbles, " Some day, my jumping-jack, your wit may cost you the leettle brains you've got."

After Lawrence has left her, Miss Travenion goes back to her room blushingly happy, and says complacently, " Papa will fix everything. Lawrence will win his mine,—and then—" and her blue eyes seem to look quite confidently into the future, for she has supreme faith in her father.

Every time he had come to New York on his various visits, he had brought happiness to her ; she remembers the joy of his arrival, the little *fêtes* prepared for her as a school girl, and the magnificent presents lavished upon her from Tiffany's and Kirkpatrick's when she was old enough for such things, and thinking of her absent dear one, she grows anxious as to Mr. Kruger's promise, sending to the office several times to ask if any one has called upon her, or asked for her, but the answer always comes back, " No ! " Then she takes to reading Ralph Travenion's last letter to her, a thing she has done a dozen times during the past few days, and while occupied in this, there is a knock on the door, and springing up and tripping lightly to it, she opens it, crying, " Papa ! at last ! " but is disappointed, for it is only Ferdie's laughing face.

He says to her, " I have not brought your father, but Mr. Kruger wants to see you."

" Indeed ? Is he down-stairs ? " asks Erma eagerly.

" No, but he gave me a message for you. He has

10

invited us all to go up and see a little Mormon Sunday-school festival."

"What has the Mormon Sunday-school performance to do with me?"

"Oh, nothing; but I thought it would be fun, and Mr. Kruger—Bishop Kruger, I beg his pardon—told me to tell you that he would be there and had not forgotten his promise. Your father will be in town to-night."

"God bless you for the news!" cries the girl, then laughs, "Do you know, I was really becoming anxious. Bishop Kruger has something to tell to me. Thanks for your invitation. I'll go. At what time?"

"About eight o'clock," answers Mr. Chauncey.

But, on arriving at the dinner-table, Miss Travenion finds that the Livingstons have made other plans for the evening. Mr. Bandman, a theatrical celebrity, at that time on his travelling tour, is to appear as Narcisse, and Mrs. Livingston has tickets for the theatre, and is anxious to go.

"I am sorry I cannot accompany you," answers Erma.

"No? Why not?"

"Because Ferdie and I are going to a Mormon Sunday-school festival. Mr. Kruger wishes to see me there. He has received word from my father. My father will be in Salt Lake, probably, to-night."

"Indeed?" says Mrs. Livingston complacently. "I am delighted to hear that; then we can shorten our visit to Salt Lake," for she has grown rather tired of the town, and is anxious to proceed on her journey. "Please give your father my compliments, Erma, and tell Mr. Travenion he must breakfast with me—at ten to-morrow morning." Then she says diplomatically, "Ferdie, wouldn't you like to see Mr. Bandman?"

"Quite well," answers that gentleman; "they say he has a very pretty leading lady."

"Then you had better come with us. I hardly dare trust Miss Travenion to you in a Mormon assemblage. You make careless remarks that excite their rage." She now comes to the point to which she has been working, and suggests: "Oliver, you had better take Erma," and is pleased to hear her son remark: "I will do so with pleasure."

"Thank you," says the girl in so grateful a tone that Mrs. Livingston, who has heard of Captain Lawrence's call during the afternoon, and has been fearful as to its effect in regard to Oliver's chances with the heiress, goes very complacently away from her dinner, and taking Ferdie and Louise, proceeds to the Salt Lake Theatre.

Then Miss Travenion, very much excited, takes carriage, and, escorted by Mr. Oliver Livingston, drives to the Sunday-school festival in the little Mormon meeting-house of the Twenty-fifth Ward.

"Papa will be in town to-night," she says in happy tones. "Fancy, I have not seen him for eight months. And Mr. Kruger says he is well."

"I shall be very happy to see him, also," returns Livingston cordially. "I have not met a man in this crude community yet to whom I cared to talk. Your father's old Unity Club anecdotes will seem to me like an echo of New York."

"I am glad to hear that papa's small talk pleases you," laughs the young lady, and a moment after says: "We are here."

Assisting her from the carriage, Oliver cries to the hackman: "Be back in an hour!" for a carriage at a Mormon ward meeting is so unusual that it attracts the attention of the crowd of Latter-Day Saints who are entering the building. Then he adds: "You need not stop in front of this place. Just draw up about a quarter of a square from here!"

And the man driving away, they mingle with the

crowd, and are scarcely noticed again, as Miss Travenion, thoughtful of the place to which she has come, has dressed herself in her most unpretentious gown, and has covered her bonnet and face with a veil so as not to attract attention by any contrast of toilet with the surrounding congregation. The hall is already almost filled, and they only find seats in the back row unoccupied. On these they sit down, and Miss Travenion's eyes go wandering over the assemblage searching for Mr. Kruger.

But they only see a very plain meeting-room, filled with the average hard-featured men and women of this Mormon city, dressed in their best, which means for the women gowns that would be a horror to a French dressmaker, and for the men, clothes that would be a nightmare to a Broadway tailor—and children—lots of them—most of them white-headed, but happy. The stage, moreover, is filled with them, dressed in the best their mothers can put upon them, chiefly bright calicoes and ginghams ; some of them looking quite pretty in these, for youth is nearly always beautiful, and Mormon tots are generally as happy as other children. Over their heads hangs a piece of white calico in festoons, bearing this peculiar motto : " UTAH'S BEST CROP IS CHILDREN."

Miss Travenion has just completed her survey, when the man she is looking for comes from a side door on to the platform, and makes the stereotyped Mormon address for such occasions, but says : " There is a better talker coming after me. I refer to the bishop of this ward, the Counsellor of our President, Bishop R. H. Tranyon, who, after the children have sung a hymn, will hold forth on what is the duty of the up-growing generation of this Sect and people, in order to become true Mormons, in the faith of Joseph Smith and Hyrum, his brother."

But all the time Kruger is speaking his eyes rove around the assembly, as if seeking some one, and finally, lighting upon the graceful form of Erma, he appears satisfied, and triumph and joy coming into his voice, his audience think it is the glory of Zion inspiring him, and applaud him as he sits down ; a Mormon girl, just in front of Miss Travenion, remarking, "Bishop Kruger seems to have his talking-coat on this evening !"

After that there is music from a melodeon, and the children sing the Mormon song,

> "I want to be a Mormon,
> And with the Mormons stand,"

and give it with as much fervor, Erma cannot help noticing, as the Sunday-schools in the East sing the beautiful hymn, "I want to be an angel," on which this is an awful parody.

Then stillness falls upon the audience, for the big gun of the evening is coming—the man who stands upon the right hand of the prophet and obtains his inspiration from him ; the man who has expounded to them during a number of years the doctrines of their creed, revealed by the Almighty to Joseph Smith, their founder.

A moment after Kruger announces, a peculiar thrill in his voice, "BISHOP TRANYON !"

As he says this, Erma, bending forward to get a better view, clenches her little hands together and thinks to herself, "This is the wretch who is Lawrence's enemy, and would destroy his happiness and mine !"

Then onto the platform comes a figure, wearing his clothes with a grace strange in a Mormon community, and whose broadcloth is finer than the sect is wont to wear, and whose gray eyes are familiar, and whose soft gestures are those she has been longing for—and whose grizzled moustache, now joined to a mighty beard, has caressed her lips. Gazing at him with all her might, something suddenly snaps in the girl's head, for he is speaking, and the incisive, smooth, cynical voice now crying the glory of the Mormon Church, the sanctity of plural, polygamous marriage—the voice now crying out the glory of what she thinks unutterable indignity and degradation to her sex, is that of—God help her !—no, she will not believe it, but still does—HER FATHER !

In one awful flash comes to her the thought, " If he is what he is, then what am I ? " and merciful insensibility comes with it.

As for Mr. Livingston, he has listened to the preliminary proceedings in a perfunctory, philosophical kind of way, sometimes scoffing inwardly. Then his mind, as the children sing their hymn, running upon other churches, finally comes to his own ; he has got to carelessly looking over the choristers, and trying to select from them youths who he thinks would make good altar-boys in his Episcopal Church.

He is hardly awakened from this when Bishop Tranyon is announced, and looking carelessly at him, thinks, " There's something curiously familiar in the old Mormon—he has a little of the New York club style about him. Good gracious ! that gesture—where have I seen it ? " and rubs his glasses and inspects him more closely. And then, remembering Travenion, the old New York swell, having known him as a boy, and seen him on his visits to New York, Ollie gets excited, for the eyes seem familiar to him, and the voice is the same that he has heard several times in the smoking-rooms of the Unity and Stuyvesant Clubs, though for a moment he cannot reconcile himself to believe what his memory tells him.

But just here, Erma's body falls a dead weight upon him and her head droops on his shoulder.

Looking at her, he sees that she has fainted so
quietly that he has not noticed it, and an awful shock
coming upon this conventional and orthodox young
man, he gasps to himself, " Good Gad, Erma's father ! "
and is so paralyzed and petrified that he makes no
effort to revive the girl, but simply looks on in a horrified kind of wonder as the festival proceeds.

In a daze, he hears the old New York club man play
his *rôle* of Mormon exhorter and apostle, and do it
very well, for he has just brought forward five children
of assorted sizes and sexes, and has proclaimed with
sanctimonious voice to the uncouth Saints assembled
about him : " These are my hostages to the State of
Deseret ; these are my pledges to the Zion of our
Lord ! " And taking up the smallest of his family—
a babe with Erma's eyes—this evangelist continues :
" This tot I have named Brigham after our well-
loved President, and Joseph for our first Prophet, and
Hyrum after his sainted brother, who was murdered
with him—unto the glory of our true religion and the
damnation of our unbelieving enemies." So, holding
the little one on his arm he cries, " LET US PRAY ! "

And he does pray—so earnestly, so impressively, so
tremendously that Oliver, gazing at him with agitated
eyes, begins to pray himself, thinking affrightedly :
" What shall I do ? My God, I am here with a Mormon's daughter ! "

Then he would make an effort to arouse the girl
to consciousness, and perhaps cause a scene, but he
suddenly thinks, " If I disturb the meeting, they may
treat me roughly. These infidels do not believe in
Gentile interruptions to their religious ceremonies ; "
and so sits quietly by the side of the unconscious
girl, till Bishop Tranyon, of Salt Lake City, ex-Ralph
Travenion, the New York exquisite, dandy and club
man, finishes his harangue, and the people crowd about

the platform and congratulate him on his great speech, to the glory of God and Brigham Young, his prophet.

But looking at Bishop Tranyon now, Oliver thinks he sees the cynic scoff of the Manhattan swell, as if, fight it how he will, he can't keep down a sneer at the religion that he preaches.

Just then, heart-breaking consciousness and recollection coming to the girl, she says in a low, faltering voice, placing a feeble though pleading hand upon his arm, "Take me away!"

In the confusion and hilarity of the festival, the melodeon playing loudly and the children singing that well-known Utah Sunday-school hymn,

"Say, Daddy, I'm a Mormon!"

unnoticed by all save Kruger, who knows his arrow has struck its shining mark, Oliver gets Erma out of the hall and to the carriage, which fortunately has returned.

Lifting her in, he cries, in feeble agitation, "The Townsend House! Quick!" for he fears his charge will faint again in the carriage. But she is beyond fainting now.

She whispers hoarsely : "You recognized him also?" then wrings her hands, and gasps, "My God! my father!" next bursts out : "That was the reason I did not meet him. That is the reason he never wanted me to come West to live with him—among his concubines he calls wives—he, my father, who once called *my* mother wife!"

Then to Oliver Livingston comes the opportunity of his life—his one supreme moment to win this woman, who is more beautiful in her agony even than in her joy; for the girl has fallen sobbing on his shoulder, and had he but treated her as if he loved her— aye, even pitied her—she would have given unto him gratitude so potent it might have grown to love, and so made her his.

But his puny heart is too small for such magnanimity, and to her tears and her mutterings, "What will the world think of me now?" he replies : "This is awful. This is a terrible thing for you. It will take you a long time to live this down. You had better retire from society for a time. Prayer and repent—"

And so his opportunity forever leaves him. The girl cuts short his last word with a shudder, then draws herself up, and says, a desperate gleam in her eyes : "Don't dare to talk to me as if the sin of my father was my sin. That kind of innuendo I will not permit!" next mutters : "I asked for sympathy and you gave me a sermon!" A moment after, she says, in measured tones, "We are at the hotel. You need not help me down. The touch of the polygamist's daughter might sully you, Mr. Immaculate!"

CHAPTER XI

"FOR BUSINESS PURPOSES."

THEN, unheeding his proffered aid, Erma descends from the carriage, and going into the house, he following her, she turns, and says haughtily : "I wish to see your mother as soon as she comes from the theatre ; but, before that, I must see *him*," and mutters, "If it is not too much of a service to me, in my extremity, go back to the meeting and tell my father to come to me at once. It may be the last favor I shall *ever ask* of you," and strides to her room.

So, he leaves her to go on her errand ; but chancing to pass a barroom, he goes in, a thing which is unusual for him, and, calling for a glass of brandy, gulps it down, his hands trembling a little.

Thinking the matter over as he drinks, he concludes his mother should be told first, and going to the Salt Lake Theatre, purchases a ticket.

It is fortunately an *entr'acte*, and he very shortly finds Mrs. Livingston's seat. Walking down the aisle to her, he whispers, "Bring Louise and Ferdie at once. Something terrible has happened!"

Looking at the white face of her offspring, the widow suddenly gasps, "Good Heavens! Erma has eloped with that awful Captain Lawrence, the Vigilante," and grabs helplessly for her wraps.

"No," he says grimly, as he supports her to the door, Ferdie and Louise following them; "but it is almost as bad."

"Tell me," whispers his mother, and seeing that he does not answer, goes on hysterically: "Tell me or I shall faint right here." But he finally gets her to the sidewalk, where the breezy air cools her nervous system, and putting her into the carriage he has brought with him, where, if she so elects, she can faint comfortably, he tells her in a few words what has happened.

Then, unheeding her exclamations of surprise and horror, as likewise those of Louise and Ferdie, he whispers, "Go back to the hotel. I am going to find this Mormon and bring him there," and leaving the carriage to drive back to the Townsend House, starts on foot for the meeting in the Twenty-fifth Ward.

But Salt Lake City blocks are long, and Mr. Livingston's episode at the theatre has taken some time. When he reaches the meeting-house, its windows are dark, the festival has ended, and there is nothing left him but to return to the hotel.

On his way back, however, his mind being on other things than his footsteps, he wanders into one of the streams that flow in this peculiar city where gutters would be in ordinary towns, and it being knee-deep, comes out of it in a very bad humor. This is not decreased by the dust which settles upon his immaculate inexpressibles, and gives him a very sorry appearance.

As he enters the hotel, Louise comes to meet him with a frightened face, and whispers, " Mamma is talking to her in her parlor," then suddenly cries out, " Goodness ! Have you been fighting with her father ? "

At which he snaps at her, " Go to bed, you little idiot," and pushing past her, enters his mother's sitting-room in by no means the frame of mind to properly meet, even for his own interest, the situation before him.

The room is but slightly illuminated,—the Townsend House gas, manufactured on the premises, being only strong in odor.

By it he can see Miss Travenion standing near the centre of the apartment, so white she would seem a statue, were it not for the dazzling brilliancy of her eyes, that appear to have burnt up the tears that were in them, and a slight nervous twitching of the hands, such as comes to us when hope is no more.

Mrs. Livingston, seated on a sofa, is speaking in a tremulous sort of way, for the girl's manner just at this time frightens her.

She is saying, " You had best leave this awful place to-morrow morning, and come with us to California. I have ordered your maid to pack your trunks. My maid is doing the same." Then she turns to her son, remarking, " You think it will be best, also, Oliver ? "

But Erma prevents his reply. She cries, taking a step towards him, " My father ! " and seeing no one behind him, gasps, " What have you done to him, or what has he done to you ? " for Mr. Livingston's pale face and disfigured trousers suggest ideas of combat that would make her laugh at other and happier times.

To this he replies curtly, " Nothing ; I could not find him."

"Why not?"

"Their blasphemous meeting-house was closed." Then he says in a nasty, sneering tone, for the young lady's manner has added to his anger, "Your father and his Mormon brats had gone away."

"His Mormon brats?" This comes from both Mrs. Livingston and Erma, though one gives it with a shriek and the other with a shudder.

"Yes, your five little brothers and sisters," he sneers at Erma. "Didn't you see them? They got the Sunday-school prizes, I think. They look like your father, and one of the girls has your eyes," and would go on with some more such scoffing pleasantries, did not his mother spring to him and whisper, "Idiot!" for the girl has sunk down sobbing upon a chair and is wringing her hands at this last cruel revelation.

Not liking his mother's word, Oliver grows more angry, and says sternly, "Remember, I am the head of the family, and shall take this matter into my own hands." To this, Mrs. Livingston, who since his father's death has grown to look upon him as the director of the family, saying nothing, he continues: "Erma, I have been thinking this matter over as I returned. Your father's crimes have placed him outside the laws of this land. Under these circumstances, I feel it incumbent on me to take charge of your life." This peculiar assumption of power he makes very placidly, turning to the young lady, who answers him not, his last revelation still overcoming her.

Noting this, Mr. Complaisant thinks: "My manner has subdued her. Crushed by this blow, Miss Haughty, who has defied and jeered me for the last few days, is now submissive to my authority," and the pangs of jealousy and rage that had been administered by Harry Lawrence come into his small mind to make him take a smaller revenge.

He says, "I think it is best, mother, that we postpone our visit to California, and immediately return to the East, until I can make proper arrangements for Erma. It will take her a long time to live this scandal down."

"Ah, you are very kind to the friendless daughter of a Mormon," interjects the girl, sarcastically ; but he being full of himself, does not heed her, and continues : "A proper retirement from society is due to it."

"Retirement !" she exclaims, "to expiate my father's crimes !" then says sadly : "You seem to think that I am sullied by his sin ; " next sneers, "Perhaps you imagine a reform school or a convent would be the proper place for me, Mr. Livingston."

"Not exactly that."

"No, but something like it," cries Erma, and rising, she towers above him, and goes on in mighty scorn : "And you dare arrogate authority over me ? You are neither my guardian nor my trustee ; " next jeers at him, for her torture makes her cruel : "If every girl in New York society expiated their father's social crimes, how many would escape ? Little Louise, for instance—eh ? "

This awful shot brings tears to Mrs. Livingston's eyes, for her dead spouse had been of such a peculiar social nature that he had been known by his intimates as "Mormon Livingston."

"Hush ! Your father's sins are open ones," says Oliver.

But she turns on him, crying : "It is not your place to criticise him. If atonement is in order, atone for yourself, Mr. Immaculate !" and this is another facer for Oliver, who has had his weak moments in which he has listened to sirens' voices, as many men in New York society have.

Then, a second after, the girl says, slowly : "You go on with your trip, Mrs. Livingston, as if nothing had happened."

"But you?" asks the widow, who, knowing that Miss Travenion's remarks have been made in frenzy, forgives her and pities her.

"I go to my father."

"To do what?"

"To DRAG HIM FROM HIS INIQUITY! Good-night, and —*good-bye*," and saying this, the young lady sweeps from the room, brushing past Louise, who is standing outside the door in childish astonishment and dismay.

But Mrs. Livingston is whispering to Ollie. "Idiot! You have driven her and her million away from us. Think of Louise and me."

To this he answers surlily, "I don't believe it wise to wed a girl society will look down upon."

"Fool!" cries his mother. "How long do you think it will take in New York society for a girl with sixty thousand dollars a year to live anything down?" and leaving him to digest this truthful platitude, she pursues Miss Travenion, overtaking her at the entrance of that young lady's room.

Here, diplomat as she is, she makes a mistake. Louise has also followed, and Erma impulsively seizes the girl, whom she loves very well, and kisses her tenderly and whispers, "Good-bye!"

Coming upon this, Mrs. Livingston, anxious for uninterrupted interview, thoughtlessly says: "Louise, go to bed at once! We leave on the early train to-morrow morning!"

At this, Erma, whom humiliation makes sensitive, draws back and mutters, "Do you fear my touch will contaminate her?"

"Not at all," says Mrs. Livingston. "You mistake me, dear Erma. I want to beg you to come with us to California. You mustn't think of what Ollie in his agitation said to you."

"I don't," answers Erma. "Thank God that wounded

my pride, but not my heart!" For in all this cruel
humiliation she has been conscious of one joy—that
any chance of union with Oliver Livingston is now forever ended.

"You must reconsider your rash determination," en-
treats the widow.

"Impossible!"

"In your present excited state you had better not
see your father."

"Now it is necessary that I see my father—more so
than ever."

"You cannot live with him with those awful women."

"Oh, don't fear for me," says the girl. "There are
others who will protect me here, if he will not."

"Who?" gasps the widow.

"*The man I love!*" And opening her door, Erma
Travenion flies in and locks it; then starts aghast! and
cries in a hoarse and rasping voice, "Tranyon!—Bishop
Tranyon! the *wretch Tranyon!* who has ruined him!
My God! what will Harry Lawrence think of Tranyon
the Mormon's daughter?" And sinking down upon the
bed, she writhes and moans, for at this thought, which
has been mercifully kept from her till the last, nothing
seems left her in this world.

During this time, Ferdie has been abstractedly sitting in a neighboring barroom, every once in a while
walking up to the barkeeper and whispering "Brandy!"
then muttering to himself over it, "Miss Mormon is
having a high old time with auntie and Ollie." The
rest of his time he whistles meditatively. Just about
midnight, he thinks: "She is through with Mrs. Livingston. I wonder if I could not do anything to
help her?"

So, there comes a knock upon Miss Travenion's door,
and she opening it herself, for she has not undressed,
finds Mr. Chauncey, who looks sheepishly at her and

says in confused tones: " Oliver has told me your determination. We are going to San Francisco to-morrow
morning. You remain here to see your father."

" Yes, Ferdie," answers the young lady.

" Any way, you are better off away from that prig
till he gets over the shock," replies the boy. Then he
laughs a little, and says suggestively, " You can have
him back whenever you want, I imagine," nodding
towards Mr. Livingston's apartment.

" I don't want him back."

" No, I presume not," returns Mr. Chauncey, trying
to smooth matters, " not since you have seen our hero,
Captain Lawrence." So he unwittingly gives the girl
another stab, but tries to correct it by muttering :

" By Jove, I had forgotten ! Your dad is the man
who is busting him. Harry isn't stuck after Tranyon,
is he ?" To this getting no reply, he goes on hastily :
" If you want me, I will stay here and look after you.
I don't care to go to California."

" Oh," says Erma, " don't fear for me. My father
has taken care of me till now. You don't suppose he
would injure a hair of my head ?" then sobs, " And he
was so good to me. I expected such joy at meeting
him."

Here Ferdie desperately turns the subject, for girls'
tears always embarrass him.

He says, " Can't I do anything for you ? Tell me—
just anything."

" Yes," says the young lady, shortly. Then she considers a moment and asks :

" You know where this Bishop Kruger lives ?"

" No, but I can easily find out."

" Very well. Will you take a note to him for
me ?"

" With pleasure !" he cries, as if glad she has given
him a chance to do her service. So, sitting down, she

writes a few lines hurriedly, and gives the epistle to Mr. Chauncey.

Half an hour afterward he returns, and knocks on her door. She is engaged with her maid, who has become frightened at being left behind the Livingston party, and says she wishes to return to New York.

Answering his summons, Erma asks anxiously, "Did you deliver it?"

"Yes; he was in his shirt sleeves, but he read it, and said he would be down in the morning. He seemed to chuckle over it. I don't think I would trust your father's friend any too much," suggests the boy.

"Thank you," cries the girl, "for your advice and your kindness," and being desperately grateful for this one act of consideration shown to her this night, she says to him suddenly: "Good-bye. God bless you, Ferdie!" and gives him an impetuous kiss—the sweetest he has ever had in his life, though with it she leaves a tear upon his cheek.

Then she comes in and says with business-like directness to her faltering abigail, "You wish to leave me, Marie, here alone?"

"Yes, I am afraid. Mademoiselle will pardon me."

"Certainly. Here are your wages! Here is money for your ticket to New York. Now go."

"Mademoiselle will pardon me?"

"Yes, leave me," and Marie departing, Erma Travenion feels that she is indeed alone in a strange country, for she hears the noise of the Livingstons' trunks as they are packing them and getting ready to depart in a hurry that does not seem altogether flattering to her.

Early the next morning, the widow, Louise, Mr. Livingston, and Ferdie depart for Ogden, though the California train does not start from that town until the evening; they are so desperately anxious to shake the dust of Salt Lake City from their feet.

11

At the depot, Ferdie notices Bishop Kruger, who gazes at the party as they board the train, and approaching Mr. Chauncey, remarks, "I'll see Miss Ermie up at the hotel. She ain't going with ye, *sure?*" peering about with curious eyes, as if to be certain of this fact. Then the train runs out, bearing the Livingstons toward the Pacific Coast, and Bishop Kruger, about eight o'clock on this day, finds Miss Travenion waiting for him at the Townsend House.

The girl comes down into the parlor very simply dressed, but perhaps more beautiful than ever, to his pastoral eyes, for he remarks to himself, "Be Gosh! She looks homelike and domestic."

"My father!" she says shortly. Then gazing round, she goes on impetuously: "He is not here—he feared to see me—he is ashamed!"

"What! that he's a Mormon?" yells Kruger, savagely. "A true man glories in that; so does your daddy. Perhaps some day you'll jine him."

"Hush!" says Erma. "Don't speak of it," and she shudders. Then she asks, "Where's my father now?"

"In town! But I ain't told him you was here yit. I thought he might be——"

"Ashamed!" cries the girl, but suddenly pauses. Kruger's looks alarm her.

"If I thought as how R. H. Travenion was ashamed of the holy Church of our Latter-Day Saints, I'd cut him off root and branch in this world and the next," he says, the wild gleam of fanaticism coming into his deep eyes. "I swear it, by the Book of Mormon!" Erma knows this man means his words, for Lot Kruger is a fanatic, and believes in his creed and in Joseph Smith, as truly as the Dervish believes in Allah and Mahomet. "Your daddy is in town," he goes on more calmly, "but I feared he might be flustered if he knew you had come upon him, as it were, in the night, and so I kept my mouth shut."

"Will you bring him to me now?"

"Yes, in an hour!"

So, Mr. Kruger departs on his errand, but shortly reappears, and says, "We have missed him agin. Your daddy's left for Tintic on the stage this morning at eight o'clock."

"Very well," answers Miss Travenion shortly. "I'll go to Tintic also."

This suggestion pleases Bishop Kruger so much that he cries, "Right you are! Ye're true grit, Sissy! You'd better go down by private conveyance. It'll be much more pleasant for ladies."

"Oh, I am alone now; my maid has left me," answers Miss Travenion; and this remark delights her auditor more than he would like her to guess. He goes on happily, "It's only seventy-five or eighty or perhaps ninety miles from here. You can drive down in a day with a good, tough bronco-team, but still you had better take it slowly and stop over night at Milo Johnson's."

"Alone in a Mormon house?" shudders the girl.

"Oh, you'll be as safe thar as if you were in your bed on Fifth Avenue. You can travel all over here, provided you do not hurt our feelings, as safe as if you was in Connecticut—more so—we don't have no burglars around here!" says Lot, reassuringly.

Making inquiries at the hotel office, Miss Travenion finds that the Mormon bishop's advice has been good. Then, being provided at the hotel with a private team, she comes down at ten o'clock in the day, to depart for Tintic, and is surprised to see the attentive Kruger ready to assist her into the light wagon, which has a top to keep off dust and sun.

"You didn't expect any one to see you off!" he remarks.

"But most every one here would do a heap for Bishop Tranyon's darter." Then he chuckles: "Ye're kind o' one o' us now!" and drives the iron into Erma's soul.

"Thank you. I suppose you mean it for a compliment," she says, attempting lightness, though her lip twitches. "But I am a little different still, to a Mormon girl!" and gets into the carriage before he can aid her.

"So you are! Ye're a prize-book picture," he mutters, looking at her till his eyes blink from some subtle passion, for Miss Travenion is dressed in a cool, gray linen travelling costume, that fits her charming figure with a "riding habit" fit, till it reaches white cuffs and snowy collar, and a little foot, that in its French kid boot looks as if it had come out of a fashion plate. Thus attired, she makes a very breezy, attractive picture; though there is no one to enjoy it, save Kruger, for the heat, even on this October day, has driven loungers from the sidewalk.

Then turning from her, as she drives down the State road, this Mormon fanatic remarks: "Gee hoss! Don't this give the Church a pull upon the daddy, and Lot Kruger a hold upon the darter!" and so goes to a little building on South Temple Street devoted to the business affairs of the Latter-Day Saints.

Miss Travenion, raising a little sunshade over a face made beautiful by conflicting emotions, journeys down the State road, which leads towards the south—past the Utah Southern Railway, that is now being graded, and after a dusty seven hours' ride comes to the Point-of-the-Mountain. Here she is very hospitably entertained, and well treated, by one of the many wives of Milo Johnson, who lives at this place.

Then the next morning, so as to travel in the cool portion of the day, leaving almost at daylight, after a hot breakfast, and taking her lunch with her, she crosses the ford of the Jordan—the river that runs from the fresh lake of Utah to its salt inland sea. So coming to its western shore, she journeys along the banks of beautiful Utah Lake—placid as a mirror— leaving Ophir and Camp Floyd and Tooele far to her west.

To the east, across the limpid waters, she notes, buried in their orchards, the Mormon towns of Provo, Springfield, Payson, and Spanish Fork. Behind them the great Wahsatch range, and, further to the south, the great mountain that they call "Nebo," which rises snow-capped, dominating the scene.

About midway down the west side of the lake, she and the driver of the carriage eat their lunch. Then proceeding onward till almost at the upper end of this quiet water, she leaves its banks, and, after two or three miles of sage brush, enters a little cañon, with a brawling stream running down it. Very shortly to her comes the odor of garlic and arsenic from the smelting works at Homansville, whose great furnaces she soon sees, giving out clouds of smoke.

Passing these, three miles further up the valley she comes to Eureka. Here, making inquiry at the store of Baxter & Butterfield, she is directed to the Zion's Co-operative Mining Institution, whose works stand a mile or more beyond, towards Silver City.

So, in another half an hour Miss Travenion, turning from the main road and driving up a little spur of the mountain, past one or two dug-outs and miner's cabins, gets out of the wagon at the door of a house built of rough lumber, and says nervously to a man in high, muddy boots and blue shirt, greasy with candle drippings: "Is Bishop Tranyon in?"

"Yes, he is in the back room," and, pointing to the door, the miner goes off to his work.

She enters, and seated upon a wooden chair, looking

over some accounts at a deal table, is the man they call Bishop Tranyon, and she says to him :—" FATHER !"

At her word, Ralph Travenion, once New York exquisite, now Mormon bishop, staggers up, trembles, and, gazing on her, cries : "Erma ! my God ! YOU here ?"

Then, forcing back some awful emotion, his voice grows tender as he says : "Why, this is a surprise, darling ! You have travelled all the way from New York to see your father. God bless you, child of my heart !" and there are tears in his deep eyes, and he would approach her and put his arms about her, giving her a father's kiss.

But she starts from him, shudders, and gasps : "Don't dare to kiss me !"

"Why not ?"

"*Because I know what you are.*"

"My God ! You know—" and the strong man turns from her, and hides his face in his quivering hands.

Then she goes on, faltering a little over the words, but still goes on : "Why have you disgraced our name? Why have you become a Mormon—a POLYGAMIST ?"

Here he astonishes her by whispering, with white lips, these curious words : "I did it that I might settle upon you a million ! For your sake I became Mormon—for your sake I became polygamist. I DID IT FOR BUSINESS PURPOSES !"

CHAPTER XII.

A DAUGHTER OF THE CHURCH.

FOR a moment, Erma believes this extraordinary statement, and falters, seeming almost to invite his caresses, at least not to repulse them.

Seeing this, Ralph Travenion mutters, "Thank God,

you believe me!" and flies to take her in his arms; but suddenly her dead mother's face seems to the girl to rise between her father and herself. She shudders, turns away from him, and says coldly: "You ask me to believe this monstrous thing,—that for my sake you became a Mormon?"

"Yes, as God is above me!—to make you rich,—to place you above the care of poverty,—to surround you with luxury,—the thing that has been my one thought in life."

"Was that your thought?" cries the girl suddenly, with a face that to him is beautiful as an angel's, but just as that of the angel's God—"was that your thought when you entered into polygamous marriage with those women down there? Oh, don't attempt to deny it!" for he is about to open his lips. "I saw two of them. I was at the Sunday-school meeting of the Twenty-fifth Ward, and beheld your hostages to your faith—five little ones, I believe. One of them, a girl, Mr. Oliver Livingston was kind enough to say, looked like me."

To this, for a moment, he does not reply. Then suddenly, forcing his tongue to do his wish, he repeats: "For your sake I did that also!"

"For my sake?" gasps Erma, astounded, then cries out: "Absurd! Impossible!" and having exhausted tears two days before, mocks him with unbelieving laugh.

"As God is above me!"

"Prove it!"

"I will!" And so, being driven to his defence, and knowing that he is pleading for his own happiness—for this child of his *other* life is to Ralph Travenion, once club man of New York City, but now Mormon bishop of Salt Lake, the thing he loves best in this world—he begins to tell his story, earnestly, as a man struggling to win the lost respect and esteem of the one woman whose respect and esteem he must have,—pathetically, as a father striving to keep his daughter's love.

His voice trembles slightly as he begins : "In New York, Wall Street practically ruined me. The ample fortune that I had determined to devote to your happiness and your life, Erma, my daughter, had passed from me. I had, after leaving sufficient for your education, but a few thousand dollars to take with me to this Western world. I had promised my old friend to settle a million dollars on you, so that if he kept his contract to make over a like amount to his son, you could wed Oliver Livingston and take the place in New York society to which you had been born. To keep this promise, I left the old life that was pleas- ant to me, and came, God help me, to *this !*" He looks about the bare room, with its rough furniture, its un- carpeted floor, its pioneer discomfort, and out through the open window over the long waste that covers the West Tintic Valley. And she looks also, and sees naught but sage brush, unrelieved save by a few floating clouds of dust that, thick and heavy, mark the course of ore- teams from the Scotia mine, making their hot and alkaline way towards the furnaces in Homansville.

Then Ralph iterates, "I came to this life for your sake," a far-away look getting into his eyes, for recol- lections of his old club life and the friends and com- panions and chums of other days, and pretty yachting excursions on the Sound, and gay opera and dinner parties and *fêtes* at fashionable Newport, come to this exile.

Noting this, some idea of what is in his mind comes also to his daughter, and makes her tender to him, and this change in her face gives him courage.

He goes on, " For your sake I did this ! "

" For my sake it was not necessary to be a Mormon."

" To make a fortune it was ! " he cries. " I wandered about the Mississippi for a year. At the end of that time, I was poorer than when I left New York. St. Louis and Chicago did not seem to me a quick enough opportunity. I came further West. I had a wild hope of making money in furs, in some stage line, as Indian trader, but found no chance, and so, in pursuit of one will-o'-the-wisp and another, I journeyed on until I found myself in Salt Lake City. Here I saw a fortune for a man of ability. The Transcontinental Telegraph Company was building its line. A contract to supply them with telegraph poles, properly handled, would make me rich. But it could be so handled only by a Mormon, and I joined the Church of Latter-Day Saints,—a stern sect, who will have no wavering disciples, no half-way apostates in its ranks. By that contract I made a considerable sum. Then the building of the Union Pacific Railway came, and by it I made a fortune, because I was a Mormon."

" A Gentile might also have succeeded," suggests his daughter.

" Impossible ! As a Mormon, and only as a Mormon, I could hire thousands of Mormon laborers at one dollar and fifty cents per day,—and pay them by store orders on Zion's Co-operative Mercantile Institution, who liquidated them in goods at, practically, fifty cents on the dollar. Mormon labor cost me seventy-five cents per day against Gentile labor at three or four dollars ; as a Latter-Day Saint I could command the cheap article. That is why I joined the Mormon Church—for your fortune and your happiness."

" Was it for my happiness that you accepted their infamous creed for the degradation of my sex—that you entered into plural marriage—that you are now surrounded by children of polygamy ? " asks the girl, a bitter sarcasm dominating her voice.

"THAT WAS TO SAVE MY LIFE!"

"To save your life? What nonsense!"

"Hush! Listen to me!" and Ralph Travenion speaks
very low, as if he almost feared the walls would hear
him. "A year after I had joined it, it was spoken unto
me by the President that the Church doubted my sin-
cerity because I had not entered into polygamy. To
be doubted in those days,—in 1865 and '66,—meant the
atonement of blood, such as was carried out on Almon,
Babbitt and the Parrishes—it meant being cut off 'below
the ears.' Had I died here then, my fortune would have
never been accumulated for you. You would not now
have a million to give you prestige,—to give you
power,—to make you reign beauty as you are. You
would not now be called Miss Dividends," and the old
man would put his arms about his daughter to caress
her, and take her to his heart—for her loveliness has
made him, her father, very proud.

But Erma cries to him hoarsely, "What kind of a
dividend have you given me? *The dividend of shame!*
Society shudders and turns from me. The Livingstons
have already done so."

To this he answers, "My God, what do you mean?"
sinking upon a candle-box that does duty as a chair
in this uncouth department.

"I mean this," cries Erma, "that when they discovered that I was the daughter of a Mormon, that I
had little illegitimate half-brothers and sisters, they
fled from me as if I were tainted and left me to the
kindness of Bishop Kruger."

"KRUGER KNOWS YOU ARE HERE?" This is a wail of
anguish from Travenion that makes his daughter start.

She answers him, though the old man's agitation
frightens her. "Certainly. He learnt of my coming in
New York, and returned on the same train with the
Livingstons and myself to Salt Lake City. He——"

But Erma pauses, astonished and horrified, the effect of her simple words upon her father is so tremendous.

He is wringing his hands and muttering, " They have me now. My heart is in their hands !" Then he steps quickly to the door, and she hears him speak to the man who has driven her from Salt Lake. " Take your horses to the stable at Eureka. Feed and water them and be ready to return this evening at seven o'clock."

" I don't see as I can, bishop," answers the driver. " The team won't stand it. They are putty nigh tuckered out now."

" Then be ready to-morrow morning," he says hurriedly, and returns to the room where Erma still sits, and sighs to himself, " I don't suppose it would be much use. If they know you are here, they know that they have my heart in their hands."

" Your heart in their hands ? What do you mean by that ?" whispers the young lady.

" I mean *you !* You are my heart,—you. My darling ! My pet ! My treasure ! Who has put peril upon herself because she loved her old papa !" and before she can prevent it, he has her in his arms and is pressing her to his heart, and caressing her, and crying over her the tears of a strong man in his extremity.

And now she struggles not, for his kisses bring remembrance of his other kisses in happier days, in faraway New York, when she has looked for his coming at her school, and afterwards as a young lady has flown to this heart, that she knows has always beat for her.

After a moment, his agitation and words make her ask, " What latent danger is there to me ?"

" Nothing immediate," he answers. " Perhaps none at all—perhaps I am a fool ; for in 1871 there are many Gentiles in this Territory, and United States troops at

Camp Douglas. *But I remember!* And the thought of what once was, makes me fear what may now be." Then he says suddenly and impressively, as if some new idea alarmed him, "Tell me about your trip from New York. Omit no details. *Minutiæ* may mean safety for us both. But first—" And it now being the dusk of the evening, he illuminates the room with the flicker of a coal-oil lamp and the yellow glow of a tallow dip, and places her very tenderly on the only chair in the room.

Seated on this, she tells him her story, he interrupting her now and then to ask pertinent questions, most of them in regard to the actions of Kruger. And getting answers that he doesn't like, he seems to grow more despondent the more her words indicate the Mormon bishop has taken interest in her movements.

But as she tells about Harry Lawrence, and the trouble the injunction on his mine has brought upon the young man, the old man's eyes gleam and he chuckles: " Yes, I rather think I have put that bantam into a business hole he won't get out of ! "

He seems so happy and so triumphant over this affair, that Erma, his daughter as she is, almost hates him.

This brings her to her contribution to Harry's bank account, to defeat Bishop Tranyon of Salt Lake and Zion's Co-operative Mining Institution, and telling this with some embarrassment and pauses and blushes, she notes her father's face grow long and his features puzzled.

Then, as she describes her visit to the Twenty-fifth Ward meeting, and Oliver Livingston's treatment of her after his discovery that she is the daughter of a polygamist, he mutters sadly : "To see you married to Livingston—a man of your own rank and place in New York society—has been the hope of my old age ! "

Here the girl astonishes him. She answers : " Had you been the greatest saint this earth has ever seen,

Oliver Livingston would never have had me for his wife. Besides "—and she laughs airily—" I could have Mr. Ollie back at my side in a week. He loves my million well enough to take me for it."

" Then bring him back ! "

" Never ! "

" Never ! Why not ? " This last almost savagely.

" Because *I* will not marry *him !* "

There is an enthusiasm and determination in the girl's manner that makes this gentleman—who is well accustomed to reading men, and perhaps has had some experience, in his plural marriages, of women—suddenly cry out : " No, you will not wed Livingston because you love another ! "

" Who is that ? " says the girl, attempting a laugh, but her face becoming very red in the dim light of flickering tallow and kerosene oil.

" Harry Lawrence, who hates Bishop Tranyon of Salt Lake so much that I hardly think he will marry the daughter of Ralph Travenion of New York ! " returns her father easily.

But Erma does not answer this. She has turned away to the window, and is looking down the hill and over the alkaline plains, and her blushes are only seen by a jack-rabbit who peers at her from behind a sage bush.

Then she faces her father and cries : " No matter what comes, you shall do justice to Harry Lawrence ! You shall withdraw your claim to his property ! "

" Oh ho ! " laughs the Mormon. " Give up what I am on the point of winning? Bishop Tranyon of Salt Lake will never do that. That is not his style."

" No," cries the girl ; " but my father, Ralph Travenion, of New York, who was once worthy the love of all who knew him, will do justice to a wronged man, because he still loves the daughter who has travelled over two thousand miles to meet him here, and who he says has brought peril upon herself, for love of him!" And looking on him, her eyes grow soft and tender as they used to gaze at him when she was proud of him at party and *fête* in far-away New York, as she murmurs: "What will Ralph Travenion do for his daughter?"

"For his daughter's sake, Ralph Travenion will do anything!" mutters the old man; then says pathetically, almost brokenly: "For God's sake, give me one kiss of your own will! You have spoken to me an hour, and as yet no daughter's kiss!"

With that the girl comes to him, puts her arms about him, and kisses him, as she used to when she was a child, and before she knew he was a Mormon and a polygamist.

"Do with me what you will!" he continues. "What do you want for this young man, who I can see is getting the first place in your heart?"

"Justice!" cries Erma. "I want you to telegraph your lawyer to stipulate that the injunction on his mine be removed."

"And what more?"

"Resign your claim to his property."

"But Kruger also owns stock in the Zion Co-operative Mining Institution."

"Buy his stock!"

"Very well, though you are robbing yourself!" mutters the man. "I'll do it!—if—if you'll forgive me."

"I'll forgive you, if you'll let me lead you away from this awful place—away from sin!" cries Erma.

But here he astonishes and horrifies her, for he whispers to her: "*Yes, if we can get away alive!*"

"What is to stop us?" falters the young lady.

Before answering her, Ralph takes up the light,

walks into the other room, examines it ; goes up the ladder, into the loft overhead, and finally inspects the outside of the house ; then he returns, saying : "No one is within hearing !" comes up to her, and whispers :

"The Mormon Church !"

"What authority has the Mormon Church over me ?" asks the young lady, raising her voice a little.

"Hush ! Not so loud !" he returns. "The Mormon Church claims authority over the children, by virtue of their authority over the parent. In ordinary cases they perhaps would not at this late date exercise it, but in my case it is different. I am so prominent. They know to lose me would be a blow to them. At present they have lost several rich members, and they are desperate ! And I"—here his lips approach her ear, and form rather than say the words—his voice is so low, his lips so trembling—"and I have been making arrangements to *apostatize !*"

"God bless you for that !" cries Erma.

To this he whispers : "You don't suppose that I ever swallowed the dogmas of Joe Smith, which I preached as Mormon bishop? I joined them to desert them the moment I had made what money I wanted out of these Latter-Day Saints !" And, forgetting himself, he gives out two or three jeering scoffs. But the next moment his face grows frightened, and he mutters : "I have been "—his voice is very low again—"making arrangements to withdraw all my property from this Territory. I have now in New York, besides the million settled on you, a very large sum of money ; but I have also such a block of stock of the Utah Central Railway that, if I sell it to the right parties, the Mormon Church will lose control of the road ; that I have not yet been able to remove. But they suspect me !" he goes on dolefully. "I have been asked to immediately pay my tithing,

which they figure at one hundred thousand dollars for
this year, claiming that I have made a million. I have
hidden the stock and I was about to refuse, but your
coming here has made that, I fear, impossible."

Then he wrings his hands, and says : "When an apostate is cut off, he is destroyed—root and branch. The
family suffer as well as the man, and you—and *you*,
Erma—YOU !"

"Your stock ! Is it near here ?" asks the girl eagerly.

"Certainly." Here he whispers to her : "In case of
anything happening to me, it is hidden in the level
running from Shaft No. 2 in the mine, on this hillside.
It is in a tin box under the fourth set of timbers to the
right of the incline. Remember it !"

"Why not take it? Leave to-night—fly on horseback."

"Where ?"

"To the Pacific Railroad."

He laughs grimly, and taking her to the window,
cries : "This is a fine country to get out of !" Then
he points over the sage brush and explains : " To the
west is the Tintic Valley—thirty miles of alkali ; but,
beyond it, hills and one spring ; then one hundred miles
of desert, burning sand, and no water that man or
beast can drink. Could we travel over that and live to
reach the railroad ? To the south,—Mormon settlements on the Servier River—Beaver, Parowan, the very
hot-bed of Mormonism. Beyond them, Lee's Ferry on
the Colorado !" And he shudders as he mentions the
name of John D. Lee, not as yet sacrificed by the Mormon Church, for whom he murdered one hundred and
thirty-three men, women, and children, at Mountain
Meadows. "After Lee's Ferry, deserts and the Apache.
To the east, Mormon settlements—Santaquin, Nephi,
Juab, Manti—and, back of them, the impassable desert-
plateaus and mountain ranges of the Rockies—mighty

rivers that foam through gorges thousands of feet deep
—and Ute Indians!"

"But to the north, father—the way I came—hardly
one hundred miles!"

"That is our only path," mutters the man. Then he
says, doubtingly: "But still all Mormon. We may
never reach Salt Lake City."

"Who'll stop us?"

"That will never be known! But it is our one
chance, and, once in Salt Lake, I think they dare not
touch me. I'll make arrangements to take you up to-
morrow. Come with me now to the hotel."

"Why cannot I stay with you?"

"Humph!" he laughs. "The hotel is better than
this. There is only one bed here. Besides, some
one would say," he chuckles rather grimly, "Bishop
Tranyon has taken another wife! And I do not wish it
to be generally known you are my daughter. Then,
too, I have a telegram to send."

"Oh, yes!" cries the girl, "for Captain Lawrence!"
And she accompanies him down the trail that winds to
the road coming from Silver City to Eureka.

So, in about half an hour, Miss Travenion finds
herself seated at a comfortable supper in the hotel.
And some time after—her father having gone off to
send the promised telegram—being very tired, she goes
up to her room, where she finds a clean cot bed, and
goes to rest, thinking: "If my life is ruined, his life has
been, perhaps, made more happy by this day's work—
he will be rich."

So, pondering of the absent man, who is not yet her
lover, yet whom she now knows she loves, she murmurs: "He will come here to put men at work once
more upon his mine; he will learn that I am the daughter
of Tranyon, the Mormon bishop!" and shudders and
writhes at the thought. Next she says more hopefully:

12

"Perhaps when he finds his property his own once more he will not hate the Mormon bishop so much as he did yesterday," and this seems to comfort her a little, for she goes to sleep.

Early next morning, Erma is awakened by her father's sharp knock upon the door. He whispers to her: "Quick! You must be ready to start soon!"

But, a few minutes after, coming into the hall, she hears: "Wall, bishop, did Miss Ermie arrive all right? I saw her off in good style, and I've come down here, first to look after the mine, and then to consult ye on some church business. What a beautiful lamb of Zion your darter is!"

It is the voice of Kruger, the Mormon! And Miss Travenion grows pale as marble, for she knows that the Church of Latter-Day Saints has its eye on Tranyon, its bishop, and Erma, his daughter, last season's prize-beauty in New York society, and Newport's latest summer craze; but now regarded by the Prophet Brigham and his Council of Seventy, as one of the elect of Zion, whom God has given into their hands to save, or lose—to elect, or to cut off, even unto the atonement of blood.

CHAPTER XIII.

THE LOVE OF A BISHOP.

THE very telegram Erma thinks may bring Harry Lawrence to her side, curiously enough keeps him from her.

It comes about in two little episodes—one of sorrow, one of joy.

On the day Miss Travenion left Salt Lake City, at eleven o'clock, the young man calls at the Townsend House, to keep the appointment Erma has made for him with her father. He comes up to the office of that hotel, rather light-hearted, considering his desperate straits financially. He is about to see the girl he loves—she who, in wild moments, since her generosity of yesterday, he thinks may have some interest in him; for otherwise why should she take such pains to have him see her father?

He asks lightly: "Is Miss Travenion in?"

"Miss Travenion has gone," says the clerk, a little curtly, for the sudden departure of the Livingstons has not altogether pleased the hotel office.

"And the Livingstons—" asks Lawrence, hurriedly.

"The whole party went to California this morning at five o'clock, on the Ogden train," answers the youth behind the counter indifferently, for Mormon hotel clerks are quite often as careless as Gentile hotel clerks.

After a moment of blank astonishment, Harry suggests: "Any letter for Captain Lawrence?"

"Yes," replies the clerk, and hands him an envelope, the feminine handwriting on which he knows, and it gives back to him hope,—for one moment. Stepping aside a little, he opens it; and the sun, shining so

brilliantly this bright October day, goes out of the
heavens—for him. For he sees a lady's visiting card
which looks like this :

I have seen my father,
Good bye

Miss Erma L. Travenion

18 Madison Square North

Crushing the fragile pasteboard in his hand, his moustache twitches with pain, and he mutters bitterly:
"Oliver Livingston was right! My darling has seen
her father ; he wishes her to still wed that washed-out
aristocrat ! "

A minute after he thinks : " She wished to bid me
good-bye, also ! Did she do it easily ? " and inspects
the card he has almost thrown away, to see if the
handwriting shows emotion in its lines. Doing this,
a little hope comes to him, for he sees a splash such as
a tear-drop might make upon the delicate tint of the
cardboard.

Putting the missive away reverently in his pocket-
book, he meditates, and reason tells him he has lost
her. It says to him, She is not of your class and people.
Her father wishes her to wed in her station, among the
exclusives of Fifth Avenue and Murray Hill, and she
obeys him. What are you that you should hope for her ?
If your mine was sold and you had nearly five hundred
thousand dollars in your pocket, you might make an

effort to win this butterfly, who has come into your mannish frontier life to make it brilliant for a day or two. You were happy before you saw her ; be so without her !

To this he cries, resolution fighting against conviction and common sense: " No more joy for me without her ! I'll win her yet ! " and goes on his way to see his lawyers about getting the injunction on his mine removed.

But his attorneys, Messrs. Parshall & Garter, do not give him very much hope of immediate success, and common sense is a very hard party to down in argument ; consequently Harry Lawrence makes a very sombre day of it, and a more sombre night.

Two days after, however, cometh joy. He is in his lawyers' offices, trying to think if any one in this wide world will go on his bond to raise the injunction that paralyzes him financially, when Garter comes excitedly in, and slapping him on the back, cries enthusiastically : " Here's luck for Harry Lawrence. I've just received a stipulation from Judge Smith, Zion's Co-operative Mining Co.'s attorney, agreeing to raise your injunction ! "

" Impossible ! "

" Fact ! "

" What reason did Smith give for this curious concession ? "

" Nothing ; only that Tranyon telegraphed instructions to that effect last night, and he thought there must be a mistake and had wired asking reasons ; that Tranyon had replied, his only reason was that he wished it, and was going to have it done. Smith thinks the Mormon bishop has gone crazy. However, I've got the stipulation and you can go to work to-morrow," answers Garter, showing to Harry Lawrence's wondering eyes the document.

That day he begins arrangements for his return to Tintic, but he has a great deal to do and many mining supplies to order and ship, and this delays him. The Sunday intervenes. But Monday, hurrying his preparations, he is ready to start so as to make half the drive that day, and is even in his buckboard, ready to leave, when Garter himself comes, out of breath, to stop him, crying: " I've got more good news for you. My boy, you're rich!" and slaps Lawrence heartily on the back.

" Rich!" echoes Harry. Then he goes on more slowly, a lump coming suddenly into his throat, " What do you mean?"

" What I say! You're rich. I have within the hour received from Tranyon a quit-claim deed to you of the Mineral Hill locations from the Zion's Co-operative Mining Co. of Tintic. Look!" cries Garter, and displays the document.

" It can't be so!" gasps Lawrence.

" It is—and what's more, the deed's in proper form. It arrived by special messenger from Eureka, with a note from Bishop Tranyon, saying that on careful examination of the matter, he had concluded that the location was properly yours."

" How do you explain it?" asks Harry, who can't believe.

" Well," replies Garter, " Tranyon writes that he is moved by love of Zion to discontinue the suit—but I think it was fear of Parshall & Garter," goes on the modest Western lawyer. " The bishop heard you had engaged us. Anyway, your title to your Mineral Hill Mine is without contest. It's as clear as mine to my caput."

" Then the Mineral Hill's as good as sold to the English company. The deed's in escrow in Wells, Fargo & Co.'s. Telegraph Southmead in New York, and get the cash as soon as you can for me, Garter," answers Lawrence. "I leave town this afternoon. I've other business to attend to!" his face lighting up with something that it has not had in it since he read Erma Travenion's card.

"You go to Tintic, I suppose," asks the lawyer, as he gives Lawrence a farewell grip of congratulation.

"No! to San Francisco," is the answer, and leaving the astounded Garter gazing at him, Harry drives straight to his bank, cashes a check, and just catches the afternoon train for Ogden.

Arriving at this place, and walking over from the Utah Central to the junction depot, Lawrence is greeted suddenly and heartily by, "How are you, Cap?" and looking up, sees Buck Powers.

"How are you, Buck? Doing pretty well?" he remarks heartily to this youth.

"First rate! The news company made a kick about dat collection Miss Beauty took up for me. Dey wanted half of it, but I stood them off," returns Buck in explanation. Then he continues suddenly, "Say, boss, she was here four days ago."

"Ah! you saw her?" asks Harry eagerly.

"No—I was on de road—but that cripple Mormon who sells newspapers told me dat de whole swell Livingston outfit went West on the Central, Thursday."

This information is what Lawrence has expected; he goes into the office and gets his sleeping berth, Buck Powers greeting this transaction with a sly wink and a *sotto voce* remark: "I guessed you wouldn't be long after her. You knows the purtiest girl as ever come over the road, you do, Cap."

.So at six in the evening, Harry Lawrence, his pulse bounding with revivified hope, his eyes sparkling with eagerness, his heart filled with a great love, is speeding towards the Pacific in pursuit of the girl he has sworn shall be his and no other's: while every throb of the locomotive that he fondly thinks brings him nearer to her, bears him away from Erma Travenion.

*   *   *   *   *   *   *   *

And she upon whom his thoughts are, is sitting by the side of the mine cabin, looking over the sage brush plain of the West Tintic Valley, and listening to the low murmur of her father's and Kruger's voices coming to her through the open doorway, and thinking: "Harry has the news now.—To-morrow he will be here to work his mine.—To-morrow he will learn what I have done for him.—To-morrow he will know I am Tranyon's daughter.—Will he be generous enough to forget my father's shame?" Then she sighs: "These are curious thoughts for me, whom they called a belle at Newport six weeks ago—'Miss Dividends,' whose bonds have made her the bond-maiden of the Mormon Church!" And mocking herself with these jeering words, Erma Travenion goes in to meet Bishop Kruger and treat him with respect, if not cordiality—for now she fears him, not altogether for her father's sake but for her own, for in the last four days she has grown to feel that Kruger, Mormon fanatic and bishop, has an interest in her that is not all for Mother Church.

This idea has entered the young lady's mind, not from one but from several incidents.

Immediately after hearing Lot's voice on the morning of his arrival, her father had come to her and hurriedly whispered, "Not a word to Kruger of our leaving. Flight would now be useless if they mean to stop us."

"But where shall we go?" asks the girl anxiously.

"Nowhere! We are safest here for the present," replies Travenion. Then, seeing astonishment in Erma's mobile face, he continues, "This and the other mining camps are chiefly Gentile. Here we would be protected by the hardy men who have come in from California, Nevada and Colorado. It is in travelling through the farming settlements that our trouble will come to us. I have told him," he indicates by a gesture Mr. Kruger, who is looking to the comfort of his team outside, "that you will remain with me here for some weeks. As you love me and yourself, do not arouse his suspicions."

"You may trust me," whispers his daughter earnestly, for her father's manner is very impressive.

A few minutes after they are all at breakfast together, Kruger greeting Miss Travenion in a more familiar and off-hand manner than he has so far assumed to her, saying, "Wall, Sissy, did your dad look natural as a miner? Stoggie boots aren't quite as nice as patent-leathers, and flannel shirts ain't quite so high-falutin' as b'iled ones, but he's daddy all the same, ain't he?" Then, chuckling at his own remark, he prevents reply by turning to Travenion and saying, "Bishop, she's too likely a gal to let go out agin to the ranks of the unrighteous. You ought to persuade her to take her endowments."

"Pooh!" answers Ralph lightly. "Erma is too devout an Episcopalian for me to hope to convert her." But Miss Travenion notes her father suffers at the mere suggestion that she, whom he loves and honors, should be even mentioned in connection with this sect of which he is bishop and apostle.

The next second Travenion has changed the subject, saying, "I'm glad you've come down, Lot; otherwise I should have had to write to you about our mine."

"Indeed! What's new since we fixed them Gentiles with an injunction?" asks Kruger, easily.

"Come up to the shaft and see," replies Ralph. Then he says to his daughter: "You won't mind a little walk?"

" No," answers the young lady. " In this Tintic air I feel as if I could climb mountains."

" Wall, ye can find plenty of mountains round here to climb !" laughs Lot.

So they all come out of the hotel into the main and only street of this mining camp—where many of the men look with by no means kindly eyes on the two Mormon bishops, for Tranyon's injunction has closed Lawrence's mine, which promised to develop into a great property which would furnish lots of work for the "boys." But on seeing the young lady who accompanies the two apostles, the hats and caps of the delvers after gold and silver come off with that respect for all women, young or old, beautiful or plain-faced, that the miners of the Pacific have since " Forty-nine," when in California they learned to value sweethearts and wives, because they had none. A chivalry they have not yet—thank God—forgotten.

But aside from her womanhood, Erma's beauty is so overpowering to these gentlemen of the pick and drill that they would follow her, were it polite, and one Pat- sey Bolivar remarks : "Good Lord, if she's a Mormon, she must be the angel that brings Brigham his revela- tions from Heaven." To this another, Pioche George, answers : "She ain't no Mormon girl—she's a lady and wears high-heeled boots and has a back-action panier that comes from Par*ie*."

After a little they are out of the town, and leaving the road, make up the hill for the mining shaft ; and Kruger, walking behind, notices the tender care with which Travenion assists his daughter over the rough places in the trail, and is rather surprised at it, for Mormons, as a rule, have but little consideration and less respect for their womankind, the very doctrines of their polygamous church preventing that—though he remembers Tranyon has been considered a light hand with his wives, leaving them a good deal to themselves, and not exacting any great account of their outgoings and incomings.

While pondering upon this, and noticing the light grace of the girl as she steps from rock to rock in the trail, and the beauty of every movement and poise of her figure, he suddenly thinks: "It's right lucky Ermie ain't been seen up at the Lion House! The prophet would have been having 'revealing from Heaven' that she was to be sealed to him."

A moment after, as Miss Travenion ethereally springs over a small tree that has fallen across the path, this Mormon gentleman suddenly exclaims to himself: "Great Enoch! They would have cost in our co-op. up in Heber nigh onto five dollars a pair in farm produce. I'll see if Miss Highfalutin' will wear silk stockings when——"

He doesn't complete this sentence, though it produces a very definite idea—though a wild one—in his mind: for what was to him an "IF," as he looked upon the rare loveliness of Miss Travenion, the Newport butter-fly, on the Union Pacific train, has become to this Mormon fanatic a "WHEN," now she is in the valley of Tintic, the daughter of a Mormon bishop—cut off from Gentile friends and surroundings.

This "WHEN" seems to please him so much that Lot Kruger quickens his steps, and comes alongside of this attractive young lady, and for some unknown reason begins to be "reel cute," and cavorts about, showing his agility, skipping over boulders, remarking during his acrobatic performances: "Yes, I feel reel boyish. I allus do when gals are about! You ask Bishop Tran-yon there, Miss Ermie."

On this frivolity, Ralph, for some occult reason, looks with an evil eye. It seems to make him gloomy, but Erma rather laughs at the antics of this Mormon ecclesiastic, who seems to wish to make her forget that he is fifty years of age, and by no means lovely or engaging.

After a little, however, he chances, during some of his prattle, to call her "Miss Tranyon," and this puts the girl into such a rage, that did he but know it, she would like to annihilate him. She draws herself up very haughtily, and says : "Excuse me! I am always addressed as Miss *Travenion*, and have never been christened 'Sissy' or Miss *Tranyon!*"

"Oh, no offence, Sissy—I mean Miss Travenion!" answers Kruger. "But I didn't suppose you would be ashamed of the name your daddy answers to, and which is respected in this community."

To this, Ralph says in explanation, perhaps apology : "When I came here, every one seemed to mistake my name, and call me Tranyon. I did not take the trouble to alter their pronunciation."

But his daughter, in whom anger now overcomes prudence, says sneeringly: "Pshaw! You were ashamed! You were afraid your Eastern friends would learn you had become a Mormon!" Then quickening her steps, she reaches the works and dump of the Co-operative Company ahead of her escorts, and seating herself on a pile of timber, looks about upon the operations of the miners, which being novel, create some interest even in her present state of agitation.

This changes into almost a sneer of indifference as her father and Kruger arrive on the dump pile, and she sees Ralph very shortly thereafter euchre his brother apostle out of his share in the Zion Co-operative Mining Company, which is quite small in comparison to Tranyon's ; all the rest of his fellow Saints having already fallen victims to his imported Wall Street methods.

Kruger looking about the place, suddenly says: "Why, bishop! we've hardly any one to work!"

"Of course not!" replies Travenion easily. "We'll be enjoined Monday. This is Saturday—so I'm laying the men off, and putting things in shape to stop operations."

"Enjined! How's that?"

"Well, I suppose if we can get an injunction on the Mineral Hill, they can do the same to us."

"I reckon you're right," returns Lot, wiping his forehead, and looking glum. "But I thought we claimed their mine—not that they claimed ourn."

"Besides," adds Ralph, "it is about as well for us. We have got no pay ore. It is the Mineral Hill we want, I imagine." Here he gives Kruger a significant wink, and continues: "You'd better walk down our incline, and see how our prospects are, and then come up and tell me if you think there is any chance of our finding anything where we're working now. I'd like your opinion on that. It won't take you half an hour, bishop."

"Wall, there's nuthin' like seein'," replies Kruger, and descends the shaft, which is not difficult, it being an inclined one, and can be walked down if necessary, as it pitches into the hill at an angle of not over forty-five degrees.

There are two ore-cars running on tracks in this shaft, to the lower level of the mine, which is about one hundred feet from the surface. These are hauled up and let down by a horse whim, that at present, in contradiction to its name, is moved by a long-eared, strong-kicking mule, that Erma notices is called Marcho.

Kruger, instead of using his feet, prefers mule locomotion, and goes down on one of these cars; the other shortly thereafter making its appearance at the surface, is unloaded of some waste rock and a few dulled drills and other débris of the mine.

Another surface employee is engaged in turning a

circular hand fan, which through a large tin pipe forces fresh air to the miners working in the lower level.

These facts are easily and accurately explained by Ralph to his daughter, as they watch Mr. Kruger's descent.

A few moments after Lot has disappeared, he suggests: "Wouldn't you like to see the interior of the mine, Erma?"

"Is it safe?" asks the young lady.

"Certainly. Do you suppose I would knowingly take you into danger?"

"Oh, I referred to my costume, not myself," says Miss Travenion lightly, who is apparently determined to throw off care as much as possible this day.

"Dust will not hurt linen," replies her father. "There is no seepage at this season, and we are way above the water level. So you have only a little dust to fear, and the descent is not long nor dangerous."

Some expression in his face makes his daughter say "Yes" to his proposal.

A few moments after, the two are alone together in the car descending the dark incline, and Ralph Travenion whispers: "Watch me! The stock is below the set of timbers on which I shall place my hand."

To which Erma murmurs: "I understand!" knowing now that it is for this reason her father wishes her to go down the Zion Co-operative mine.

At the foot of the incline they find a level running from it in two directions: one towards the Mineral Hill, the other directly away from it. This last has been only continued about forty feet, and is apparently deserted. The first, which seems to be of much greater extent, is in operation, sounds of sledge on drill being heard coming from it, and the lights of the miners being seen as they work on its face far away from the incline.

Assisted by her father, Erma is led into the working portion of the mine, where she finds Mr. Kruger making his inspection of the same with the aid of a tallow candle, and, apparently, not exceedingly pleased with what he sees.

"You don't find very much mineral, do you, bishop?" remarks Travenion. "No," replies Lot, surlily. "There ain't enough in this vein to silver a tea-pot." Then he says suddenly : "But we have only got one hundred feet more to run to the Mineral Hill——"

"Which we won't travel in a hurry, when we're enjoined," jeers Ralph.

With this, he explains to his daughter the methods of mining that are employed, showing her the air as it rushes out of the tin air-pipe, to give life and vitality to the miners employed below.

This inspection doesn't take long, and, a few minutes after, they return to the station, followed by Lot.

Just here, however, Travenion says : "I haven't had a look at this other drift for a good while. I think I'll make a little examination of it now," and goes into the unused level.

When he reaches the fourth set of timbers from the shaft, by the light of his candle, Erma sees him put his hands on them, and lean against them, as he examines the face of the drift.

"Would you like to come in, Kruger?" he asks. "I find nothing."

"Seein's believin'!" cries Kruger, and makes an examination also. Then the two men come back to the station.

Erma notices that Lot has left his genial spirits in the bottom of the mine, for when they are hoisted to the surface he turns round and says : "Tranyon, unless we get the Mineral Hill, we don't get anything."

"And for that we have got to fight them," answers

Ralph. Then he continues : "By the bye, you know Captain Lawrence has engaged Parshall & Garter. We have got a big fight on our hands, and I suspect I'll have to assess you."

"How much ?" gasps Kruger.

"Well, I guess about twenty-five hundred dollars will do for your share, as a starter."

"As a starter !" screams Lot, who, though comfortably off for a Mormon, is not rich like Travenion.

"Yes, for just a little bit of a starter. It's going to cost me one hundred thousand dollars, perhaps more, to fight this case, and you don't suppose I'm going to spend *all* the money, do you, bishop ?"

"Great Zion ! You talk of money as if it was water !" groans Kruger. Then he mutters to himself : "I wish I could get out of this thing !"

Leaving him to digest this unpleasant communication, Travenion takes his daughter's arm, and they walk to the end of the dump pile. Here he points out to her various mining locations and things of interest on the scene.

Up to the right, about a mile, is the big ledge of the Eureka Mining Company, then in litigation also. Across the West Tintic Valley, over thirty miles of sage brush, is the Scotia Mine. To the left, Silver City and Diamond.

"But where is Captain Lawrence's mine, the Mineral Hill ?" asks the young lady eagerly.

"Just up a little and further to our right—about three hundred feet ;" and Travenion pointing out the spot, Erma places such anxious eyes upon it that her father whispers : "No hope of seeing your young man now ! He doesn't know yet his injunction is discontinued. He'll be down in a day or two !" and pats her cheek, and laughs as if he had hopes himself from this enterprising young Gentile Philistine.

Just here they are interrupted by Kruger, who comes up suddenly and mumbles: "Bishop, I'd like to sell out!"

"Who to?" jeers Ralph. "Law-suits are too plenty around here for most people to want to buy them."

"To you!" says Lot. "You're the only man can handle this thing properly. Then you'll have the whole of it."

"I think I have enough now, considering I've rather an expensive family," returns Travenion, and his eyes regard his daughter laughingly but lovingly.

"You won't buy my stock?" appeals Kruger again.

"Not unless you name a *very* low figure, bishop."

"So I will," cries Lot. "I ain't no good at mining, nohow. If 'twas cattle, or farmin', I'd stand any man off!"

Then he names so low a sum that Travenion says: "All right! We'll draw up a deed this afternoon," and with that gives the foreman the necessary orders for closing the mine.

They all start down the hill together, though before leaving, Ralph gets a very grateful glance from his daughter, who, coming close to him, whispers: "You bought Kruger's stock so as to make the deed to Captain Lawrence. God bless you, father, for doing him justice!"

So they come down the trail, towards the main road, all apparently happy—Erma because she thinks Travenion's justice may make Harry Lawrence forget she is Tranyon's daughter; Kruger because he has got out of what he thinks a bad speculation with some little money; Ralph because his daughter's eyes are brighter and her step is lighter than at any time since she has known he was a Mormon.

As they are passing a pile of rocks that borders the trail, a sudden sound, like that of a dozen locusts, comes to them. Erma, with a little cry, gathers her skirts about her, and springs upon a near-by boulder. Travenion looks hurriedly about for a stick.

The next instant, Lot, who has lived all his life in wild places, has guessed the matter, and coming up, cries : "Why, it's a pesky rattler!" and with a handy rock smashes the head of a serpent that has coiled itself upon the trail, a little ahead of them.

"A rattlesnake ! Oh, mercy !" screams Miss Travenion, scrambling higher up on her boulder of safety.

"You can come down, now, Erma," says her father. But she stands poised on her eyrie, and discusses the matter, making a picture that causes Lot's sturdy heart to beat harder than it did when climbing the mountain.

"Not yet—I have read of them. They travel in pairs !" she gasps.

"Wall, this critter is dead, any way," suggests Kruger. " He has bitten himself twice since I ' rocked' him. It's all-fired queer how these varmints commit suicide when wounded."

"There's no danger," says Travenion.

"I'll toss him out of the path ; then you'll come down, Sissy !" remarks the gallant Lot. For somehow the beauty of this young lady—so different from the other women this man has met—makes him wish to soothe fears he would be indifferent to, perhaps condemn, even in one of the many wives of his bosom.

"Oh, please do. I'll thank you so much, Mr. Kruger," answers Erma.

Then she ejaculates : "Do it *quick!* I don't like to look at it !" For the Mormon bishop seems to be awkward over his work, perchance because Miss Travenion, in her agitated pose, displays an ankle that might daze any lover of the beautiful.

A moment after, he has flung the reptile away, and Erma descends, a little nervous yet, as she falters :

"Are there many of them about?" and manifests a disposition to run down the hill.

"This is the first I have seen this year," says Ralph, reassuringly.

"Yes, these critters are scarce round here," adds Lot ; " but over thar in Provo Cañon, fifty miles away " —he points northeast—" ye can't go one hundred yards without hearing 'em. And up at the head of it, there war thousands of 'em, but we all turned out, couple o' years ago, and burnt 'em up in a cave they 'denned' in. It's a marvellous place, the top of Provo Cañon," he continues. "There's springs of writing-ink up there, and green and red colored water, and ice-cold fountains and b'iling hot fountains, all coming out of pot-shaped domes."

"It must be very curious, Mr. Kruger," returns Erma, who thinks she must appear grateful to him for killing the snake.

"Perhaps ye'll see it some time, yerself, Sissy," remarks Lot. "I have got as pretty a ranch as is seen in Utah, up the Kammas Prairie on the head-waters of Provo River. I have got as fine cattle and sheep, and four as likely——"

He checks himself suddenly here, but Ralph sarcastically adds : "Wives—why don't you say it at once, bishop? Four as likely *wives* as there is in Utah, as well as a fifth at Provo, and a sixth in Cache Valley." Then he chuckles : "You're too bashful, Kruger !"

For that gentleman has suddenly grown red, and guffaws : "Git out ! Bishop Tranyon ! Yer givin' me away to your darter !"

"Pish !" cries Ralph. "You were never diffident about it before. I have heard you brag about your women folks and big family to a dozen girls, at a dance in Provo."

"Stop, bishop!" interjects Kruger, interrupting him. "You have scared Ermie plump off!"

Which is true, for Miss Travenion has suddenly displayed a desire for rapid movement that has carried her well ahead of the gentlemen, down the trail.

Her refined mind resents her father's laughing allusions to polygamy, which make her shudder. Anxious to avoid the subject entirely, she walks on so rapidly that her escorts do not overtake her till she has reached the hotel.

As she walks, two ideas force themselves upon her. Her father wishes her to know that Kruger is a married man. Kruger does not care that she should learn the fact. Why is he confused and diffident over her knowledge of what he has boasted to a dozen Mormon girls at a time?

She can't think of any answer to this for a little while, but just as she reaches the door of the hotel, a great wave of color flies over her face, followed by an unnatural pallor, and shivering as if struck by the ague, she sinks on to an empty box that stands near the door.

A moment after her father is by her side, whispering: "You are faint!"

And Kruger coming up cries: "This high air up here is too much for ye!"

"I'll be better in a moment!" whispers the girl. "Could not you get me a drink of water?"

Her father going on this errand, Lot laughingly suggests: "I reckon it must have been the sight of the snake that weakened ye!"

"Yes—I think it was—the sight of the snake—" shudders Erma.

Then Ralph brings the water to her and she drinks it as if there were a fever in her veins, and her eyes seem to follow Kruger, the Mormon bishop, as if he were the rattlesnake—only they look on him with more loathing than they did on the reptile.

CHAPTER XIV.

A RARE CLUB STORY.

THEN, under the plea of illness, Miss Travenion seeks her little room in the hotel, to get away from the sight of this man whom she has suddenly grown to loathe—she hardly fears him—the idea that has come to her about him seems so preposterous.

Some two hours afterwards, her father knocking on her door, asks if she is well enough to see him. Being told to enter, he does so, whispering to her: "Speak low! Sound passes easily from one room to another."

Then he informs her he has received his deed from Kruger, and has forwarded the deed of Zion's Co-operative Mining Company to Captain Lawrence, remarking: "This will bring your young springald down here very suddenly, I imagine," playfully chuckling Erma under the chin with a father's pride.

"Do not deceive yourself!" answers the girl. "Captain Lawrence is not engaged to me. He has never said one word of love to me. He will now probably never say one of love to me. YOU ARE MY FATHER!" This last with a sigh is a fearful reproach to this Mormon bishop, who in the misery of his child is repenting of his sins.

A moment after he whispers: "Be careful of what you say before Kruger. Though we have travelled together for many a day and many a night, I fear in case of apostasy that to Lot Kruger's hand is given my cutting off."

With this caution he leaves her.

In this case, Travenion's subtle mind has guessed the truth. For the heads of the Mormon Church have thought it wise to place this matter entirely in Kruger's hands. They fear the apostasy of R. H. Tranyon.

They fear *more*, the loss of the vote of his stock in the Utah Central Railway—that will lose them the control in that road. They have determined to prevent it.

But with the Jesuitism that has always governed the policy of the Mormon theocracy, they have told Kruger—whom they have had on such business before, together with his old chum Danites, Porter Rockwell and Bill Hickman—to take the affair in his hands, and if he finds beyond peradventure and doubt that R. H. Tranyon, capitalist and bishop, is going to apostatize, to do "*what the Lord tells him to do*," which they know means Tranyon's destruction, because Kruger is an old-time Mormon fanatic, and will do the work of the Lord, by the old methods of the days of the so-called Reformation, when "blood atonement" was preached openly from their pulpits, and death followed all who doubted or apostatized. They have also made up their minds, if trouble comes to them through what Kruger does, to sacrifice him to Gentile justice, and, if necessary, secure Mormon witnesses that will bear evidence against him, and a Mormon jury who will convict him, as they are making ready to do with Kruger's old friend and associate, Bishop John D. Lee, of the Mountain Meadow massacre.

This commission delights Lot very much. He doesn't think his friend Tranyon an apostate, but he does think Tranyon's daughter, this Eastern butterfly, as beautiful as the angels of paradise, and he has accepted his mission gleefully.

All the way driving down to Tintic, he has been rubbing his hands and muttering to himself: "It's lucky they didn't see her in the Tithing Office or the Endowment House, or there would have been a rush of apostles for this beauty, who shall become a lamb of Zion, and be sealed by the Lord in plural marriage unto Lot Kruger."

It is with this idea that he has come to Tintic, and, still believing Tranyon to be Mormon zealot like himself, thinks Ralph will regard it as no more dishonor to give his daughter into polygamy to a brother bishop ; than he, Lot Kruger, would think, of turning over any of his numerous progeny to make an additional help-mate to any of his co-apostles.

Being confident of this, Lot imagines he can wait patiently till " Ermie sees the good that is in him."

Therefore, they all sit down to a waiting game ; for Tranyon believes himself safer in this mining camp than anywhere else in Utah, and dare not leave so long as Kruger is by his side.

This delay is not utterly unbearable to Miss Trave-nion, because every day she thinks the incoming stage, or some private buckboard, or light wagon, will bear into town the man she is looking for—Captain Harry Law-rence—who, at least, should come filled with gratitude to Ralph Travenion, though he may despise Bishop Tranyon.

So she passes her time, driving to Silver City, Diamond and Homansville with her father, who, under the pretence of settling various demands of business, lingers in Tintic Mining District ; now and then reading a novel, for Ralph has thoughtfully sent to Salt Lake and provided her with some books. Altogether, she is not uncomfortable, as she has brought a sufficiency of clothing with her, though most of her trunks have been left at the Townsend House. Her father, who has never forgotten his old sybaritic life, sees that their table is supplied with every luxury which can be obtained in the place, sending Mormon boys to Utah Lake for trout, and to Payson for late fruits, and securing from Salt Lake City wines of the best vintages of France.

The air is fresh, and growing colder, and the young lady's cheeks are very rosy, though they have been browned by the sun. There is some little excitement in the place, also. The litigation between the Big Eureka and the King David has come to trial by battle, and these companies have each imported armed fighters from Pioche, Nevada, the most ferocious mining camp in the West.

Thus time runs into November, but the girl's heart is getting heavier and heavier, for the man she is looking for, and who has occupied most of her thoughts for the last six weeks, has not yet arrived.

Then one day, quite late in the month, she gets a shock, for she hears he has left the Territory, having sold his mine to an English company for a large sum of money, and that they have even now come to take possession of it.

Travenion, having also got the same news, says to her, shortly : " Generosity did not do much good with young Mr. Harry Ingrate—did it ? "

And she, being stung with misery, jeers her father, and herself also, for that matter, " Yes, the daughter of Tranyon, the Mormon bishop, has no longer a hold upon the Gentile's heart ! Perchance he thinks I should wed in my own faith ? "

Then she falters out of the house, and, alone by herself, among some piñon-pines that grow on the hillside, tears come into her lovely eyes, for she feels herself cut off forever from the bright world in which she once lived, and mutters : " Is this rough mining camp a dream ; or were Newport yachting parties and Delmonico balls hallucinations ? "

But this brings the matter first to climax and then to catastrophe. The girl treats with great *hauteur* and angry scorn Kruger, who would be devoted to her, if she would but let him, for, curiously enough, this old polygamist, for the first time in his life, is in love, as much as a Mormon can be, with this elusive butterfly who dodges his net and mocks his pursuit. Under the plea of business he suddenly goes away.

Then Ralph, coming to Erma, says: "Now is our time. We leave in a day or two!"

But before they have completed their preparations, Kruger, who has driven rapidly to Salt Lake City, and as rapidly returned, comes suddenly into Travenion's mining office, where he and his daughter have been discussing their preparations for departure.

Perhaps some evidences of their intentions are about the room, for Lot jovially remarks: "Packing up, Ralph! That's right; they will be wanting ye in Salt Lake soon. I've brought a communication from the head of the Church."

"Oh!" says Travenion, feigning a lightness that he does not feel. "What does the Lord say, through Brigham Young, his prophet? Erma, just wait for me outside. I'll go down with you to the hotel in a moment."

Acting on the hint, Miss Travenion leaves the house, and stands waiting for her father; and waits, and waits until darkness comes upon the scene, and voices in excitement come out of the thinly boarded building. Actuated by an anxious curiosity she cannot control, the young lady draws nearer to the house, and through its thin walls come to her these words: "It's no good discussin' the matter further, Bishop Tranyon. The Church orders you two things. One is to pay the one hundred thousand dollars tithing you owe to it——"

"Haven't I told you that I have no ready money?" cries Ralph. "Isn't this lawsuit taking every cent I can spare?"

"Yer duty to yer Church is fust, my friend!" answers Lot. "Besides, what yer tellin' me ain't true. Up at the city they know you've discontinued the lawsuit, and have given that d—mned Captain Lawrence "—he grinds the words out between his clenched teeth—"a quit-claim deed to his mine. Perhaps you thought you'd give him yer darter also ; but he's gone away to Europe, I reckon, and busted that plan."

Ralph does not answer him, and he goes on : "The Church says it will take yer one hundred thousand dollars tithing in stock of the Utah Central at fifty."

"At fifty !" screams Travenion, forgetting himself in rage. "Why, it's worth one hundred and fifty. I've been offered that for it by the—" But he remembers, and says no more.

"By the Union Pacific Railway !" ejaculates Kruger sternly. "Ye've been dickering with them for that stock ! Ye want to sell the Church out of control of that road !"

"As God is above me, that is not true !"

"Swear it, R. H. Tranyon ! Swear it by Joseph Smith, the prophet of the Lord !" cries Kruger, in his fanaticism prescribing an oath that is very easy for Travenion to take.

"I do," he answers, "by Joseph Smith, the prophet of the Lord !"

"Then I believe ye. No one could take that affidavit and lie !" says Lot, devoutly.

A second after, he goes on suddenly and suspiciously : "But it is reported, among the Saints in the city, you're getting lukewarm in the faith, R. H."

"And you, Lot—what did you say ?" asks Travenion anxiously.

"I said it was a confounded lie ! That there wa'n't a truer Mormon than R. H. Tranyon on the 'arth ! Tell me so yerself ;" and the voice of the man becomes pleading as he continues : "We have been pards so long I wouldn't like to cut ye off."

"I swear it !" gasps Ralph. "I'm a true Mormon !" For now he is sure that the man appointed to be his destroying angel stands before him.

"You can prove it !"

" How ? "

" You've a little lamb down here——"

" My God ! "

" Make a sacrifice of her to the Lord ! Let Ermie take her endowments, and the Church and I will believe ye're true to the faith of Joseph Smith, the prophet, and Hyrum, his brother."

To this Tranyon makes no reply for one second. Then he mutters suddenly and brokenly : " Tell them I'll pay my tithing with the Utah Central stock."

" At fifty ? "

" Yes, at any figure they like ; only, for God's sake, leave my daughter out of this business. I'll bring it with me ! "

" Ah, that 'ere stock's down here ! " says Kruger suddenly. " Now you're coming round, bishop, to the demands of the Church, I'll tell you some good news I have for you. They're goin' to make you a missionary to England ! "

" Aha ! before the election in the Utah Central ? "

" Yes ; the Church will vote the rest of yer stock for ye."

" But my daughter ! " falters Travenion. " I can't leave her ! "

" Don't have no fear for her, bishop ! I'll look after her as if she was my own." And Kruger's orbs light with sudden passion. " I've been keepin' my eyes on her. She's a——"

But he says no more, for Erma Travenion sweeps in between the men, with such a look in her blazing eyes that they both fall back from her.

She cries, " Father, you pay *no* tithing to the Mormon Church. Your daughter takes *none* of its vile mysteries of endowment ! "

" Quit yer blasphemy of the Church of Zion ! " yells Kruger to the girl. Then he turns on Travenion and rebukes him sternly, "Bishop, your darter's been brought up wrong! She's too high-spir'ted and wayward! I never 'low no woman in my household—wife or darter—to lift up her voice ag'in me and my doin's. If Miss Upity were my gal I'd take the blaspheming out of her with a heavy hand."

But here astonishment comes on Erma. Her father says: "Kruger, you're right! My daughter has been brought up wrong! I now see my error in not bringing her into the true faith. She shall take her endowments!"

"First kill me!" cries the girl, who cannot believe what she hears.

"Kill ye!" answers Lot. "Why, it will be the making of ye. Saving yer soul from perdition, is yer daddy's duty, my child."

"Saving my soul?" screams Erma. "Saving my soul?—by making me one of your horrible sect that degrades both women and men also by its bestial creed!" And indignation makes her beauty greater than it was before—so great that fanatic Lot's eyes grow as bright as hers, though with a different gleam.

But her father stops more, by saying hastily: "Kruger, go up to Salt Lake. Tell them I'll pay my tithing in the Central stock at their figure. Tell them I'll vote the balance as they please, and my daughter *shall* take her endowments!"

"Swear 't as you hope for Heaven!" cries Lot.

"As I hope for the Mormon paradise!" answers Travenion.

At this the girl gives two awful gasps; one—"Deserted by the man I once thought loved me!"—the other—"Betrayed by my father."

And the two men leaving her, she sinks down, dumb with despair. After a moment their footsteps pass down the trail.

In a few minutes, thought and movement coming to their victim, she rises, and staggering to the door to make some wild effort to fly, is met by her father, who whispers to her : " Forgive me ! "

" Promising me to the degradation of the Mormon Church. How can I forgive that?" Then she sighs, " How could my father do this? "

" For both our lives ! " he whispers. " Kruger has gone to Salt Lake. I have a certain plan for our escape ; " and would put his arms about her and soothe her.

But the girl bursts from him, sobbing wildly. And he bends over her, trying to comfort her, and sobbing also: " It was for both our lives ! Erma, darling, could you not see it ? Don't you know that I would die for you ! " Then he mutters, " It would have been a pity if, for a few words, we had lost our opportunity to—defeat this Mormon rustic—we, whose intellects have been sharpened in the outside world. What is pride against success ? Be a woman of sense as well as of emotions. Pardon me using diplomacy in my extremity. Aid me to carry out my plan ! "

And she remembering that this man is her father and has, up to the present time, treated her as the daughter of his pride and love, queries, " How ? What plan ? " then mutters despairingly : " What matter ; you have given him your oath."

" Pish ! By my hope of the Mormon Heaven," he jeers ; then whispers in a voice whose earnestness compels attention : " Kruger has gone to Salt Lake to tell them of my submission. To-morrow morning you leave, *without me*, for Salt Lake City ; with you shall go my stock in the Utah Central Railroad. When there, express that stock to my order at San Francisco, by Wells, Fargo & Co., taking their receipt for the same by certificate numbers and valuing it at five hundred

thousand dollars   I'll risk W. F. & Co. standing the
Mormon Church off for half a million, for I'll pay no
more tithing to Brigham Young."   And he grinds his
teeth, thinking of what he has already paid.

"But I may be cut off on the road!" falters Erma.

"No, there is no chance of that," he answers ; next
cries : "Good God! you don't think I would put peril
on you! Listen how I have guarded you."   Then he
hastily explains that she is to travel *via* Tooele, which
will prevent any chance of Kruger's meeting her as
he returns from his errand—for Lot always comes to
Tintic by the shorter Lake road; that two Gentile
miners, whom Ralph can trust, will guard her to Salt
Lake City ; that Kruger, on his return to Eureka, will
find them both gone, and will try to follow his, Travenion's, track, for he will, of course, imagine they have
fled *together;* that he will be sure to follow him, for
Bishop R. H. Tranyon can be easily tracked, being well
known all over the Territory, having time and again
preached at Conference to Mormons who have come to
the Tabernacle from the south and the north, the east
and the west.   "In finding me he will think to find you
—so you at least will be safe," chuckles Ralph.   Then
he says earnestly: "As soon as you are in Salt Lake,
take the train to Ogden, and then the U. P. Railroad,
and get to New York as quickly as you can.   There I
will meet you!"

"But you—what of you? While I seek safety, you
sacrifice yourself?" dissents the young lady, noting
her father's idea tends to her escape, not his.

"That is the craftiness of my plan!" grins Travenion.   "When Lot returns to Tintic I shall have also
disappeared!"

"Where?"

"Into the bottom of my deserted mine!" chuckles
her father.   "No one will think of looking for me

there. I have already stored the place with all the luxuries and comforts of life. While Kruger is seeking for me all over the Territory, arousing his Mormon fanatics to inflict upon me 'the vengeance of the Lord,' I shall be having a very comfortable time of it," sneers Ralph. "After he has gone, perhaps to the far southern settlements, to cut me off there, I shall come out and drive very quietly to the railroad, and take train for California or Omaha, whichever seems most safe."

"But they may recognize you in Salt Lake City!" suggests Erma.

"Hardly. I shall travel at night the entire way to Ogden, not even entering Salt Lake. Besides, the Church has put this matter into Kruger's hands, and will not interfere in his business, and Kruger will be away. I know the peculiar methods my saintly associates have in these affairs—they want to punish only at second hand. No suspicion must fall upon apostles' heads; that might mean punishment from the government of the United States. Now," he says shortly, "will you do what I have explained to you for my sake—for your own safety?"

And the girl cries eagerly: "Yes! Anything to escape from this accursed land."

That night Ralph makes his preparations, and before daylight next morning he says to his daughter, who has already breakfasted, "Come with me. The wagon is at the foot of the hill."

Getting into the street, which is dark and deserted at this early hour and has quite a little fall of snow on it, November having far advanced, and Thanksgiving day being already celebrated, they move along the road towards Silver City; the only noise coming to them being occasional firing from Eureka Hill, where the fighting men of that company are exchanging playful shots with the guards of the King David, just to remind their employers that a raise in their salaries will be agreeable.

After fifteen minutes' walk they come to the hill on which the Zion's Co-operative deserted mine is located. At the foot of this is Travenion's light express wagon, drawn by a strange team of broncos, two men standing by it. Then Ralph says easily : " This is Patsey Bolivar, and this, Pioche George. Gentlemen, this is my daughter whom you have promised to take care of."

" We'll see the young lady through," remarks Patsey, taking off his hat.

And noting Erma has started back, for she has recognized her selected escorts as two of the most ferocious fighters in the camp, Pioche George, as he doffs his sombrero, remarks : " We look a leetle rough, miss, but you'll find us very tender of you, and very tough to your enemies—eh, Patsey ? "

To which Bolivar cries cheerily : " No coppers on us ! "

" Oh, papa's selection proves that," says Miss Travenion, who has looked into these gentlemen's eyes and feels confident of them as she gives these two fighting men her hand, so affably and trustfully that she binds them to her—even to life and death.

Then Ralph remarks : " I wish to take my daughter with me up to my mine ; would one of you come with us to take her down ? I shall bid her good-bye, there."

" With pleasure, bishop," replies one desperado.

But the other laughs, " Quit calling him bishop. He's repented and become a Christian like us ! "

For Travenion has been compelled to take these men partially into his trust, which he has done quite confidently, knowing he has paid them well, and after having taken his money they can be bought by no one else, the code of morals of the Western mine fighter being very definite on this point.

So, followed by Pioche George, Patsey Bolivar remaining to look after the team, Ralph assists Erma up the hill.

In a few minutes father and daughter are standing in the ore house on the dump pile of the now deserted Zion's Co-operative Mine, their accompanying fighting man remaining outside, "to give 'em a chance to be confidential."

Ralph whispers, " I'll go down and get the stock."

But Erma says suddenly, "Let me go with you. I must see that you are comfortable during your retreat from the world."

"I rather think I've looked out for myself pretty thoroughly," laughs Travenion, who seems in very good spirits, the strain of waiting having passed from his mind. Then he goes on earnestly, "God bless you, Erma, for thinking of me. Come down and see what I've done for myself. I can give you the stock there just as well as here."

So, lighting a candle for her, and guiding her steps very carefully, Ralph assists his daughter down the incline, and the two shortly come to the station, and turning along the level that runs away from the Mineral Hill Mine, Ralph pauses at the fourth set of timbers and laughs, " What do you say to this for a bachelor's apartment ? "

To this his daughter cries, " Oh, sybarite !—you've even got champagne and dried buffalo tongues."

As he has, a dozen pints of Veuve Clicquot, likewise Château Margaux, as well as a couple of boxes of rare Havanas, and canned provisions ; a soft mattress and warm blankets ; a chair to sit upon, half a dozen novels and some current literature to kill time with, lots of candles to illuminate his retreat, and plenty of water in a small barrel.

" I'll be pretty comfortable here, I imagine," he says, contemplatively.

14

"No, you'll be cold," answers the young lady.

"Cold?—a hundred feet under the ground? This depth is the perfection of climate. It is neither too warm in summer nor too frigid in winter. I shall be very snug down here," he remarks; then chuckles, "while my friend Kruger is hunting for me through snow-storms and blizzards on the outer earth."

"Still it seems horrible," mutters the girl with a shudder, "for you to be buried under the ground. The air——"

"Is excellent!" interrupts Ralph, tapping the tin air-pipe with his hand. "This is a natural draught—not enough for twenty or thirty men working down here unless the fan is in operation, but lots for two or three. See how brightly my candles burn!" Then he says sharply, "We've no time to lose. Pioche George will be getting impatient up-stairs. Hold a candle for me, my darling!"

With a pick-axe he has brought down with him, he exhumes from underneath the fourth set of timbers a small iron box, strongly secured by padlock, and giving it with its key to Erma, says: "Do as I have directed with this. It is the Utah Central stock."

Then, for the parting is coming, she falters: "Father, when will you join me?"

"As soon as you are surely safe and out of this accursed Territory, and Kruger has disappeared, pursuing me with his Mormon bloodhounds."

A second after, he bursts out, as if a great relief has come upon him, from throwing off the bonds that have held him so long: "Oh, how I have scoffed them in my heart, as I have preached their religious bosh at Conference and ward meeting, all these years. Won't this be a great story to tell in the Unity Club, New York, to my old chums, De Punster and Van Beekman, Travis and Larry Jerry, and the rest of the boys? How they will shriek at Ralph Travenion, the swell, having been a Mormon! Won't the champagne flow to my plural marriages? Egad! it's worth while to take these risks, to have such a royal story to tell!"

"Hush!" cries his daughter, sternly. "Remember the poor women you are deserting." A moment after she says more slowly, "They must be provided for as soon as you are safe."

"Oh, they will have plenty," answers Ralph. Then he bursts out again, "I leave too much behind. When I think of what I have paid, year by year, as tithing to the infernal Mormon Church, I curse it. But they are tricked at the last. I'll sell the control of their pet railroad out of their hands. Hang them, I could dance for joy!"

With these words, the old beau skips with a waltz step to the bottom of the incline. Then they ascend, the rope aiding their steps, and the pitch not being very steep, to the outer air, and the time has come to say farewell.

Pointing to a white-topped wagon at the bottom of the hill, Travenion says: "Quick! Give your father a kiss, and pray for his safety."

The girl answers: "One hundred!" and throws herself into his arms, and murmuring: "You are the only man who ever loved me—the only one! Mormon that you have been—polygamist that you are—you are the only one who's left to me!"

For she has been looking at the shaft of the Mineral Hill Mine, upon which the English company are now commencing to work, and her thoughts are on the man who she feels has deserted her.

Then, as Ralph embraces her, a shudder runs through her; but it is not of cold, though snow is falling, but it is the chill of her heart as she thinks: "But for this man, whose lips are now pressed to mine, Harry Lawrence would not despise me!"

But Travenion mutters in her ear :   It is late now—
you must leave at once, for the days are quite short ! "
and beckons Pioche George to approach.

"You can trust us, bishop, to take her through,"
George remarks, noticing the old man's agitation as he
gives the daughter of his heart his last kiss.

Then Erma hurries down the hill, and he, sitting on
the deserted dump pile of his mine, watches her until
Pioche George lifts her into the wagon and it drives
away over the snow-white road, making across the West
Tintic Valley, and so towards Ophir and Tooele, for
Travenion has directed them to go by this somewhat
roundabout road, to avoid any chance of meeting
Kruger, perhaps even now returning from his errand to
the heads of the Mormon theocracy in Salt Lake.

Looking on this he says : "She is safe ! " and laughs :
"I will be safe myself, shortly ! Now for my bachelor
quarters ! " and goes slowly again into the mine.

About half way down the incline he starts, pauses,
and listens, muttering : "I thought I heard a noise."
then sneers at himself, "Some stone touched by your
foot—you're weak-kneed, Ralph."

Continuing his descent and holding his candle in
front of him, he comes to his quarters, where he says,
looking about : "This is a pretty comfortable spot
to kill time by champagne, a weed, and a novel."

Which he does, lighting one or two more candles, to
give him better illumination, then gently sipping the
Clicquot, between puffs of a Bouquet Especial, as he
turns over the leaves of a new French romance, which
seems to amuse him greatly.

And all the while, from the darkness of the level,
beyond the incline, two red eyes glare at this sybarite
as he chuckles over the jokes of Monsieur Paul de
Kock.

Turning his back to the incline, in order to get a

better light upon his novel, Ralph sits chuckling over the queer conceits of the gifted Frenchman—the red eyes all the while coming nearer to him.

As Travenion laughs again, a heavy step sounds behind him, and the great red eyes are at his shoulder, looking over the volume with him, and he springs up with a shriek, for Kruger's voice is in his ears crying, "Doomed by the Church!"

Then this Mormon fanatic is upon him, seizing his arms, and bruising his more tender flesh, chuckling: "What's champagne muscle to grass-fed muscle, you dainty cur of New York!"

And though Travenion fights as men only fight who are fighting for their lives, he pinions him and makes him helpless, and dashes him brutally down.

Looking at him, the old club man, who was once a Mormon bishop, tries his last diplomacy. He gasps between white lips and chattering teeth: "This—to a man who has been your chum—your companion—who is your brother in the Church."

"Who *was* my brother in the Church!" cries Lot. "But we'll discuss the affair a leetle. With ye're permission, I'll liquor."

Knocking the head off a bottle of Clicquot, he quaffs it greedily; the one Ralph was drinking from having been thrown down in the struggle.

Throwing the bottle away; as it crashes to the other end of the level, he remarks with a hideous leer: "Now we'll come to biz once more!"

But Ralph answers him nothing.

Then Lot laughs: "You walked into yer own trap. You thought I'd gone to Salt Lake, but I reckoned from yer break-out of last night that yer Utah Central stock, which the Mormon Church needs and will have, was here in yer possession, an' made up my mind to locate it. I knew it wa'n't in yer safe, 'cause I'd seen that open too often lately. I reckoned it was right in this mine, and I'd been hunting over this place all night without success. But in the mornin' I heard a noise on the trail, and I seed ye and yer darter comin' up, an' I knowed what yer'd come for! An' when yer come down in the mine, I come down a *leetle* ahead of yer, and spied on yer from that drift, an' seed yer give that stock to Ermie to take away. But I'll 'tend to her afterwards."

To this Travenion sighs: "My daughter!"

But Kruger goes on savagely: "I would have shot yer while yer were profanin', if it hadn't been I didn't want to shock her by her seein' yer die. But now, I love yer so well, R. H. Tranyon, I'm goin' to fix ye!"

With this, he takes the case of wine and hurls it to the other end of the incline. There's a crash, and Margaux and Clicquot trickle over the stones of the mine.

Then he cries: "Yer won't need this!" and throwing over the keg of water, it runs to waste upon the earth.

"Neither will ye want pervisions!" and he tosses the old club man's dainties into the sink of the mine at the bottom of the incline, keeping a big buffalo tongue, which he bites and eats, talking after this, with his mouth full, which makes him more hideous and awful, as he jeers: "I ain't had no breakfast —I'm foragin' on the enemy of the Lord."

"My God! What do you mean to do?" gasps Travenion, who has looked on with eyes that are growing bloodshot.

"Cut ye off behind the ears—make a blood atonement of ye! You've been so crafty about this, no one will ever know you're down here to hunt ye up."

Then running up the incline, Lot loads the two cars standing at the surface, with great masses of rock and boulders, fanaticism giving him increased strength.

Letting them run down, he unloads them, and once more does the same, unheeding the cries of the man helpless in the level below.

When he has done enough of this, he cuts the cars loose at the surface, and they come crashing down, and block up the incline. Then he comes down again himself and piles the boulders he has already let down, on top of the wrecked cars, blocking Travenion from the outer world.

Noting his purpose, Ralph staggers up, bound as he is, and prays: "Not that! Shoot me—kill me another way! For God's sake, NOT THAT!"

But Kruger cries: "Powder and lead cost money! The Church is too poor to give ye an easy atonement." And he piles the rocks up to the pleading wretch's shoulders.

A moment after, he blows out every candle, save one, to light him in the finishing touches of his awful work; when, desperately struggling, Travenion drags himself to the barrier, and screams: "My God! You are mad—you don't know what you do! I'm your old friend and chum!"

"I'm sacrificin' you here on the altar, where I heerd ye blaspheme your religion an' your prophets! That's what I'm doin'!"

"Mercy! Not this death!" gasp the white lips, and bloodshot eyes beseech the executioner, looking over the barrier rising steadily between them.

"Ye've been given into my hands by Jehovah and Brigham, both of whom ye've blasphemed!" cries Kruger, piling the barrier up to the shuddering man's neck.

Then he goes on in savage mockery. "Ye'll tell no funny anecdotes and sacrilegious jokes about our president, Brigham Young, and our prophet, Joseph Smith! Champagne won't flow over yer infamous apostasy, in the Unity Club. It will be a rare tale to tell yer chums Von Punster and De Beekman, and Travis, an' Larry Jerry, of how yer made a mockery of our sainted religion, an' jeered us, even when ye preached from our altars! But ye'll never tell it! 'DEAD MEN TELL NO TALES!'"

Then the barrier is up to Ralph Travenion's face, which is now pale as the flickering candle that lights its agonies. Over this face comes one pang more cruel than the others, and the white lips sigh, "My daughter!"

"Yer darter—that's the p'int! I'll look after her salvation. She shall be a lamb of Zion. I'll take her right into my sheepfold."

"Powers of Heaven! What do you mean?" And the wall now rises above his mouth.

"I sha'n't be hard on her," mocks Kruger. "I'll spare her herding and cattle work. She shall do chores round the house. I'll be light on her, I will, bishop, for I mean—" He whispers three words into the fainting wretch's ear, who reels back from him and shrieks: "MY GOD! NOT THAT!"

To his scream, the crashing sounds of rocks and a big boulder make answer, and the light of this outer world leaves Ralph Travenion, and footsteps are heard passing away along the echoing level, and up the incline, and the old club exquisite, bound and helpless, is left alone in darkness—not to the torture of hunger, for of that he thinks not—not to the torment of thirst, for of that he cares not—not to the despair of certain death, though that has come upon him—but to the agony of fearing that the daughter of his heart may by some art or trick taste the awful degradation of plural marriage, such as he as Mormon bishop has preached and sanctified and has meted out to the daughters of other men.

BOOK III.

Out of a Strange Country

CHAPTER XV.

THE SNOW-BOUND PULLMAN.

As this horror is taking place inside the earth, Miss Travenion and her two escorts on its surface are speeding over the snow towards Tooele.

The consideration and respect with which she is treated by these two rough-and-ready fighters of many a desperate mining battle is almost oppressive : they are so exceedingly polite.

Every time he addresses her, Patsey Bolivar takes off his hat. Chancing in one of his remarks to use the word " infernal " (which is a very mild expression for this gentleman), Pioche George suavely suggests : " Don't ye mind Patsey's high-flown remarks, miss. I've told him if he uses any stronger expression than a plain ' damn ' in yer presence, that I'll perforate him."

" Would you rob me of one of my guards ? " gasps the girl.

" No," replies George. " Patsey an' I have arranged that any discussion between us shall take place after we've seen ye safe through—as we will ; though I reckon we've more to fear from snow than anything else on this trip, for it seems as if a blizzard was a-blowin' up."

So Miss Travenion journeys on, Patsey sitting on the front seat and driving, and Pioche George, who is beside him, turning round to her and regaling Erma with anecdotes of his frontier experience, some of which are amusing, and nearly all of them horrible.

About two hours after, Kruger also drives furiously out of Eureka, but does not travel the same route as the young lady he is in pursuit of—going up through Homansville towards Salt Lake City—the most direct route—but, strange to say, leaving it, and taking the road to his right, which leads on to Goshen, then Payson and Provo, for he intends to go up the Provo Cañon to Heber City, having some curious affidavits to make that he dare only indulge in before a Mormon judge. From this place he will journey rapidly as horseflesh can take him to Park City, and then to Echo Station on the Union Pacific Railway, which is also in the Territory of Utah, and subject to the domination of its judges.

He expects to encounter Miss Travenion at that point, though the snow that delays her on her trip will hinder him a great deal more, going up Provo Cañon and over the divide to Heber City. But he is a sturdy old Mormon, and though it means an all-night drive— part of the way, perhaps, in a sleigh—he does not care much for the storm, for he has a plot in his head that makes him rub his hands and chuckle, even when the wind blows the fiercest and the snow drifts the strongest.

Shortly after he has turned from the main road to Salt Lake, a wagon coming down from that city carries Harry Lawrence, who is very happy, and Ferdinand Chauncey, who is very tired: for they have made an all-night drive, and had they been five minutes earlier, would have encountered Kruger, to his astonishment, and, perhaps, to theirs.

As they come up to the cañon leading to Homansville,

Harry cries: "Ferdie, in half an hour I'll see her!" then mutters: "My Heaven! what a monster of ingratitude she must think me now!"

"Oh, I'll fix that for you, easy enough!" says Ferdie confidently. "I'll tell her how you've been wandering all over California after us, thinking she was in our party. I think my word will carry you through."

Curiously enough, this is the fact. Lawrence, full of hope, has reached San Francisco, to find the Livingston party is not there. They have gone to Belmont to spend a few days, the clerk at the Grand Hotel informs him, at the house of Mr. Ralston, the banker; a gentleman who, at this time, was pouring out hospitality with a lavish hand to prominent visitors to California.

Not having an invitation, Harry is compelled to remain, and await their return, but they come not. After a week or two, he discovers that they have gone straight from Belmont to the Yosemite, which is a long trip, as there are few railroads in the State at this time.

Notwithstanding this, he follows them, and after four days of staging and rough riding, finds he has missed them entirely; for now he cannot discover where they have gone, on leaving the valley of the cataracts. As a matter of fact, they have journeyed to Southern California, and have spent a couple of weeks at the great cattle ranch of Mr. Beale, near the Tejon Pass.

So, after a fruitless visit to the Big Trees, Lawrence concludes to return to San Francisco, knowing that the Livingston party must ultimately find their way there, before they return to the East.

In this place, which was just beginning to get excited over the great mining boom in the Belcher and Crown Point, which three years afterwards gave way to the still greater one of the Consolidated Virginia and

California, in which many fortunes were won, and more fine ones were lost, he passes two anxious weeks.

Being known to several mining men, and receiving telegram from Garter that the first one hundred thousand dollars had been paid upon his mine by the English company, and he can draw on him for fifty thousand dollars at sight, he goes to driving away thoughts of his errant sweetheart, by taking flyers in the securities of the San Francisco Stock Board, and one afternoon, purchasing a couple of hundred shares of "Belcher" at about fifty—its ruling price in the market at that time—he pays for them, and puts them in his pocket, hoping to sell them on the morrow at a few dollars a share advance, and strolls up to the Grand Hotel, for that is where the Livingstons have stopped before, and will probably stay on their return to San Francisco. Therefore he makes it his headquarters.

Here he is delighted to find Mr. Ferdinand Chauncey playing billiards.

"By Jove, Harry! What are you doing here?" cries this young gentleman, who has become very familiar with the man who has saved his life.

"Hunting for you," replies Lawrence, returning Ferdie's warm grip very cordially.

"Ah, you've come to tell us the news, I suppose," laughs Mr. Chauncey. Then he amazes Lawrence with the query: "How is she?"

"Who?"

"Erma Travenion, of course—how is she getting along with her many step-mammas?"

"What do you mean?" ejaculates Harry, thinking Mr. Chauncey has gone daft.

"I mean what I say. Innocence won't do. Has old Tranyon given you his mine as well as his daughter? Ollie and his mother quarrel every day over his desertion of the heiress. The widow says that she and

Louise won't be able to live on their income now, and
Oliver has turned sullen, and says if they can't, Louise
can go into a Protestant nunnery. So that young lady
is in despair."

"What the dickens do you mean?" gasps Harry.
Then he says: "Are you crazy?" and looking into
Ferdie's face, and seeing sanity there, suddenly seizes
him, leads him apart, and commands: "Tell me what
you're driving at!"

Then Mr. Chauncey, guessing from Lawrence's manner that he does not know what has happened, tells him
what took place in Salt Lake the evening before their
departure, to which Harry listens with staring eyes.

As Ferdie closes, he suddenly breaks out: "Now I
understand!—Tranyon's deed to me—it was that angel's
doing!" Then mutters: "My God! She'll think me
a monster of ingratitude! A prig, like that scalliwag
up-stairs;" he turns up his thumb towards where Mr.
Livingston is supposed to be.

To this Mr. Chauncey says nothing, though his eyes
have grown very large.

After a second's thought, Lawrence continues very
earnestly: "You say I saved your life. May I ask you
a favor in return?"

"Anything!" cries Ferdie.

"Very well! You can explain this matter to Erma
Travenion, so that she will know that I followed her
for love, all over California, and did not desert her for
pride, because she was the daughter of a Mormon, in
Utah. Will you come with me, and make that explanation?"

"Yes—when?"

"Now! The train leaves in an hour."

"I will," cries Ferdie. "I only want fifteen minutes
to pack my trunk and explain my sudden departure to
the Livingstons."

Which he does, and the two make their exit from San Francisco on the afternoon train, and two days afterwards find themselves in Salt Lake City, where Ferdinand would like to lay over for a night, but Lawrence says, "No rest while she thinks me ungrateful!"

Despite some demur on the part of Mr. Chauncey, he puts him into a light wagon, and the two drive all night so as to make Eureka in the morning, which they do, some two hours after Mr. Kruger has left it.

At the hotel, seeing neither Tranyon nor his daughter, Lawrence drags Ferdie, who is very tired, with him up the trail to the office of Zion's Co-operative Mine, and says: "You go in, my young diplomat, and tell her; I'll wait down here out of the way."

Which he does; but a few minutes after Chauncey comes back and reports: " There's no one there!"

"Nobody?"

"Not a living soul!"

Lawrence investigating this and finding it true, they return to the hotel again; but to Harry's anxious inquiries, no one can give him any information of the whereabouts this day of Bishop Tranyon or his daughter till, after two hours' search, some one suggests: "They may be up at the mine."

"They're not working that now?" says Harry.

"No, but I saw the bishop and his daughter go that way very early this morning."

This information is enough for the impetuous Lawrence, and he again drags Mr. Chauncey up the trail with him, past the office; and one hundred yards beyond they come to the dump of the Zion's Co-operative Mine, but the place seems deserted.

"I expect, with your usual luck," suggests Ferdie, "the bishop and his daughter have gone back to Salt Lake City, and we have missed them on the way. Miss Erma seems a pretty hard butterfly for you to track."

But Lawrence suddenly interrupts him, whispering : "Listen ! There's some one in the mine. Perhaps they're down below."

"What makes you think that ? "

"I hear them."

"I don't."

"But I do ! Right through this air-pipe," cries Harry, and he springs to it, and disconnecting the fan from it, puts his ear to it. A moment afterwards he exclaims : "There's somebody in trouble down there ! " and the next moment, disregarding the danger of foul air, is well on his way down the incline.

Three minutes after, he reappears, and says : "There's been an accident of some kind. Cars have broken loose and are smashed down there at the bottom, and boulders and loose rock are piled up, cutting off somebody. He's alive yet ! I heard him moaning."

Then he suddenly whispers, growing very pale : "My God—if it is she ! " Lovers are always fearful. Next he cries : "Run, Ferdie, up to the Mineral Hill—it's only three hundred feet from here—tell them to send down half a dozen miners like lightning ! "

And Chauncey flying on his errand, a sudden idea coming into Lawrence's mind, he steps to the air-pipe, and using it as a speaking-tube, shouts down : "Halloo there ! Who are you ? Are you too much injured to speak ? "

And listening, there comes up to him from the depths faintly, through the tube : "I'm uninjured, but am bound and helpless."

"Who are you ? "

"R. H. Tranyon."

To this, Harry suddenly screams back : "Your daughter !—for God's sake, tell me where she is ! "

"Why should I tell you that ? "

"Because I'm Harry Lawrence ! "

And through the tube comes faintly up to him :
"Thank God! You are here to save her!"

"From what? My Heaven! From what?" shrieks
Lawrence down the tube.

"From Lot Kruger, bishop in the Mormon Church,
who has buried me here—who is now pursuing her!"

"Good God! For what?"

"To marry her!"

"Don't fear for that!" cries Harry. Then he
grinds out between his clenched teeth : "The accursed
polygamist 'll be dead before that happens!" A second
after he shouts down : "Give me the particulars," and
gets them up the tube. Finally he says : "How long
have you been there?"

"I can't tell. It seems days. I was buried here on
December 1st, early in the morning."

"Why," cries Harry, joyfully : "it's December 1st
now. You haven't been there five hours." Then he
goes on : "Kruger's only four hours ahead of me. You
rest quietly. The miners will have you out in two or
three hours. You make up your mind your daughter's
safe, if it's in human power! She might die, but never
marry Kruger."

Here Ferdie, coming back with some miners, is very
much astonished to hear Lawrence say hurriedly to him :
"Get the men down that incline. Remove the rocks
and get Tranyon out!"

"And you," cries Chauncey, "where are you going?"
for Harry has already turned to leave the dump
pile.

"To save his daughter!" And before the last word
is out of his mouth, Lawrence is speeding down the
trail to Eureka, where in twenty minutes he gets a fresh
team, and driving through the storm, which has now
become blinding, and through the night, which comes
on too soon, and being compelled to go very slowly,

for the snow is drifting heavily, he makes Salt Lake City early in the morning.

Going straight to the Townsend House, Harry says to the clerk: "Don't make any mistake this time, young man, in your information. Miss Travenion is here?"

"No, not here!"

"Good Heavens!"

"She was here last night," says the clerk, with a grin, "but drove away, five minutes ago, to catch the train for Ogden," and is astonished at the hurried "Thank you" he gets, as Lawrence runs out to his wagon again.

Clapping a ten dollar bill into the sleepy driver's hands, Harry cries: "That'll wake you up! Utah Central depot like lightning!"

He gets there just in time to board the train as it runs out of the station, to make connection with the Union Pacific that will leave Ogden this morning.

She is not in his car, but Harry looks into the next one, and seeing the young lady asleep, mutters: "She is tired also. I'll not wake her," then suddenly thinks: "By George! How shall I begin the business? She must despise me now!" and wishes he had brought Ferdie with him; though he laughs to himself: "I suppose it would have killed that future Harvard athlete— two nights' steady driving and no rest between!"

Sitting down to think over this matter, and being overcome with weariness himself, sleep comes upon Harry also, and he doesn't wake even after the train has arrived at Ogden, till he is roused by the brakeman. Looking about him, he gives a start. Miss Travenion has disappeared.

Muttering to himself: "I'm a faithful guardian—I keep my word to her father well! I have a very sharp eye out on my sweetheart!" he runs across to the

15

Union depot, and is relieved to see that the young lady is in the office of Wells, Fargo & Co., expressing a package.

This has come about in this way : Erma Travenion had arrived safely in Salt Lake City at ten o'clock on the night before. Wells, Fargo & Co. being of course closed, she could not deposit the Utah Central stock that night.

Knowing that speed is vital to her, and that she must have money for her trip East, she drives to the house of Mr. Bussey, the banker, and he very kindly rushes about town for her and gleans up from friends of his sufficient for her trip East, charging her for same on her letter of credit.

Asking his advice about an express package that she wishes to send—though Erma doesn't state its contents —he says : " Take it with you, my child, to Ogden. At that time, before the Union Pacific train leaves, Wells, Fargo & Co. will be open. Express it from there. Their receipt will be just as good in Ogden as in Salt Lake City."

This she is doing while Lawrence is looking at her. Her appearance makes him sigh. Not that she isn't as beautiful as when he last saw her, for she is more lovely, only so much more ethereal. Her eyes are too brilliant, and there is a little apprehension in them, and a few lines of pain on her face, some of which, Harry has a wild hope, are perhaps caused by him ; though he grieves over them just the same.

As she comes out of Wells, Fargo's, having finished her business with the express company—which has taken some five minutes, the transaction being a heavy one, and the receipt very formal—Lawrence, with rapture in his heart, and love in his eye, approaches to speak to his divinity, and to his intense chagrin, gets the very neatest kind of a cut. The girl looks him straight in the face—with haughty eyes that never flinch, though there is no recognition in them.

So passing on her way, she buys her tickets, and makes arrangements for her sleeping-car.

This catastrophe has been brought about as follows : While standing waiting for the receipt from Wells, Fargo & Co., Erma has caught the conversation of two men who are standing just outside its door.

One of them says : "Who is she ?" for Miss Travenion's beauty has attracted his attention.

The other, a mining man who has seen her with the bishop in Eureka, answers : "Tranyon the boss Mormon's daughter."

"Impossible !"

"Fact, I assure you," laughs the second man. "From the airs she puts on, you'd think she was a New York or St. Louis belle. But I believe she's booked for the seventh wife of old Kruger. These Mormon girls have no brains ! I guess readin', writin', an' 'rithmetic's about the extent of her education."

This decidedly slurring description of the belle of Newport's last season makes the girl think every one despises her ; and seeing Lawrence, and remembering his desertion, she sighs : "He despises me also—but he shall never show it to me—NEVER !" And so passes him as if she had never seen him.

Striving to eat, but finding she has no appetite, Erma goes almost timidly to the train, where she has engaged a stateroom, for she thinks the whole world is talking about her father and herself, in about the same language she has heard, and shrinks from public gaze and public scoff. She is happy to get to the privacy of her stateroom unnoticed—which is not difficult, every one about the station being excited and busy.

The snow is still falling heavily on the tracks, and the Central Pacific is behind time. Finally, getting a telegram that the train on the more western road has been detained by snow on the Sierra Nevada and Pequop Mountains, and is ten hours late, the Union Pacific pulls out of the station, one hour behind its time.

Just then the privacy of Miss Travenion's stateroom is invaded by Buck Powers, on his business tour through the train.

He says in resonant voice: "How are you off for peanuts? They're the only fruit that's in season now."

"I don't wish any," she replies, quietly.

"Won't you have some candy, or chewing gum? You look as if you needed somethin'."

Seeing this is declined by a shake of the head, he suggests: "That fire must have given you the blues, like it did me."

"What do you mean?" asks Erma, a little startled.

"Why," cries Buck, "don't you know it's been burnt down six weeks? There ain't no Chicago, but it made the highest old fire the world has ever seen."

"Oh, that's what you're referring to!" murmurs the young lady, who in her own troubles has failed to remember the destruction of the great Western city. Then she astounds the news-agent by adding, "I had forgotten that it was burnt."

"You—had—forgotten—the Chicago fire! Great Scott! You'd do for a museum!" he gasps. Then he says interrogatively: "You remember me, Buck Powers, don't you?"

She answers: "Yes, very well,—you're the news-boy who was injured by accident on the train. Captain Lawrence saved you."

"Well, I'm relieved that you ain't forgot everything!" he returns, and a moment after leers at her and says: "The Cap's on the train. I reckoned when I saw you he wouldn't be very far away," and goes off whistling merrily, though he leaves a sad heart behind him.

As for Lawrence, for one moment he has savagely thought, " She is safe on this Union Pacific train. Why should I follow her, to get more cuts ? " But the next second he remembers : " She does not know,—she thinks me worse than Livingston, for he is only a prig to her, while I seem an ingrate. She practically gave me fortune. Shall I desert her for a snub that she thinks I deserve ? Never ! "

After a little, joy comes to him again ; he remembers : " Her father said ' Thank God ! ' when he heard my name. She told him of me six weeks ago. She shall think of me again ! "

So he has bought tickets for the East, and boarded the train, which is now running up Weber Cañon rather slowly, as the grade is quite heavy, and the snow-drifts are multiplying and piling up on the road at a great rate.

An hour afterwards, going into the smoking-car, to kill time by a cigar, Harry looks out of the window, and they are at Echo.

As the train begins to move again he suddenly starts and mutters : " By George ! I did right to come ! He *is* on her track ! "

For just as the train is pulling out of this station, he sees dashing down the old stage road from Park City a sleigh drawn by two horses, in which four men are gesticulating for the conductor to hold up. But that official, who is standing near Lawrence, says grimly : " What ! Pull the check line for Mormon mossbacks who'll get off at the next station, when the train is two hours late and snow-drifts ahead—not much ! " And the train rolls on, followed by some very savage curses from the men in the sleigh.

One of these, Harry notes, is Kruger, and he chuckles

to himself : " Left behind ! He won't overtake us this side of Chicago ! However, it's just as well I'm on board ! "

An hour after they pass the Utah line, and come into Evanston two and a half hours late. Here they take dinner, and meet the train from the East that left Green River in the morning. This reports very heavy snows on Aspen Hill.

Lawrence, however, makes no attempt at further communication with Miss Travenion, reflecting savagely : " Perhaps before this trip is over, Miss Haughty may need my aid, and call on me, and then I'll explain."

So they pass up the valley of the Bear, the storm getting wilder, and the snow deeper, as they pull up the heavy grades, and it is night before they reach Aspen, though they have two strong locomotives dragging them.

Then they come to the Aspen Y, which is the top of the divide, and from which there is a down grade running almost to Green River.

But this part of the road is a difficult one to get over. Two locomotives are not considered too much for its grade when there is no snow on the track ; now they can just handle the train, the track being slippery, and the snow-drifts heavy and increasing.

It is usual to make a flying switch at this point—one engine detaching itself from the train and entering the Y, leaving one locomotive, which is amply sufficient under ordinary circumstances, to take care of a train on the steep down grade, which begins at this place.

To-night the two locomotives should both remain attached to the train, and pull it entirely over the divide together—the helping engine being compelled, of course, to go on as far as the next station, Piedmont.

But the conductor, being a man of routine, does it in his ordinary summer way, by the flying switch, and sends the helping locomotive away. This giving its warning toot, uncouples from the second engine, runs ahead of it, and making a switch into the Y, is ready for its return to Evanston.

But the single locomotive now attached to the train has not steam to carry it over the divide; its wheels gradually revolve more slowly, the efforts of the great iron beast become more and more labored, and finally the train comes to a dead standstill, fifty yards from where the grade commences to descend.

Then, when too late, the other locomotive comes back and goes to its assistance; but the train has stopped— the drifts gradually closing in round the wheels—and now both locomotives cannot move what they could have together carried certainly over the mountain.

Though the attempt is made again and again, the train is stalled, and the snow comes down faster and faster and drifts deeper and deeper. Fortunately, the failure of the Central Pacific to connect, has produced a very light passenger list. Harry notices there are only three in his sleeper—a consumptive, going to Colorado, and a lady tourist and her child, a boy of about ten, who have been seeing Salt Lake City.

On the Pullman occupied by Miss Travenion there is only one other traveller—a young girl who is being forwarded to an Eastern school by Gentile parents connected with the Union Pacific Railway, in Ogden.

These, however, after a little, set up a wail. It is for supper, which the conductor grimly informs them is waiting for them at Green River, ninety miles away.

Then comes the triumph of Chicago business methods, and Buck Powers, issuing from the baggage car, cries dominantly: "PIES!! Beefsteak pies!—Mutton pies'—Dried-apple pies! PIES!!"

Going to him, Lawrence says anxiously: "Have you looked after her?"

"Do you think I'd let Miss Beauty starve?" utters the boy in stern reproach. "I have provisioned her stateroom for two days. She's got three beefsteak pies, two mutton hash pasties, two pork turnovers, and six assorted jam and fruit tarts, as well as a dozen apples. I have done my duty to her, though you haven't. You've left her alone all to-day—you ain't been near to jolly her up. She needs chinning, she does. I have had to step into your shoes and comfort her!"

"Oh, you have, have you?" returns Harry. "Thank you!"

"Well, I'm right glad you're grateful!" remarks Buck. "More so, perhaps, than she is, for when I asked her if she'd seen Brother Brigham at Salt Lake, and how she thought she'd like to be a Mormon—I always ask these questions of tourists coming from Salt Lake—she rose up, a kind of mixture of the Statue of Liberty and my old schoolmarm in Indianie, and said, 'Please continue your business tour at once!' So I got a move on, quick. The next time I passed by, her eyes were red, as if she'd been crying. I don't think you've been doing your duty, Cap!"

With this the boy goes on his way, leaving Lawrence rather elated at his information, for he shrewdly guesses that if Miss Travenion is in any very great trouble, she is more likely to call upon him than any one else to help her out of it. Knowing that she is well provisioned and taken care of, some hour or two after this, he having nothing else to do, goes to bed, something the other passengers have already done.

Next morning, looking out of the car window, Harry finds the snow deeper than ever, and still falling, and the train stalled more hopelessly than ever at the Aspen Y, now known on railroad maps as Tapioca.

CHAPTER XVI.

"TO THE GIRL I LOVE!"

GETTING dressed, Lawrence negotiates with Buck Powers for another pie for breakfast.

That worthy informs him that "provisions has riz" during the night. "There ain't enough for another round," he says. "If you weren't the Cap I should charge you double."

"Then we shall all be hungry soon—unless relief comes?" asks Harry, as he briskly attacks a pork turn-over, for the crisp, snowy air produces a mountain appetite.

"All but her," remarks Buck. "She's fixed as I told you!"

Thinking he will see what chance there is of immediate relief from their present predicament, Lawrence lights a cigar, and steps off the train into a snow-drift. A hasty examination shows there is no chance of the train being moved, until it is shovelled out by hand, though he is pleased to note that the sun has come out, shining brightly, and the snow has ceased falling for the present.

A moment after, he gives an exclamation of delight, for the view is a very beautiful one.

To the south, standing out against the horizon, and looking much nearer than they are, stand the Uintah Mountains, dark blue at their base line with pine forests, and white with eternal snow on their peaks. From them, right to his feet, an unbroken tableland of one solid mass of white. Midway between these mountains and himself, runs the Utah line, and some-how—though the idea hardly forms itself in his mind—he would sooner, on account of the young lady he is protecting, it were further away, especially when he remembers that it is but very little over twenty miles by the railroad over which they have come, from the boundaries of the Mormon Territory. He doesn't think long of this, as he gets interested in watching the movements of the locomotives.

These are now both switched on the Y and are moving about slowly, with a view of keeping themselves what is technically called "alive"—that is, their steam up, sufficient to give them power of motion. Every now and again one is run off the Y and down the main track towards Green River and the east, keeping that portion of the road open, as far as the mouth of a long snow shed, which begins a little way from where Harry stands, and disappears in the distance towards Piedmont.

Towards the east and north he can see a long distance, as the descent is quite rapid to the big plateaus that run to Green River, but there is nothing given to his eye save snow—snow everywhere.

A moment after, the conductor comes tramping through the drifts, and knowing Captain Lawrence by reputation, stops to speak to him.

"I presume," says Harry, "you wired our situation to Evanston last night."

"Of course, and a nice tramp I had of it to the telegraph station. It's over a mile back, and the drifts made it seem five. Every one from here to Ogden, along the track, by this time knows our position."

"I suppose they'll be sending up a relief train soon."

"I hardly think so, before to-morrow," replies the conductor. "They have got all they can take care of, down below at Evanston, just at present. In fact, I imagine we've not seen the worst of it."

And this is a shrewd prediction, because, though he doesn't know it, this is just the beginning of the great snow blockade of '71 and '72, on the Union Pacific

Railway, when some trains were delayed for thirty days between Ogden and Omaha—the usual time being less than three.

"Fortunately, we've not got a heavy train to move," remarks Lawrence, who is anxious to look on the best side of everything.

"And, thank God! no great amount of passengers," replies the conductor. "Otherwise there would have been a howl for grub before now. We've only got two outside those on the sleepers, and one is a woman, and the other a little girl, the daughter of the engineer of the helping locomotive. He's got her in his arms now, as he stands by his engine. Come over and see what he thinks," adds the autocrat of the train, as he trudges off through the snow towards one of the locomotives on the Y.

Harry has taken a step to follow him, when he suddenly pauses.

He is just outside Miss Travenion's Pullman car, and now, through a window that is slightly open, comes the voice of his divinity, who is seated at one of the organs those cars sometimes had in those days.

Curiously enough, the girl whom Buck had reported as having the blues last night, is singing the brightest and merriest of ditties this morning.

"By George! It must be because she has plenty to eat," cogitates Lawrence, lighting another cigar on the question.

But a few minutes after, in his own car, Mr. Powers chancing to come along, he gets some information which he thinks elucidates the matter.

"She's kind o' joyous in there, ain't she, Cap?" says Buck, with a grin. "An' I reckon I did it!"

"How?"

"Well, this morning, even over her breakfast, which was a long way ahead of any one else's on the train, she didn't have no appetite, and seemed in the dumps; whereupon, I suggested that I had hinted to you that she'd kind o' like company probably."

"You infernal—!" cries Lawrence, fire coming into his eye.

"If you take hold o' me, Cap, I won't tell you the rest!" remarks the boy, retreating a little before Harry's anger. Then he goes on: "She took it something like you—she got red in the face and said: 'Please don't mention the matter!' quite haughty. Whereupon I thought I'd guessed the p'int, and suggested: 'You an' the Cap must have been havin' a smash-up in California!' And then she got real anxious and nervous, and cried out at me: 'In California!—what do you mean?' So I told her how I'd seen you at Ogden, four or five days after her party left for California, and that I'd told you she'd gone West, and you took the journey, I reckoned, to catch up to her."

"And she—" says Lawrence, eagerly.

"Oh, she kept on questioning, and the more I told her, the better pleased she looked, and since then she has been quite chirpy, so I reckon I produced her high spirits."

"God bless you, Buck!" cries Harry, slapping the boy on the shoulder, and the astonished Arab of the railway moves off with a five-dollar greenback in his hand, wondering what made the Cap so liberal.

As for Lawrence, it has suddenly occurred to him that Buck Powers has given Miss Travenion the exact information he had taken Ferdie from California to tell her.

A moment's cogitation and he says to himself: "She was wounded because I hadn't come to Tintic after her. I'll chance a walk through the car, and see if the darling 'll cut me again."

Acting on this impulse, he gets off the train, and

walks to the forward end of her car, Miss Travenion's stateroom being at its rear.

"I'll give her the length of the car to meditate upon me," he thinks.

As he enters the main portion of the Pullman, her stateroom door is open, and as he comes down the aisle, Erma rises. He knows she has seen him—something in her face tells him that.

Then intense surprise falls upon him :—the young lady steps out with extended hand, and says brightly : "So you have discovered I was on the train *at last?* I had been expecting a visit from you all yesterday."

At this tremendous but most feminine prevarication, Lawrence fairly gasps. A second after, he discovers the wonderful tact displayed in it, which calls for an explanation from him, and does not require one from her.

However, he is too awfully happy to stand on little points, and seizing the taper fingers of the young lady, and giving her tact for tact, and prevarication for prevarication, remarks : "You most certainly would have, Miss Travenion, but I only discovered that you were on board this morning, from Buck Powers."

"Why," cries Erma, "I saw you at—" She checks herself suddenly, biting her lips a little, and then goes on : "We've been near each other a whole day, and have not spoken."

"That's a great pity ! But we'll make up for lost time, now !" answers Lawrence, gallantly. Then he suggests : "What did you breakfast on ?"

"Pies !"

"So did I—our tastes are similar," he laughs, for there is something in the radiant face looking into his that makes him think this snow blockade, privations and all, is the very nicest thing that has come into his life.

A moment after, for he is too earnest for any more

light comedy fencing, he comes to the point with masculine abruptness, remarking : " Mr. Powers told you
—God bless him !—that I have been in California ? "

" Yes."

" I got this little note "—he produces her card with
the " I have seen my father. Good-bye " sentence on
it—" in Salt Lake City, and presumed you had gone
to California with the Livingstons. I was then poor.
Four days afterwards, I suddenly found myself astounded and rich. I did not ask how it came—I was
too anxious to make use of my money. I thought a
tour of ' the Golden State ' would please me."

Then he goes on hurriedly and tells her of his wan-
derings in pursuit of the Livingston party, and his un-
expected interview with Ferdie at the Grand Hotel,
omitting, however, his journey to Tintic and his rescue
of her father, as he doesn't wish to alarm or make Erma
think she is under obligation to him.

" Ah ! " falters the girl, very pale, and turning her face
away from him. " Then you know—I'm the daughter
of Tranyon—the Mormon bishop ? "

" Yes," he cries ; " that is what brought me from
California in such a hurry ; I wanted to thank you for
giving me what I would probably have never got without you—a fortune."

" Oh ! it was gratitude," murmurs the young lady,
" that brought you from California ? " A moment after
she coldly says : " That sentiment need not actuate
you. I simply induced my father to do you justice,"
and from now on is very icy ; for Erma Travenion demands the love, not the gratitude, of this young gentleman beside her.

This sudden change in his divinity astounds Lawrence, who has not been a student of woman's ways.
Inadvertently he puts himself right again, for he suddenly says : " Did I know that I had anything to be

grateful to you for, when I wandered about California seeking you—six weeks?"

"Oh!" cries the young lady, "that was *before* you knew my father was R. H. Tranyon, the Mormon bishop?" This last quite haughtily, for she has grown fearfully sensitive on this point since the conversation of the two mining gentlemen in Ogden.

"But," remarks Lawrence, "I know that *now*." Then, growing desperate, he blurts out : "Shall I tell you why I went to California?" and his voice grows very tender.

But the girl, suddenly rising, says with a curious mixture of haughtiness and humility, perhaps shame : "To whom do you wish to tell your tale?—Erma Travenion, of New York, or to Miss Tranyon, who has been called a Mormon 'gal,' and who is reported to be booked as the seventh wife of Bishop Kruger of Kammas Prairie?" Then she cries mockingly, almost savagely, "Which are you talking to?"

"To the girl I love!" cries Lawrence.

"O-oh!"

"To the girl I'd make my wife if she were the daughter of Beelzebub, and booked for the seventh consort of Satan!"

"O-o-o-oh!" With this sigh Erma sinks on the seat again ; a moment after she suddenly smiles and murmurs : "Don't make my pedigree worse than it is!"

"Would you like to hear the tale I took with me to California, and have carried ever since in my heart?" says Harry, bending over this young lady, whose face is hiding its blushes, turned towards the car window, upon whose frosted panes her white finger is making figures.

"Y-e-s!"

Then he tells her how he has loved her since the night he first saw her at Delmonico's, and mutters : "Give me your answer!"

"My answer;" murmurs Erma, turning a face to him that is half hope, half uncertainty, all love, "if I were what I was that evening in New York, would be——"

"Yes!" he cries, and has his hasty frontier arm half round the fairy waist of last summer's Newport belle; for there is something in her lovely eyes that many men have looked for, but no one has ever seen till now.

But she rises and falters, "Wait!"

"How long?"

"Wait till I know you're sure you will never feel ashamed of the Mormon's daughter! Oh!—oh! can't you wait one min—!" For Harry has not waited, and the girl's last word as it issues from her rosy mouth is smothered by an audacious black moustache that she can parry no longer. And perchance those lovely coral lips return his betrothal kiss—a very little:—at least Harry thinks so. A moment after he knows it; for Erma Travenion, though very hard to win, having given her hand does not hesitate to make her sweetheart very sure he has also her heart.

CHAPTER XVII.

A VOICE IN THE NIGHT.

INTO this Elysium, Buck Powers, who has been one of its architects, breaks with news-boy rapidity. The girl passenger is in the other car gossiping with the lady tourist, and Harry and Erma have forgotten there are other people in this world. Entering rapidly, the banging car door, and an excited and astounded "Gee whiz!" calls the lady and gentleman from heaven to earth.

"What do you want here?" cries Lawrence, and he pounces upon the flying Buck and leads him to the forward compartment, while Erma suddenly discovers that the outside landscape is a thing of most immediate interest.

"I—I didn't mean to run in on you, Cap," gasps the fleeing Buck. Then he smiles on Harry suddenly and grins : "Have you made a through connection at last? Are you switched on the main track now?"

"Stop your infernal conundrums!" laughs Harry. "Take a five-dollar greenback and go away, and don't you tell a living soul that Miss Travenion is going to be Mrs. Lawrence!"

"I'll take a five-dollar greenback," answers the boy, "because you're the luckiest man I ever seed, and it's business. But I've got somethin' to tell your young lady!"

"Very well," answers Harry, and leads Buck back to Erma's side. Here the youth remarks with a snicker that brings blushes upon Miss Travenion, "I hear as how the Cap has just been elected president of the road!" A moment after he continues : "I come to tell you the grub's all out. Somehow, since they got an idea that they might run short, our passengers has eaten so as to make 'em run short. I haven't had a pie to sell for four hours, and there's a little gal, the daughter of the engineer of the helper, has got hungry and is screaming for food——"

"Screaming for food?" cries Erma. "Thank you, Buck, for telling me," and the next minute she is in her stateroom.

"Gracious! you'll be short yourself," expostulates Buck as she returns. "You ain't carrying grub to a giantess!" for she has a beef pie, three fruit tarts, and a couple of apples.

"Perhaps the child's father is hungry also," replies Miss Travenion, who seems very benevolent this after-noon.

16

"Very well!" says Mr. Powers, "I'll bring the engineer, only don't stint yourself!" and goes on his errand.

A minute after, Erma and Harry are on the platform and the man of the throttle-valve comes to them, carrying his little daughter, who looks pale, and has hungry eyes. Seeing her bounty, the engineer cries, "God bless you, miss." Then he mutters, "You'll rob yourself."

"Oh, I've more left," answers Miss Travenion; "besides, she needs it," for the child has already gone to work ravenously on the fruit tarts.

"God bless you, just the same," cries the engineer. "Thank the lady, Susie."

But Susie, looking at her benefactress, forgets gratitude in admiration, and babbles, "Beau'ful, beau'ful," extending a fruity hand and putting up two lips embellished with jam.

"Don't, she'll spoil your dress," says the father. But Erma has her already in her arms, giving the little one a kiss, and playing with her and doing some small things to make her happy.

And doing small things for the baby does great things for herself, though she does not know it, for it gains the engineer's heart.

The man wipes a grimy eye with a more grimy sleeve, and mutters, "I was afraid my little one would get sick from starving, and she's all that's left me of her mother, who's buried in Green River—God bless your kind heart and beautiful face, miss!" and so going away, spreads the news of the beautiful girl's bounty through the train.

But this brings requests from other hungry ones to Miss Travenion, who has a little that they will eat—if she will give it them.

Consequently, about five in the afternoon Lawrence,

who does not know of this raid on his beloved's commissariat, and is in the smoking-car pondering over the problem whether the knowledge of the awful death to which Kruger had doomed and from which he had rescued her father, will not make Erma too anxious and too nervous about Ralph Travenion's further fate, finds himself disturbed by Mr. Powers.

The boy comes hurriedly to him and says : "She ain't got nothin' to eat, and she's hungry."

"What do you mean ?" cries Harry. "Didn't you say that you had provisioned her for two days ?"

"Yes ! but she's given it all away to the women in the way-cars."

"No relief train yet ?"

"No, an' I don't see any chance of one."

"Very well," remarks Lawrence, putting on his overcoat, "I'll see what I can do."

He steps out of the car, and the best he can think of is to tramp to the telegraph station, and see if there is anything left there. It is over a mile and a half, but a beaten track has been pretty well made in the snow by the brakemen and conductor on some of their visits to that point, so he gets there in a little over half an hour.

Here, the conductor is talking to the telegraph operator, and they seem to be excited over something.

"What's the matter ?" asks Harry.

"Nothing, only the line's down between here and Evanston !" says the operator. "It was working twenty minutes ago, but I can't get the Evanston or any other Western office now."

"What was the last news from there ?"

"Bad !" replies the man. "They can't get a locomotive or relief train to us till to-morrow. They'll have to pick and shovel their way through a lot of drifts."

"Meantime we have nothing to eat !" grumbles the captain.

"Oh," remarks the conductor, "they telegraphed me this morning that they would send up provisions in sleighs. Some teamsters will bring them up. They ought to be due here to-night. They can make the eighteen miles, I reckon, in nine hours."

"There is no danger of a train coming from the other way to bring more hungry people?" asks Lawrence earnestly.

"Oh, no!" answers the operator. "That's all fixed. I heard Evanston telegraph Green River this morning, for all passenger trains bound west to be held at that point—they can feed them there—and all freight to be stopped at Bridger."

"You are sure?"

"Certain!—the order was from Hilliard, the train dispatcher of this division. There's only one passenger train side-tracked at Granger, and a freight switched off at Carter and another at Bridger, between us and Green River."

"Very well!" says Lawrence. "Have you got anything to eat?"

"You're welcome to the best I can do, Cap," replies the man of the wire, who knows Harry by sight, as most of the employees of the road do. But the best that Lawrence can obtain for his sweetheart is some pork and beans, and some bread made of middlings. These he wraps up in an old newspaper—nothing else being handy—and turns to go, but pauses a moment, and says : "Haven't you got any tea, or coffee, or something of that kind?"

"Tea," cries the operator. "I can accommodate you!"

So, laden with a small package of this ladies' delight, the Captain leaves the log cabin, which is the only house at Aspen, and does duty as a telegraph office, and trudging back through the snow, brings comfort and happiness to Erma, who has grown so hungry in the chill night air that she has almost repented of her generosity.

Buck Powers accommodates her with boiling water, and the Captain would leave her to her meal, but she suddenly stops him and cries : " What have you had to eat ? "

" Oh, don't mind me," says Harry.

" But I do—you have tramped through the snow for my comfort. Besides, I must take care of you—be-cause——"

" Why ? "

" Oh, well, you know "—a big blush—" what I told you to-day ! If you remember—take tea with me ! "

" With pleasure, if you put it on that ground ! " laughs Harry, who is desperately hungry, and when he has fallen to, forgets himself, and eats a good deal more than his share, though they both enjoy the meal.

But just at this moment there is a cry outside, and a faint hurrah from the negro porter inside.

It is the arrival of the teamsters, who have come, bringing with them comfort and provisions, and every-body is now in the land of plenty, though it is a very rough plenty.

Looking at them, Lawrence wonders why so many men have come with the relief sleighs ; but is told they brought them along to help the teams through the drifts.

So they pass a very happy evening—the young lady singing a song or two for her swain, more beautifully, he thinks, than any prima donna, and saying good-night to him afterwards so tenderly that Lawrence, coming to his own car, astonishes the negro porter by giving him five dollars for making up his bed in the state-room which is unoccupied, and more roomy than a section.

A moment after he murmurs to himself: "Can it be? Is it possible?"—and then cries, "Good gracious! the engagement ring—and no jeweller in sight!"

And so he goes to bed, to be awakened by a voice in the night that changes confidence into doubt, and makes joy into sorrow.

Harry has hardly been in bed an hour when there is a rap on the door of his stateroom.

"Hang you!" he cries, thinking it is the negro porter. "I've left my boots outside. What are you waking me up for at this time of night?"

"'Ssh! don't talk so loud, Cap! Let me in!"

And opening the door, Mr. Powers makes his appearance, his eyes, in the moonlight that is streaming in, large, luminous, and excited.

He gasps: "Cap—come—an' save your girl!"

As Buck speaks, Lawrence is out of bed. "Quick!" he says.

"You know in my baggage car I hear most of what's goin' on. Them teamsters that came here with the grub are camping in there to-night. I heard them talking. They're Mormons!"

"Ah!"

"Buck Mormons from Echo and Heber, and that way. One of them said to the other, 'The bishop will be along soon. The orders is, we're none of us to make a move, but to have the sleighs ready to start out quick, and one fixed with furs in it and blankets, to keep the girl warm.'"

"What makes you think they meant Miss Travenion?"

"They described her."

"Did you hear the name of the bishop?"

"Yes," answers Buck. "It was the cuss who came West with you and her!"

"Kruger!—Hush! Speak lower! Whisper to me!"

"I am a-whisperin'!" says the boy. "It's the lowest

I've got. I've spoilt my voice hollerin' as news-agent, an' I can't bring it down !"

" Are the Mormon teamsters armed ? "

" They ain't Mormon teamers. Some of them is disguised. I heard one of them call another ' Constable,' and the other chinned him as ' Sheriff.' Hadn't we better tell the conductor ? "

" No," says Lawrence, shortly, for he remembers the conductor is a routine man—and, of course, of no use in such an emergency.

A moment after, he says quietly to the boy : " Miss Travenion was very good to you, Buck. Will you help me save her ? "

" That's what I come for.".

" It may be a life and death matter."

" That's what I come for."

" Very well," replies Harry. " You go quietly about the train—they won't notice you—and find out what you can, and come and report to me, in Miss Travenion's car. I am going there."

" All right."

As Buck turns to obey his orders, Lawrence suddenly whispers : " No matter what happens, don't let any one of that gang learn I am on the train."

" I understand ! "

Then the captain asks suddenly, " How many of them ? "

" Twelve ! "

" Good God ! "

As Buck goes on his errand, Lawrence, looking carefully about to see he is not observed, slips from his car into that of Miss Travenion, which is quiet, save for a loud snoring from the gentlemen's smoking compartment, which indicates that the Ethiopian porter is making a very comfortable night of it.

A lamp, partially turned up, illuminates faintly the

rear of the car. He taps lightly on Miss Travenion's door. No answer! His heart sinks; she may be already carried away from him.

Then he raps more loudly, and her voice tells him she is as yet safe.

"Who is it?" asks the girl.

"I—Harry Lawrence!"

"Is anything the matter?"

"Yes! I must see you in two minutes!"

"Impossible—I am not dressed."

"You must dress in two minutes. Throw on a wrapper or shawl."

"Oh, mercy! What is it?"

"Dress!"

"Very well!—Good gracious! where's my slippers?" This last a nervous aside.

Then the noise from inside Miss Travenion's state-room indicates she is obeying him with a vigor that shows he has impressed her.

Within the time specified she has opened her door, and stepped out to him, draped in some warm woollen wrapper, which clings about her lithe, graceful figure; and the moonlight shining through the car window gets into her unbound hair, and makes it very soft and golden.

She says hastily, but pathetically, "Now, tell me!"

"Can you be very brave?"

"Yes! Try me!"

Looking in her eyes, he knows she can be.

"Very well," he whispers, "sit down. To-day, fearing to alarm you, I did not tell you all I knew in regard to your father; but it is necessary now that you understand everything about Kruger, the Mormon bishop."

"Why, he's two hundred miles away."

"In a few minutes he will be here."

"Oh, mercy!" The girl leans against her lover, and he can feel her heart throb and pulse with apprehension. His arm goes round her waist, and seems to give her confidence, as he tells her the whole story of her father's blood atonement, from which he saved him. And she gasps: "You are not deceiving me—my father is not dead?"

"He's as safe as you are!"

"Thank God!"

"Perhaps safer!" Then he tells her of the revelation Buck Powers has made him this night.

"Ah!" Erma cries; "Kruger is coming to force me to give up that Utah Central stock."

"For more!"

"What more?"

"To force you to be his seventh wife."

But she says very quietly: "There is no fear of that. I can always die at the last."

"I know you can *die;* but for my sake you must *live!*" cries Lawrence. Then he says grimly: "If there's any dying to-night, Kruger does it!"

"Ah! that may mean your life. For my sake you must live! I've—I've only been happy for a day." And her tender arms go around him, as she sobs over him, calling him her darling, her betrothed, her future husband, and many other wild terms of endearment she might not use, did she not feel this night might take him from her.

A moment after she cries: "He is not here yet—let us fly!"

"Fly, where?" asks Lawrence. "Through those snow-drifts, over those uninhabited plains? In half an hour we should be overtaken. If not, by morning we should be dead."

"Then, how will you save me?"

"All I know is that I will save you! But to do it,

you must follow my instructions. Twelve men I shall not resist openly—except at the last. Give me your receipt from Wells, Fargo, for that stock."

She steps into the stateroom, and a moment after hands it to him.

"Now," he says, "listen to me! Each word I utter is important. When Kruger comes, you must be in your stateroom, asleep. Nothing must betray to him that you expect or fear his coming! Nothing must inform him that you know of his crime against your father ; and, above all, nothing must suggest to him that I am on your train. Our one great hope is, that he does not know I'm here, and may be—just a little careless ! Remember, you have nothing to fear as long as I live ! "

But Buck Powers breaks in on them at this moment, and mutters : "Cap, Kruger's here ! He's talkin' with the men over there ! "

" On which side of the cars ? Can he see me if I leave them this way ? "

" No ! "

" You're going ? " says the girl. And putting her arms round his neck, nestles to him, and murmurs : " Remember, your life is my life ! "

And so he leaves her, and steps cautiously out, and crouching in shadow of the cars, and looking over the white plateaus of drifted snow, he thinks :

"Fly, where ? Fight—how ? Impossible ! " Then of a sudden the snow disappears, and he remembers a hot spring day in '64, in Arkansas, when he and his Iowa boys did what was deemed impossible in war—artillery holding woodland and brush copse against infantry. He sees his cannoneers—boys with fresh young faces and fair hair, just from Western prairies and green fields—fall and die, as the musketry flashes all about them, and singing bullets bring death to them, but still stand and scourge that undergrowth and timber shelter with grape and case shot, till the gray infantry slowly draws back ; until the Yankee lumberman has built up a dam like those that float timber down Maine rivers, and so saved the Federal fleet, and thus saved the Federal army.

He mutters : " I did the impossible then for my country ; I can do the impossible now FOR MY LOVE."

And from that moment Harry Lawrence has the one great quality that makes success possible in all desperate undertakings—confidence !

CHAPTER XVIII.

THE LAST OF THE DANITES.

EVEN as he looks, hope comes, for he sees the glow of one of the locomotives on the Y, and knows that its fires are still banked—it has a little steam ; and he remembers, the line is clear of trains to Green River.

Then he whispers suddenly to Buck, who says : " I understand ! " and goes cautiously away, while Lawrence struggles through the snow-drifts to the helping locomotive, the one nearest the switch that leads to the main track running to the East.

The engineer, who is a careful man, and has a pride in his machine, is still with his engine, and Harry is delighted to see he is the one whose heart Erma has won by kindness to his child.

" I was rubbing her up a little, Cap," he says. " I want to be sure she's all ready for to-morrow's work."

" Is she ready for *to-night's* work ? "

" What do you mean ? "

" I mean," answers Lawrence, who has looked the man over, and concludes it is better to lie to him than to argue with him, "that there are road agents on the train."

For a moment the man looks at him in unbelief, then there is a little noise and commotion about the sleepers, and he cries : " My God ! my child ! "

" Your child is safe. Buck is bringing her over ! " says Harry, pointing at the figure of the boy, half leading, half carrying the little girl through the snow. " Any way," he goes on, " they would have done nothing to her ; it's the other one they want, the heiress ! "

" What ! that beautiful girl that kept my little one from starving ? We must save her ! " cries the engineer, getting hold of his own darling from Buck, who has come up.

" We will ! " whispers Lawrence. " Those road agents will only trouble her and Wells, Fargo & Co.'s express. The express must take care of itself —we'll take care of the girl ! "

" But how ? "

" By running her down to safety on your locomotive ! "

" Great goodness ! I never thought of that ! " replies the man of the throttle-valve.

A moment after, he says : " I haven't got coal to reach further than Granger."

" That'll do ! Get up steam as fast as you can, but don't let anybody see you're at work on your locomotive ! "

With these words, Lawrence goes into consultation with the engineer and Mr. Powers as to the details of the transaction.

It is arranged that Harry is to do the work of the fireman, who is on the train, and whom they dare not take the risk of arousing ; Buck is to turn the switch to put the locomotive on the main track, and to board them as they pass him, which they will do very quietly.

Leaving the engineer quietly making his preparations, Lawrence walks cautiously across, not towards Miss Travenion's car, but towards the sleeper behind it—the one he occupies.

From that he cautiously approaches the other, looks in, and finds it empty of all save Miss Travenion, who has apparently hurriedly dressed, and is seated, confronted by two men, who evidently have her in their keeping, as one says : " Don't be scared ; we'll take good care of you, even if you have been tryin' to rob the Mormon Church ! "

Catching these words in the outer darkness of the rear compartment, Lawrence knows that Kruger has already had his say, and for some reason left the girl. Harry is glad of this, for feeling the revolver in his belt, he fears he might have killed the Mormon, which would probably not have saved either himself or his sweetheart.

In this he is doubtless right. For while he has been holding conference with the engineer, Kruger, followed by four or five of his satellites, and accompanied by the conductor, who is expostulating with him, has entered the car.

" Now, ye keep quiet ! " he says to that official. " We've got a warrant for this young lady, for assistin' her daddy to run away with half a million dollars' worth of Utah Central stock. There's the documents, sworn to by the sheriff of Heber City, Utah, before a Probate Judge."

" A Utah judge has got no jurisdiction in Wyoming," answers the conductor.

" No ! But this is made returnable," says Lot, " before the United States District Judge, and Wyoming's part of his district, and that gives us authority. Don't step in the way of the law, young man. Besides "—here he looks round at his following, and remarks : " We're goin' to execute this warrant any way, an' ye ain't got the power to stop us ! I've sized ye up, an' ye've got two nigger porters, two brakesmen, an' yerself. We've twelve men armed with Winchesters, an' we've got the drop on yer train-hands, mail agent, an' Wells, Fargo's messenger, for they're surrounded and cut off from ye. Now the sheriff's goin' to serve his papers."

At this moment, the negro porter, who has just awakened, flies out of the car shrieking : "For de Lord! Road agents ! "

"Ye see how much good he'd do ye !" guffaws Kruger to the conductor. "Now," he continues, "ye step back an' let me do my business polite ! "

"Not unless you agree to report with the young lady at Evanston, before you take her into Utah," says the dethroned autocrat of the train.

"That we will do, certain ! " replies Lot, with a wink to the sheriff. "Now ye wake her up."

Thus commanded, the conductor raps upon Miss Travenion's stateroom door, and to her inquiries, asks her to dress herself, stating there are some gentlemen on business, who must see her at once.

"Very well ! Let them wait ! " answers the young lady quietly, though there is a tremor in her voice.

She keeps them waiting so long that one of the men mutters : "The gal must be rigging herself out for a dance," and Lot himself knocks on her stateroom door, saying, "Miss Ermie, come out quick ! It's Kruger, yer daddy's friend, who's talkin' to ye."

"You here?" she cries through the door. "What has happened to my father, that you come to me ? "

And he says : "The sheriff here has got a little business with ye. Yer daddy has disappeared."

"A—ah ! " And it's all she can do to keep from bursting out and upbraiding him, telling him what she knows, and so ruining the chance Lawrence is preparing for her.

"Yes, yer daddy has gone, and the Utah Central

stock that belonged to the Mormon Church has gone
with him, an' the sheriff here thinks it's in yer possession, and has sworn out a warrant agin ye, an' is here
to execute it. An' I come along with him to make it as
light for ye, as possible. He thought ye'd got clean
away from him, but heerd the train was stopped here
by snow, an' so he come on to get ye. But before he
takes ye, I want to tell ye a few little things. Come
out !"

Then hearing the noise of the moving bolt in Erma's
door, Kruger says to the men with him : " Just step
back a leetle into the smoking-room, while I talk to
the girl."

" All right, bishop !" answers the sheriff, who seems
entirely under Lot's domination.

The men withdraw as Erma comes out and stands
before Bishop Kruger, her beauty perhaps at this
moment appealing to him more than it ever did—for
excitement has added a lustre to her eye, and she seems
so helpless, and so much in his power.

He mutters, his eyes blinking a little at the radiance
that is before him : " Now, Ermie, ye can make everything quite easy for yerself !"

" Indeed—how ?" She tries very hard to conceal it,
but some scorn will get into her voice.

" By givin' up the stock quiet !"

" Ah ! then you will let me go ?"

" Oh, no ! The sheriff wouldn't do that ; but when
he takes ye back to Utah, I'll go bail for ye, an' I'll
take ye down to my home in Kammas Prairie, where
ye'll be nice an' comfortable, an' I'll look after ye."

" You are always very good to me," says the girl
with a sneer, though he doesn't detect it, and replies :
" Yes, I'll be better to ye than ye know !"

And she, trying to act her part, to prevent any suspicion in his mind, thanks him with so much appar-

ent heartiness that the old satyr loses his head, and chuckles : " Now, that's the right kind o' talk. Now yer lookin' beautiful as one o' the angels of Zion. I've been havin' my eye on ye, an' I'm goin' to exalt ye, an' take ye into my family."

" Take me into your family—as a *daughter ?* "

" No, as a *wife*, for I love ye ! "

And looking to her like an ogre, he would advance to her, whispering : " By this kiss of peace, I take ye into my family ! "

But she has forgotten to act now, and scorn is in her eye, hatred in her voice, and loathing in her shudder. She says hoarsely : " BACK ! don't dare to sully me by the touch of your finger ! I loathe you as I do your iniquitous church ! "

" Ye blasphemer ! " he cries. " This is the second time. I'll be hard on ye now, an' bring ye down from yer high horse. Where's that stock of the Utah Central ? "

" Find it ! " jeers Erma.

" I will ! " he answers, " and then I'll make ye sorry ye turned yer nose up at Lot Kruger ! "

Raising his voice, he shouts : " Sheriff, come in an' take yer prisoner, an' make a search of her baggage ! She's got the stolen goods with her, I reckon ! "

A second later the girl is placed under arrest.

But a quick though thorough search of the baggage she has with her, shows that the Utah Central stock, that Kruger knows the Mormon Church must have, is not in her possession.

He says : " Sheriff, step off a leetle ; I'll reason with this child, to see if I can't get from her the locality of the stolen goods."

So, coming to her again, he mutters : " Ye'd better take things reasonable, an' tell me where that ar' stock is ! I WILL KNOW ! "

But she laughs in his face, and cries : " Find it ! "

" Now," he says, " I ain't 'customed to bein' sassed by women. I'll have it out o' ye ! Tell me, or I'll treat ye as I do my own darters, when they disobey me ! "

His brutal hand is upraised, and in another second this exotic from far-away Murray Hill will receive what she had never felt before—a box on her dainty ear. But she, forgetting prudence, forgetting Harry's counsel, pants, " I dare you ! Do you think I have no one here to avenge me ? "

" Who ? " asks Kruger, suspiciously, his hand still lifted.

" Who ? " echoes Erma—" who ? " Then, remembering in time, she turns her speech and laughs. " That stock is safe in the hands of Wells, Fargo & Co., where you dare not touch it ! " and unwittingly paves the way for her own escape.

" Oh ho ! " guffaws Lot. " It's on the train. We'll see if we dare not touch it ! "

He calls to his men, who are in the smoking-room : " Two of ye look after her here, though there ain't any great danger of Miss Dainty's running very far in this snow. That stock is in Wells, Fargo & Co.'s safe, an' we'll have it now. It's right here on the train, boys. We've got a warrant that will hold us up in this business ! "

For some of the men have turned pale at the thought of making a raid on Wells, Fargo & Co., an institution that has gained a reputation for being implacable in its pursuit of train robbers, highwaymen, and others that raid the precious things the business community intrust to it.

Then whispering to her : " I'll come back for ye ! We'll take ye an' the stock together, back to Utah ! " he leaves the girl, followed by all but the two men, whom Lawrence sees watching her, as he peers into the gloom.

Harry is thinking of how to get these two guardians of Miss Travenion away, and has half made up his mind to kill them, when Buck Powers comes sneaking to him, and whispers : " Cap, the engine's ready ! "

" Where are Kruger and the rest of his gang ? "

" They're making a raid cn Wells, Fargo. They're demandin' some stock, or somethin' or other, an' the agent is standin' them off. He thinks they're road agents."

With these words comes an idea to Harry Lawrence.

He whispers quickly to Buck, then says : " You understand ? "

" All right, Cap, I'm on to you ! " and Mr. Powers disappears.

Thirty seconds after Buck bangs at the door of the sleeper with great noise, though he is careful not to enter, and from its end nearest to the express car, yells : "Come on ! you're needed. Wells, Fargo's agent is standin' the bishop off. The bishop says the gal's safe and he wants you ! "

" All right ! " answers one of the men, and handling their guns, the two disappear to take part in the trouble with the express agent, which is now creating a great commotion on the train, the passengers in Lawrence's Pullman crying out : " Road agents ! " and the young lady in Miss Travenion's car, who has been awakened by the noise, screaming for help.

This excitement aids Lawrence. He steps into the car, and touching his sweetheart on the shoulder, whispers : " Come ! "

And she following him to the platform, he springs into the snow-drift, and says : " I must carry you ! "

" Certainly ! " Her arms clasp themselves trustingly round his neck, as he trudges through the snow, bearing his happiness with him.

The locomotive on the Y is just moving as he

reaches it, for he crosses directly to it, not daring to carry her past Kruger and his men, who are still about Wells, Fargo & Co.'s car.

"Ah, you're going to carry me away on the locomotive!" whispers Erma, as Lawrence puts her on board.

"Yes, we'll take care of you!" mutters the engineer, giving Harry a helping hand.

In another moment they are in the cab of the locomotive, which is slowly running over the Y towards the main track, which leads to the East, and safety.

This has been kept open as far as the snow-shed, and they will probably not meet a great deal of drift until they get beyond it, but the steam is light in the engine, and it cannot move very fast.

The other locomotive stands behind them, on the Y. Lawrence notices, as they leave it, that its fires are banked, and some one is on board it, though apparently asleep.

A second after, they pass Mr. Buck Powers, who switches them to the main track, they running so slowly that he easily follows them, and jumps on board.

All this time Harry has both ears and eyes fixed on the forward end of the train, to see if their absence is discovered.

But the Wells, Fargo & Co.'s man is still standing the Mormons and their bishop off, and threatening to shoot ; and his movements interest them so much they do not notice the great mass of iron that has come on to the main track, and is now plunging away from them down the incline towards the long snow-shed.

"Now," Harry says to the engineer, giving a sigh of relief, "you can light your headlight."

Just then a cry comes out from behind them. It is that of the conductor of the train, who is screaming : "Great Scott ! who's run away with the locomotive ?"

and some of Kruger's men run shouting through the snow.

Then Lawrence cries, " Give her steam ! "

The locomotive dashes through little drifts, and drowns sound, but he knows that in a very few moments Lot Kruger will have discovered that what he values more than the stock of the Utah Central Railway is passing away from him.

The engine is already flying through the snow-shed —one of the two long ones that line the steep decline leading towards Piedmont and the East.

In it they find little snow to impede them, but at the end of the shed their trouble begins, for on this track, which has not been passed by trains for twenty-four hours, they encounter deep drifts, and once or twice the locomotive nearly stops, and the engineer tells Lawrence that if it were not for the steep down grade, they would never be able to make it.

Several times they have to back, and push on again, though the sheet-iron covered cow-catcher, which acts as a snow-plow, helps them tremendously. Still it is a long time before they reach the second big snow-shed, and looking at his watch, Lawrence finds that they have been half an hour doing what ought only to have taken them ten minutes.

But just as they are entering the second snow-shed, where the track makes an enormous bend, almost running back upon itself, in the form of a U, something comes out of the snow-shed—not much over a mile away —that they have left behind them. Something that makes Lawrence's heart jump, and then grow cold, as with hoarse voice he cries, pointing back : " My God ! what is that ? "

And the engineer sets his teeth, and says : " They're after us ! It's the headlight of the other locomotive ! They have got up steam, and they have the advantage of us, because we have to bore the way through drifts and clear the track for them. They're bound to catch us!"

"Not if steam'll beat them," mutters Harry, and assisted by Buck, he piles the engine fire with coal, and helped by the rapid descent, they forge through drift after drift, none of these being very deep in the second long snow-shed.

Then they come out of it, into the open country once more, and meet deeper drifts, into which the engine plunges with a slow thud, throwing the snow higher than its smoke-stack, as it struggles through. Here the other engine must have the best of it, for they clear its track for it, and they haven't left the second snow-shed half a mile behind when, like the eye of a demon, the glow of the yellow headlight of their pursuer comes gliding after them.

The engineer mutters : "They're goin' to catch us!"

"Never!" cries Lawrence, and piles on more coal—though his heart is cold as the snow-drifts through which the engine plunges.

"We'll be up to the Piedmont switch in a minute. I might as well stop there!" mutters the engineer. "We can't clear the track for 'em and beat 'em too!"

"Put your hand on the reversing lever and you're dead!" cries Lawrence, his pistol at the man's ear.

"Not for my sake!" screams Erma, for she has the man's child in her arms.

"For all our sakes!" answers Harry. "Keep her going—till we can move no more! Then——"

"What?" asks his sweetheart.

"Then Kruger'll trouble you no more; of that be certain!"

"But you?"

"Oh, that doesn't matter."

They are moving quite slowly now, and the girl sud-

denly cries, "Buck, where are you going?" for the
boy has just said, "Good-bye! God bless you, Miss
Beauty!"

"What are you going to do?"

"*Show you how a Chicago railroad man treats chumps!*"

And though Erma cries: "Don't! You risk your life!"
and Lawrence puts out a detaining hand, even as they
come to the Piedmont side-track, the boy jumps from
the cab, unlocks the switch, and hides himself in the
snow-drift.

"My God! He's going to run 'em off the track!
My pard's the boss of that locomotive!" screams the
engineer. "He'll be smashed to pieces!"

"Go on!" answers Lawrence, and his pistol again
threatens.

The locomotive dashes forward, for there is a roar
two hundred yards behind them, and over the noise they
hear Kruger's yell of triumph, which, even as he utters
it, is turned into a howl of rage.

There is a shriek of terror from the engineer of the
pursuing locomotive, for Buck Powers, in the moonlight, has risen up beside the switch, and turned it,
just as the engine dashes to it, not so as to side-track
it, but only half way, to dash it over ties and snow-
drifts to destruction.

As the locomotive passes, Kruger, who has his pistol
in his hand, turns it from the direction of Lawrence and
the flying locomotive straight at the breast of the boy
at the switch, and fires upon him! And Buck Powers,
giving a shriek, staggers and falls into a snow-bank,
reddening it with his blood.

But even as Buck does so, he is avenged. The locomotive, plunging forward off the track into the drifting
snow, topples over, and though the engineer and fireman jump free, Kruger, with his eye in grim triumph
on the dying boy, is thrown beneath the ponderous

mass of iron, that topples over him, crushing his body, and sending his soul to where the souls of the Danites go.

The engineer and fireman clamber out of the snow-drift unharmed, though shaken up. Three of the Mormon *posse* who have been with Kruger come out of the snow unarmed, for their Winchesters are buried deep in a white bank ; and Lawrence, knowing they are helpless, makes the engineer run his locomotive back to the switch. Springing out, he has the boy in his arms in a minute, and getting into the cab, he holds Buck Powers to his breast, while his locomotive goes on its way unhindered now, though followed by the curses of its Mormon pursuers.

Then Erma whispers to Harry, " What chance ? " But he shakes his head, for he knows what those gray-blue lips mean—he has seen them too often on battle-fields.

As he does so, the boy, whose face has already grown pallid, and upon whose forehead the dew of death is standing, gasps : " I saved ye, Miss Beauty !—Didn't I do the trick like—like a Chicago railroad man ? "

" Yes," sobs the girl, bending over him. " What can I do for you ? "

" The Cap won't be jealous—just give me one kiss—that's all. I've never been kissed—by—a—beautiful—young lady."

And two sweet lips come to his, that are already cold, and he gasps : " You're pretty as a Chicago girl—that's where I'm goin' ! "

And delirium coming on him, he laughs ; for his old life is coming back to him ! And the railroad, and the city that he loves so well and is so proud of, getting into his mind, he cries : " I'm braking on the Burlington again, an' we're bound for Chicago. Hoop ! we're at the Rock Island crossin'—we've whistled first an' got the right o' way. C. B. & Q.'s always ahead !—Two long toots and two short toots ! Town whistle ! We're goin' into Aurorie an' out of it again. Now we whiz through Hinsdale an' Riverside !—I can see the lights of the city.—Engine has whistled for the Fort Wayne crossin' ! Sixteenth Street ! Slow down ! The bell's beginning to ring—the lights are dancin'—Michigan Avenue ! We're runnin' for the old Lake Street Station ! I'm a-folding up the flags and takin' in the red lights —the bell's ringin' fainter—the whistle's blowin' for brakes—the wheels are goin' slower—slower—slower —the lights is dancin' about me—the wheels are stopped. The train is dead—the lights is goin' out ! CHI-CAGO ! ! "

And with this cry, Buck Powers goes to Heaven.

Then Erma, bending over him, and wringing her hands, and tears dropping on his dead face, whispers : " Let us take him to Chicago, Harry, and bury him in the city he loved so well ! "

And so they do, some months afterward ; and there he lies, entombed in that silent city of the dead, beside the waters of the blue lake, and that great city of the living. And no truer heart, nor nobler soul, will ever tread the streets of that grand metropolis of the West, than that of this boy, who loved it so well, and who gave his life for gratitude—now nor to come, even if it grows to have ten millions.

CHAPTER XIX.

ORANGE BLOSSOMS AMONG THE SNOW.

So holding the dead boy in his arms, the engineer contriving to do the firing, they journey slowly along the road to Bridger.

Here, finding telegraphic communication is still cut

off with Evanston, they know it is safe to run on to Carter.

From the freight train at this point they fortunately get a man to do the firing of the locomotive, Lawrence paying him for the same.

The sun is rising as they pass the Carter tank, and the engineer tells them he thinks they have got coal enough, as they are on a down grade, to take them to Granger, for the snow is not so deep here as it was up the mountain.

Finding no orders have been received at this point, they keep on, and finally, about seven o'clock in the morning, they can see the passenger train from the East, side-tracked half a mile ahead of them at Granger.

"I can't take you any further—I have got no coal—and I don't know what the company will say to my doing what I have done!" mutters the engineer, who is now apparently anxious as to what the Union Pacific will think of his night's performance.

"Here's one hundred dollars!" remarks Lawrence.

"No, I did it because the young lady had been kind to my child!" and the man shakes his head.

"You must take it!" cries Harry. "You will probably be laid off for last night's work!"

"What? For running away from road agents?"

"Running away from sheriff's officers!"

"From officers of the law?" gasps the man of the throttle. Then he cries out suddenly: "They'll discharge me! You've ruined me and my child with your infernal lies!" and he looks at Lawrence with angry eyes.

But Harry says cheerfully: "If they discharge you, this young lady will give you enough money to buy a farm in Kansas. If she doesn't, I will! Besides," he continues, hoping to soothe the man's fears, "though those fellows we escaped from were Mormon officers, they were acting as bandits, and had no more legal right to do what they were doing in Wyoming, than road agents! I'll give you a bond for the money, if necessary, when we get to the station."

This promise, and the one hundred dollars in hand, makes the engineer feel more comfortable, as they run alongside the passenger train at Granger. Here many questions are asked them, and in return they discover the wires are still down towards Evanston, and there are, of course, no orders from division headquarters.

At this place Lawrence arranges for the transportation of the boy's body to the East, for he is very anxious to get it out of Miss Travenion's sight, who sits in the locomotive cab, half dazed, though when she looks upon what was once Buck Powers, she sometimes mutters with a shudder : " This time yesterday he was alive and happy—and now he's dead—for me," and fondles the boy's cold hand.

Lawrence is thus compelled to tell the story of the night's happenings, which he does to the station agent, who acts as constable at this place. This official looks serious, and rubs his head, and says : " Hanged if I know what I'd better do ! Buck got his death killing the infernal Mormon in Uintah County, and this is Sweetwater ! I guess you'd better take the young lady on to Green River, and then if they want you back for a coroner's inquest, or to try you for murder, you can go to Evanston, if you can get there—which looks almighty dubious just about now," for another snow-storm seems to be blowing up.

Thinking it best to follow the man's advice, and a locomotive being compelled to go to Green River, though the wires are still down to division headquarters, and consequently no orders, Lawrence takes the opportunity, and succeeds, about one o'clock in the day, in getting his sweetheart to the comforts of the

Green River station, where there is quite a town, a
pleasant hotel, and plenty to eat. For all the stations
he has run by this day, at that time were but little more
than telegraph offices and water tanks, with freight-
house attachments at some of them, and have not much
increased in size or importance, even to this day.

At Green River, snow comes upon them again, and
the yard gets full of trains, though none leave for the
East ; for the Union Pacific is beginning to appreciate
what the great blockade of 1871 means.

Telegraphic communication having been restored
between Evanston and Green River, Lawrence wires
the superintendent of the division a statement of what
happened at Aspen and Piedmont, and receives the following characteristic reply :

"Shall hold you for damage to locomotive. The homicide part
of the matter is not our business."

A day or so after this, a passenger train gets through
from the West to Green River, and walking out to meet
it, Harry is astonished but delighted to see Mr. Ferdinand Chauncey step out of one of its sleepers.

This gentleman, being brought in to see Miss Travenion, informs her of her father's safety.

"I got him out of the mine within two hours," he
says, "of Lawrence's leaving. Together we sneaked
down through Mormondom to Ogden, where your papa
concealed himself on a Central Pacific train, and is now
in California, I imagine, unless the snow-drifts on the
C. P. are as bad as on this ! "

Relieved from anxiety about her father, Erma begins
to pick up spirits again, for this young lady, in her
life that has been so easy up to this time, has not been
accustomed to seeing men die for her, and has not
recovered from the death of the boy at the Piedmont
switch.

A little while after, Mr. Chauncey, who has an Evanston "*Age*" in his pocket, pulls it out, and says : "Perhaps you may be interested in that!" pointing to an article in the newspaper which is an account of the inquest by coroner's jury held upon the body of Kruger at Evanston.

They had taken the evidence of some of the trainhands, and the verdict had been :

"That the boy Buck Powers killed Kruger, and Kruger killed Buck Powers! Consequently there is an all-round *nolle prosequi* in the matter."

This rather unique finding pleases Harry immensely, for now, he imagines, he will not be delayed in getting his sweetheart to civilization.

Some two or three hours after, telegraphic orders being received, they board the same train that Mr. Ferdie has come into Green River on, and depart for the East.

Passing through Rawlings in the night, early the next day they find themselves halted by the snow blockade at Medicine Bow, about one hundred miles west of Laramie ; and this time it seems to be a permanent stoppage.

Train after train comes in from the West, and none from the East, they being held there by snow, at Cooper's Lake, and tremendous drifts in the deep cuts from Laramie towards Sherman.

Fortunately they have plenty to eat. There is a grocery store, and they are the first of this snow blockade, and so they live on "the fat of the land," which means canned goods of every style, and ham and bacon *ad libitum*.

Though Ferdie rages at the delay, Lawrence, being near his sweetheart, would be content but for one thing : Erma's position, without a chaperon, and accompanied by two men, neither of them relatives, is "embarrassing."

Lawrence probably appreciates this even more than she does, as now and then remarks come to his ears, from some of the passengers on the other trains, that he would resent, if common sense did not tell him that he must in no way bring his sweetheart's name to any scandal.

It is partly this, and partly the natural impatience to call his own this being he loves so much, that he is desperately afraid some accident or chance will even now take her from him, that causes him to come to Erma one day, and explain the matter to her.

He urges : "Why should we wait for a grand wedding in New York, dear one ? As your husband, I can show you much greater attentions, and can do things for you that I could not as your betrothed, in the privations and hardships of this blockade. Why not make me happy—why not marry me here ? "

But the young lady, affecting a little laugh, murmurs : "What ? Before you have given me the engagement ring you wish to use the wedding one ? "

And he replies : "I wish to marry you ! "

"Not by a justice of the peace ! " cries the girl in horror.

"No, by a minister."

"Where will you find one ? "

"On the next train behind us—the Reverend Mr. Millroy, of St. Paul. He's anxious to do some work ; he has had no pastoral duties to perform for a month or two. Let us give him a chance—you know your father wished it ! "

This mention of her father's views perhaps actuates Erma more than she imagines—but it also reminds her of him ! She falters, " You are sure you will never repent ? Remember, I am a Mormon's daughter ! "

"So you are, and the belle of Newport and the sweetest—the dearest—the——"

But she cries, placing her patrician fingers on his moustache, "Stop!—no more compliments!"

"You consent?"

"P-e-r-haps! When do you wish it?"

"This evening!"

"Oh!" And blushes fly over her face and neck as Lawrence goes away to consult with Mr. Ferdie.

This young gentleman makes arrangements with the minister, and consents to act as best man on the occasion, crying: "Thank God, Harry, you've given me some excitement at last! I had finished my last novel and my last cigar, and thought I should die of *ennui* in this everlasting, unending, eternal snow."

But even as Mr. Ferdinand makes his preparations for the nuptial *fête*, another train from the West comes in upon the crowded railroad tracks at Medicine Bow. On it, Oliver, Mrs. Livingston, and Louise. They do not see Lawrence and Miss Travenion, as their cars are some little distance apart. But Mr. Chauncey, who has a habit of visiting from one train to another, finds them out, and after a little chuckles to himself: "This will be the ceremony of the season! I'll—I'll have some Grace Church effects for Mr. Ollie's benefit and discomfiture."

So after exchanging greeting with his aunt and her family, he gets Miss Louise to one side, and explaining something to her that makes the child's eyes grow large, bright, and excited, she suddenly gives a scream of laughter and whispers: "I'll do it—if mother puts me on bread and water for a week. It will make Ollie crazy."

"That's right! You always were a lovely child!" returns Mr. Chauncey.

After this, throughout the day, Louise acts as if under intense but concealed excitement, for she says nothing to her mother and Oliver, but every now and then gives little giggles of laughter, which so astonishes Ollie that he remarks to Mrs. Livingston : "The privations of this snow blockade have made the child deranged." Then he says severely : "If I hear another insane giggle, Louise, I'll shut you up in the stateroom ;" for this young gentleman is always happy to play the domestic tyrant.

These remarks so frighten Louise that she disappears.

About seven o'clock in the evening, Mr. Livingston remarks to Ferdie, who has dropped into his car : "It's dreadfully tiresome ! Don't you think you could join us in a game of whist ?"

"I would be delighted," replies Mr. Chauncey, "but there is going to be an entertainment in the train next to ours. Can't you come in and enjoy it ? Eight o'clock is the hour."

"What are they going to do ? "

"I don't know exactly, but I expect it's exciting."

"Well, anything is better than doing nothing," laughs Oliver, in which his mother agrees.

So it comes to pass that the two leave their Pullman and wade through the snow to another side track, where a palace car is brilliantly lighted, and apparently crowded with the *élite* of the blockaded passengers, all in their blockade best.

At the door Oliver asks the porter : "What's going on ?"

"A weddin', sah !" replies the negro. "An' they're havin' a very hard time inside ; thar wasn't no weddin' ring—but I'se just cut off one of de curtain rings to give to de groom."

"Ah, some cowboy affair," remarks Ollie, who leads his mother into the car, and then gives a gasp, and sinks down on an unoccupied seat, while Mrs. Livingston, too much overcome for words, drops beside him.

For beneath a centre cluster of red and green coal-oil railroad lamps hung up as a decoration they see Erma Travenion and Harry Lawrence being joined in holy matrimony, and Ferdie and Louise acting as best man and bridesmaid.

A moment after the ceremony is finished.

Then Mr. Chauncey announces that a wedding break-fast, or, rather, wedding supper, is served in the grocery at the side of the track.

"It is not exactly a wedding breakfast," he says, "because it's evening, but there'll be plenty of champagne, and every one is cordially invited to attend!"

Just here, social diplomat as she is, Mrs. Livingston, gathering herself together, gets on her feet, and coming to Erma, gives her a kiss of congratulation, saying, "My dear, I hear you have no proper wedding-ring—let this be your first bridal present;" and places a magnificent ruby of her own on Mrs. Lawrence's finger.

Then they all go through the snow to the grocery, which has a back room that is fitted up as a dining-room, where the champagne flows like water in Western style, and a Nevada congressman with a silver tongue makes a little address to the bride, remarking on orange blossoms in the snow. "The snow we'll keep in the West—the orange blossoms go to the East with the bride, God bless her! But a *Western man goes with her!*"

This sentiment appealing to Western hearts, and the champagne appealing to Western palates, the gentlemen of the party make a great night of it.

Three days after, the snow blockade at Sherman being broken for a little time, the trains all get under headway, and, with cheering passengers, leave Medicine Bow, run down to Laramie, and the next morning are out of the great snow blockade, and flying across Nebraska towards Omaha.

So, one evening just before Christmas, Harry Lawrence and his wife come into the Grand Central Depot, New York, Erma whispering, "Did ever girl have railroad trip like mine?—I went to find a father and found a husband!" and her eyes beam upon Harry, who is pressing her arm to his side.

From the station they drive to the Everett, where a telegram comes to them from California, announcing the safety of Ralph Travenion, and that he has shipped his Utah Central stock east by Wells, Fargo & Co., and is returning to New York via Panama, for he does not dare to trust himself in Utah.

Thirty days after this, Travenion strolls into their parlor at the Everett, and looking at him, no one would ever have thought that he was once a Mormon bishop, for he is now the same debonair exquisite of the Unity Club that he was years ago, and gives Lawrence his father's blessing, as one.

"My boy, we must make you an Eastern club man," he remarks. "I shall put you up at the Unity and Stuyvesant. We're rich enough to live in the East, and in order to make us richer, let's go over to Boston, and see the heads of the Union Pacific!"

Which they do, and sell the control of the Utah Central, out of which Brigham Young and his fellows go, with wailing and gnashing of teeth, for they know that the hand of the Union Pacific is upon them in railroad matters, and it is a grasping Gentile corporation ; in proof of which the Mormon Church does not control one railroad in Utah—though it built nearly all of them.

Some time afterwards, over their dinner-table in New York, Travenion, whose instincts are those of a business man yet, says : "I should have stayed in California. There's a fortune there ! Even while in San Francisco, I made some money in mining stocks. Belcher, for instance, had gone up very much."

" Belcher ! " cries Lawrence. " Good Heavens ! I've got two hundred shares of that stock in my pocket-book, and have forgotten all about it ! "

" Oh ! " says Erma, " that was the stock you had when you first heard that I was Bishop Tranyon's daughter—and you forgot your investment for me ! "

" Well, Providence has rewarded him for it, for I think Belcher must be up to a thousand dollars a share, by this time ! " laughs Ralph.

And telegraphing San Francisco, Lawrence finds this is the fact, and sells out his Belcher stock for something over eleven hundred dollars a share, making nearly two hundred thousand dollars by the transaction.

" Luck is upon you, young man ! " says the ex-bishop. " Your election comes up at the Unity Club to-morrow. I've no doubt you'll go in—but that Oliver Livingston may give you trouble."

" Oh, I think not ! " cries Erma, " his mother has been so very kind to me, as, in fact, have all my old friends."

For some rumors of the peculiar adventures that have made Miss Travenion Mrs. Lawrence have got into circulation, and in them Harry has been made a Western hero and a frontier demi-god. Besides, society is generally very nice to a young and beautiful woman who has sixty thousand a year of her own, a rich husband, and richer father, and who is going to have a fine mansion on Fifth Avenue, and give many dinner parties and a german or two each season.

" I differ with you, my dear," returns Ralph. " Oliver Livingston is an infamous cad."

" Why, what has he done now ? " asks Lawrence, noting the excitement in his father-in-law's manner.

" What has he done ? " cries Travenion. " The miserable sneak has told in the Unity the story of the Mor-

mon club man—tne story I risked my life to originate.
I told it to-day with graphic elaboration, and Larry
Jerry and the rest only half smiled, and said they be-
lieved Mr. Livingston had told them that yarn about a
month ago. I shall never tell it again !"

"Don't !" cries his daughter. "Don't make me
ashamed of you." Then she says more calmly : "What
have you done about your families out there ?"

"Oh, they're provided for *well !*" remarks Ralph.
"I believe one of them, the genuine Mrs. Travenion"
—he winces a little at the title—"would have made me
trouble, but I think the Church instructed her to let me
alone ; I know a few secrets of theirs that make them
quite amiable to me, now I'm out of their clutches.
Their delegate to congress, the one who has four wives
in Utah, and declares he is not a polygamist in Wash-
ington, might not like me to explain what I know of
his large family," chuckles the old gentleman.

But for all this, he does not tell the story of Bishop
Tranyon, the New York dandy, very often.

His guess about Oliver Livingston, however, was a
shrewd one. For chancing to be on the Governing
Committee of the Unity when Lawrence's name comes
up for membership, he sneaks in a black-ball, as many
another prig and coward, from envy and malice and
uncharitableness, has done before, and will do to
come.

But this doesn't count much, for Ferdie, who chances
to be its youngest member, has gone about with his winning manner and boyish frankness, and has button-holed
everybody, saying, "Hang it! You must put Harry
Lawrence through. He's the man who saved my life.
He's from the wild and woolly West, but some day he's
going to make New York howl !"

So Lawrence goes in.

Though he doesn't do quite as much as Ferdie has

promised for him—for he is too happy to be inordinately ambitious—and is contented to be a successful railroad director, and have a yacht on the water and a villa in Newport, and a town-house on the avenue, and to be the husband of Miss Dividends.

FINIS.